Project Utopia 2030

By

R. Norman Johnson

ISBN: 1-4107-0969-8 (softcover)
ISBN: 1-4107-0968-X (electronic)

Library of Congress Control Number: 2002096923

This book is printed on acid free paper.

Printed in the United States of America
Bloomington, IN

1st Books - rev. 12/31/02

Part I: Near Utopia

CHAPTER ONE: Near Utopia

The lights of the computer center dimmed as the security guard spoke to a figure crouched over a computer keyboard.

"I'll leave ya enough lights to work with Dr. Wilford. Gotta shut all the rest down though. You make sure to turn the security switch on when you leave. . . Dr. Wilford?"

The figure bending intently over the keyboard, finally half-realizing he was being addressed, looked up blankly, "What? Uh. . ."

"The security switch. . . I could get in trouble if they knew I was lettin ya stay late so please remember to turn on the security switch when ya leave . . . Okay, Doc?"

The figure gazed up at the cameras around the room absent-mindedly before realizing what was said to him. "Oh, yes, certainly Jimmy. I'll be here only briefly but I'll make sure to turn it on . . . Uh, goodnight."

Doctor Benjamin J. Wilford, at 61, more resembled the stereotyped chemist or physicist than a computer scientist. His white hair, slightly bowed back and wrinkled brow would seem to fit the description of some mad scientist from a 20th century horror flick, but one look at his warm blue eyes and kind smile assured one of his character. His calm, pleasant tone of voice immediately made one feel at home with this grandfatherly figure. All of these characteristics together were "Doc", the affectionate name given Dr. Wilford by the computer room staff.

Coming out of semi-retirement from his 30 year position at Bradford College as senior computer professor, Dr. Wilford had been hired five years earlier by the Altrex Corporation to supervise the computer center at their purchasing plant in lower Manhattan.

There he supervised the computer room and it's fifty-five technicians. These technicians quietly pecked away at their terminals for eight hours a day entering various data which came from who knows where, while the fatherly Dr. Wilford made rounds through the immense room offering kind suggestions, occasionally replacing a weary technician for a much needed eye rest. Never in Dr. Wilford's five years with the company had there been even the slightest malfunction at any of the terminals. As he understood the system, all maintenance was done automatically from a large central computer somewhere at the corporate headquarters.

Something was wrong today though. At precisely 4:15 p.m., 45 minutes before the center closed for the night all of the terminals went blank.

Dr. Wilford sat at his terminal mentally reviewing all of the information he had memorized from the computer manuals over the past five years. None of the troubleshooting processes seemed to have the slightest affect. As the evening wore on he felt no nearer to any kind of solution. He puzzled over the bizarre behavior of this normally perfect machine. It just wasn't acting right and he felt compelled to find out why!

Trying method after method as outlined in the manual, the result was always the same. Nothing. As the doctor sat puzzling over his problem, his mind slowly slipped to thoughts of home. His daughter, Andy, nearly 30 now, had been the joy of his life since the death of his wife 16 years ago. ANDY! Oh no! She'd have dinner waiting. A glance at his watch though, told him she'd long since gone to bed. It was nearly midnight. He'd give her a call in just a moment, after one more try.

Hours later, nearly exhausted, Dr. Wilford sat at the terminal no closer to a solution then when he started. He'd tried literally every method in every manual. As sleep slowly closed in upon the professor, he, in a half dream state, began to think back to his days at Bradford College. The endless hours he'd spent in his lab refining programs. Just then he sat up, wide-awake. It was a long shot, and probably wouldn't even come close to cracking this machine, but he remembered a program, designed by himself and a colleague that they used to crack problem systems. The Alpha program. A slight smile spread across the doctor's weary face as he mused at the absurdity of using a 30-year-old program to solve the problems of a state of the art computer system. Oh well, nothing to lose!

Carefully and painstakingly he resurrected from his memory each detail of the ancient program. Step upon step, string upon string, the Alpha program began to emerge as a mass of numbers and symbols filling screen after screen with it's complicated language. After half an hour of pecking at the keys, the grizzled old man had finally listed all the steps from beginning to end on the screen before him. It was all there, waiting to be entered. By this time a full smile spread across the doctor's face. Feeling both pleased with himself at having remembered such a long and complicated program and facing the total ridiculousness at using it on the TXR 47, he nearly chuckled to himself. Resigned to the inevitable, he pressed ENTER and waited for nothing to happen. For a slight moment nothing did happen. The monitor sat quiet and blank.

Braced for failure, the Dr. resigned himself to trying again tomorrow after a good night's sleep. Picking up his coat, he reached for the terminal to switch it off. A split second before he accomplished this task the screen burst into life with names, numbers and. . . and . . . Sitting down he watched as it all unfolded before his eyes and finally he stood speechless, viewing the most horrifying sight he'd seen in his life. The stunned, silent minutes brought with them the realization that what was displayed before him could change the life of literally everyone in the year 2030.

CHAPTER TWO: The Story

"We are living in the most exciting and technologically advanced age in the history of man. One need only look around to see just how fortunate we, in the Age of the Corporation, are." Zack looked over the first lines of his story with a feeling of anxious anticipation. "The boss couldn't have made a better choice in assigning someone to write on the wonders of today's technology" he thought. There was no one more excited about living in the year 2030 than Zack Murphy.

The son of a successful journalist, Zack had made a name for himself in the holovision industry before he was 25 with his keen eye for news and quick witted way of putting words together. Now at 31, Zack had become one the bright young talents of the holovision industry as a writer and occasionally as an "On the air reporter." The former he did with zeal, while the latter only at the insistence of his employer. Somehow the thought of standing, full torso, in the homes of millions of viewers left him a bit cold. The fame and notoriety of the holovision industry were not what motivated Zack, and his generally mild personality aided his aversion to the camera.

This morning was different though. His normal shyness toward being on camera had been pushed aside by his driving desire to share his excitement about the state of the world. He had lots to say.

"The past 10 years have proven, for this reporter, to have been the most exciting time since the turn of the century. One can only marvel at the advancements that we, the people of the world, have been partakers of.

"In 1997, after this planet came dangerously close to world war and total annihilation, for the third time, a dynamic organization came into being bringing peace and a new birth to societies all over the world. Out of need and the foresight of some very wise men, the World Council of Corporations was born. Together, through the United Nations, they pressured world governments into putting away their differences and joining in building a unified world dedicated to peace and the happiness of all its inhabitants. The result was that one government after another surrendered its power to the WCC, coming obediently under their authority.

"By the year 2010, nearly all hunger, pestilence and disease had been eradicated. What followed was a decade of rebuilding, a decade of remaking a warring world into a world bent on peace and unity, and but for a few small radical groups in remote parts of the globe, by 2018, this great world peace was all but achieved.

"This great world council set its sights on the year 2025. This was to be the year to reach the loftiest of goals; a final end to poverty, hunger, and unemployment. By that year each man and woman in the world would be gainfully, happily employed or at least have every opportunity to be so. Through the wisdom and hard work of the WCC, unbelievably these goals were achieved over one year ahead of schedule. What has followed has been a renaissance of social, cultural, and technological advancement.

"Now, ladies and gentlemen of the world, we are here in the most advanced, civilized time that the world has ever known. We are living in the year 2030.

"This story will deal with, in detail, many of the spectacular developments of this great time in history. I'm Zack Murphy and I invite you to join me in this look at '2030'."

Rubbing his hands across his tanned, handsome face, Zack noticed the time.

"Oh no! I'm gonna be late . . . Time for this later!"

He tapped his computer monitor lovingly as he grabbed his jacket and headed for the door. Outside his building, Zack took a loving look around at the city, once known for its violence and crime. Once clogged with traffic and contaminated with smog. Now what he saw was a city teeming with progress, free of pollution and nearly free of crime. All around him, instead of the crumbling tenements of the last century, he saw majestic buildings, clean, smooth, and shinning with the polish of fine marble.

"Mercurite!" he thought. All around he saw buildings and streets made of it. "Have to include that in the story. Let's see, how to word it." He searched momentarily as one scans a word puzzle until the phrasing came clear. "If one could choose a single element that has brought the greatest progress in the world today, it must certainly be the discovery of the mineral Mercurite, an incredible substance discovered and mined on the planet Mercury. This mineral, when processed, makes a literally indestructible building material, which is so lightweight that it is able to be used in all types of industry. These buildings show no sign of wear even though most of them were built over fifteen years ago." He imagined himself in front of the camera motioning to the very buildings he passed. "Most people don't realize why roads no longer erode and automobiles no longer dent, scratch or break down, how spacecraft have gone farther, faster, and are safer than ever dreamed possible. The answer is Mercurite." His excitement over the story grew with every step and every thought.

Pleasant smiles graced the faces of those who walked by on the street confirming in Zack's mind that this truly was the age of all ages to have been born into.

A quick trip on the subway brought images to his mind of the New York that his grandfather had known. The clean, efficient underground transport system stood in stark contrast to the terrifying subways described by his grandfather. It puzzled him that the old man would still hang lovingly onto memories of that dank, dark time. "Human nature, I suppose. Even still it's good that so many are taking advantage of the corporation retirement system. For them being able to leave here for a new life at the colonies must be attractive." He could see why. For many reasons this environment seemed ideal, but it always took time for society to change. Well, hopefully his story would help the cause of progress.

As he entered the front doors of the modern headquarters of the Corporate Broadcasting Company, several youngish people stationed at various desks throughout the lobby greeted him. Soft music lilted through gently scented air. "Mm, pine forest today," he thought as he sniffed the air. One specifically attractive young blonde called him by name.

"Hi Zack," she said with an alluring grin. "What about that dinner we keep talking about?"

"Oh, uh, yeah. . . well just as soon as I finish with this project I'm working on. I promise, Susan. . ." Mercifully the elevator doors closed. His mind was definitely not on Susan James. She was one thing about 2030 he could do without. The ride up the elevator relaxed him. Somehow the solitude of the little chamber offered solace. As he was swept smoothly and gently upwards the skyline of the clty burst before him through the transparent mercurite walls of the elevator. "Incredible", he thought, the same sentiment he expressed every day.

By the time the doors opened to the 140th floor, Zack's mind had fallen again to his story. He plotted how he might squeeze minutes out of the day to work on it.

The newsroom was buzzing with activity as he fairly skipped across the room greeting his co-workers as he went.

"Boy, aren't we in a chipper mood", chimed in one homely secretary.

Zack wove his way to the other side of the room toward his office, which was shared by two other reporters. He was greeted by his secretary.

"Good morning Zack, the chief wants to see you first thing. It sounds pretty important" she chirped not looking up from her work. Zack often wondered how someone with so little personality managed to find her way into the newsroom, which seemed to be made up of every joker in the city. This morning, though, he would not be daunted; even by Miss Snyder! He bent down and gave her a peck on the cheek.

"Thanks sweetheart!" he said as he brushed by her. She glanced up blankly until he was out of sight. She allowed a girlish blush and the hint of a smile to cross her face but momentarily regained control and went sullenly on about her work.

Three doors down, through the large glass, Zack could see the chief, Sam McDermott. He thought of him more as a father than a boss. He'd been the best friend of his own father, and when his dad was killed on an overseas assignment some years earlier, Sam stepped in to fill Zack's father's shoes. He felt it his responsibility to get young Zack through to manhood. Zack paused a moment outside the office to look at his boss. The middle aged, balding, and overweight gentleman sat engrossed in a conversation over the telephone. Zack chuckled as he thought of the frustrated callers who stared at a blank pictophone screen as they talked to Sam who refused to use anything but an ancient telephone, one you had to actually hold up to your ear and mouth to speak into. But this was Sam McDermott. He didn't really fit into the 21st century. He reminded Zack of some 20th century editor, full of emotion, constant cigar, and with a stubborn streak only matched by his soft heart.

Sam looked up as Zack entered his office. He motioned him toward a chair. Zack chose the edge of the desk instead, and watched as Sam finished his call.

"'Bout time you got here! I've got something for ya. That is if you're awake yet." he joked. "Seriously, I've got a press conference for you to cover."

"Aw, Sam" the groan showed his disapproval. "Can't ya get someone else. I was kind of hoping to have a few minutes to work on '2030'."

"No Zack, this is a pretty big deal and I want it covered right. Besides, you'll have time to write on your way. The conference is way downtown."

"Alright. What's the deal?" Zack sensed the seriousness in Sam's voice.

"Well, one of the corporate headquarters reported a high level burglary, an inside job, and the government security police have been chasing this guy for hours. I don't have any more details except they're just about to get the guy and we've all been asked NOT to send anyone until they announce his actual capture. . . at which time they'll have a press conference. That's where you fit in. Can you handle it?"

"Yeah, sure Sam, but what's the big deal? Why can't we go cover the search?" Zack asked half into the conversation as he stared out the window at the clear blue day.

"They said something about the guy being extremely dangerous. I dunno. Sounds pretty simple though."

Up until that last phrase Zack felt totally uninterested, but something about the words extremely dangerous intrigued him. Sam always said he took after his father in that regard. His editor warned that it would get him into trouble some day. Little did either of them know just how much trouble it would bring on this very day.

Just then Sam got a call. As he turned to answer his phone, Zack leaned over toward the computer monitor on Sam's desk. There he read "Fugitive last spotted around 4th & Selmer near the Space Science Complex. Government security forces closing in. Please keep reporting staff away until. . ." Sam looked up from his phone just in time to see his young adopted son whisking by his office window, and with a wink and a wave Zack disappeared into the maze of desks in the newsroom. 2814

CHAPTER THREE

Birch, poplar, and cedar trees, green and lush, surrounded the palatial mansion and grounds of the Alton estate. Its twenty acres of lavish gardens, ponds, fountains and waterfalls seemed something out of a fairy tale. Across green rolling hills of carefully manicured grass, surrounded by hedges and gardens filled with exotic plant life, stood the Alton home. Ivy-covered brick housed a spacious 40 room mansion complete with indoor pool and gymnasium, teak floors, crystal chandeliers, and wall to wall antiques, as well as the latest in the state of the art electronics and computer equipment.

James Alton sat at dinner with his family as servants closely attended them, silently slipping in and out of the room. Alton, an executive for the Altrex Corporation, was the stereotypical executive of the 21st century. He had the look of wealth about him. He was tall with deep furrows in his brow, not the kind you get from being in the sun too long, but those one gets from the constant stress of corporate management. His body showed signs of a life spent in the elite class where physical labor was unheard of unless it was for recreation or relaxation. It was obvious that Mr. Alton spent his leisure time with other than physical pursuits. His rounded soft shoulders rose weakly above a bulging midsection supported by very thin, spindly legs. His eyes were a cold steel blue with just a hint of nervousness about them as they glanced back and forth at the others seated for the meal.

"Does anyone know where Peter might be?" he said, staring at the remnants of his family sitting before him.

"I'm sure he's studying father. It seems to me that his finals are coming sometime soon at college." spoke a handsome young man seated to Mr. Alton's left.

James Jr. was a budding young executive being groomed by Altrex for corporate management. His mild temperament was a stark contrast to his father's quick temper, yet he loved and admired the older Alton. The tall, blue-eyed young man was the pride of his father who dreamed of his son's success with Altrex to continue the family tradition.

"Jimmy, you know as well as I do where Peter is. Father, if he hasn't left yet, he's getting ready to go down to lower Manhattan. To the slums. . . to work with those. . . people." Sondra Alton spoke in her usual snide tone of voice. James Alton's only daughter, an attractive 25 year old woman, Sondra enjoyed her father's wealth immensely. It supported her lifestyle of parties

18

and never ending social functions. She too admired her father but for different reasons than her older brother. She saw him as a ruthless businessman who fully realized his position as a member of the elite class of society.

At this moment, though, all three had Peter on their minds. The youngest of the Alton children, he had always been a rebel. Unlike James Jr. and Sondra, Peter was never satisfied with the role set before him as a member of the elite class. The 21 year old, dark haired youth always hated the private corporation schools he'd attended since childhood, and now as a student at Bradford College he joined every radical group that came along. . . at least long enough to find out if what they had was what his troubled mind searched for. His recent interest, springing out of a sociology class, was in a small group of people living in lower Manhattan. They were non-corporate individuals. In the age of the corporation nearly everyone worked for one of the WCC companies. But there were those, for reasons unknown to most, who chose not to. They lived mostly in inner cities and deserted suburban neighborhoods and survived on God knows what. There were no jobs outside of the corporate umbrella. Peter had become intensely interested in helping these people and on one of his visits to the area came across a small clinic where the 500 or so people received medical treatment. It was dirty, rundown, lacking in medical supplies, and run by a handful of volunteers from the outside. Their job was overwhelming as disease was rampant in the little slum area. Peter knew the instant he saw the place that he wanted to be there to help these people.

Mr. Alton looked up just in time to see young Peter clad in a leather jacket and carrying a pack on his shoulder heading out the front door.

"And where are you going young man." he said rising from the table.

"Out." replied Peter somewhat sarcastically.

Sondra broke in loudly. "Out to the slums again? Honestly Peter, don't you know how embarrassing it is? A member of this family associating with. . . with. . ."

"Go ahead and say it, sister dear. . . I associate with the scum of the earth. Well, you might try to know some of them. . . they might teach you something about being a person!"

"Stop. . ." interrupted Mr. Alton. "Peter, I'll not have you going down there. Sondra is right. The slums of Manhattan are no place for a young man of your caliber. Now sit down and eat."

"No thanks, I've lost my appetite. . . good-bye." He slammed the huge oak door as he stormed out of the house.

The old man sighed and sullenly sat back down to his dinner.

"Father, what are you going to do with Peter?. . . well. . ."

"Sondra, just relax! Father, I'll go out and find Peter and I'll talk to him." Jim got up from the table and headed for the door. "And sis, try a little tact next time. It might surprise you with its effectiveness!" With that he left the room.

CHAPTER FOUR

As he hurried through the doors of the CBC building into the sunshine, Zack mentally planned his course. It would be quicker to get to 4th and Selmer by foot but he'd have to hurry. The cool morning air was quickly giving way to warm gusts, the beginning of another hot September day. Sweat began to flow from his body as he quickly jogged toward his destination. His lean, muscular body was accustomed to running and he felt good! A smile spread across his face as he felt the invigorating excitement of the upcoming scene. He loved the thrill of shooting for a scoop, and so did his boss for that matter! Up one side street and then three blocks down, across a footbridge and then through another alley.

Nearly out of breath he finally arrived at 4th and Selmer. As he looked around he realized that he was in a primarily industrial area just a block behind the street that housed many of the corporate headquarters for the city. Across the nearly deserted street he recognized a press badge worn by a tall thin man.

"Darn" he thought, "no scoop on this story!" He wondered what news agency this man was from. He'd have to move fast he thought.

Just as he began to step out of the alley into the open, he noticed some commotion in the alley across the street. Bursting into the morning sunshine an old man in a white lab coat appeared from the entrance to the alley and paused a brief moment in the street. At first the scene puzzled Zack. It didn't make sense. This old man looked like some sort of scientist. He was small, frail and rather bald, and even from across the street Zack could see the meekness which the man emitted. It was the look in his eyes though that snapped the reporter into reality. Sheer terror showed in the old man's eyes, as if some terrible thing was pursuing him. He looked up and down the street in a panic as if trying to decide which way to go. Then all at once he noticed the reporter. Without hesitation he bolted toward the man with the obvious press badge on his lapel. Reaching the newsman the scientist seemed to be trying to say something while struggling to catch his breath.

A sharp crack split the air, and before his eyes Zack saw the old man crumble into the arms of his fellow reporter. Something told him he should step back into the protection for the alley as the horror of the situation gripped him. The old man had been shot and was dying in the arms of the tall, thin man across the street. What could be happening?

The sound of footsteps up the street was quickly followed by the appearance of five NSP troops. Their appearance brought to Zack's mind the story he'd done just a month ago on the National Security Police. What a change they'd brought with them at their inception nearly ten years ago. Replacing the ever increasingly corrupt municipal police forces around the country it took them almost no time to nearly eradicate crime throughout the nation. He had nothing but respect for these dedicated and hardworking men and women in their sharp blue and white uniforms. This made the scene harder to understand. Could this meek little man be the dangerous fugitive his boss had told him of? If so, why not apprehend him instead of killing him in the street?

At first the old man slumped limply into the tall man's arms. The look of surprise on the reporters face let Zack know that he must have been as puzzled about the situation as he was. All at once the little man raised his head, looking the thin man in the eyes. He seemed to be trying to say something. As the reporter bent low to listen, a puzzled, horrified look crossed his face. With that the old man went limp. What could the old man have said to cause such a reaction in a trained newsman? What was happening here?

Zack didn't have long to ponder these questions before a sleek NSP truck wheeled around the corner and screeched to a halt. It arrived on the scene just as the troops did. Then, in a bustle of activity, the troops took the old man from the arms of the stunned reporter, put him on a stretcher and loaded his body into the back of the truck. Someone official looking began asking the reporter questions to which he shook his head. The officer then seemed to copy the information written on the thin man's badge down in his notebook. With that he tipped his hat, wheeled around, and disappeared into the truck, which sped away with a nuclear whine. They left a rather bewildered looking reporter staring in disbelief in the direction the truck had gone.

As Zack watched the police truck disappear around a corner, the thin man spoke through a radio he had on his wrist. Zack had every intention of crossing the street to talk with the other reporter, but as he glanced back in his direction, a small car pulled up. The thin man jumped in, closed the hatch and disappeared as quickly as the police had. Futilely running after the car, Zack was finally left standing in the middle of the street feeling dazed and bewildered. His mind raced back through the scenario of events, which had just taken place. It didn't make sense.

"The press conference! I don't even know where it is! Better get back to the office. No, better yet, I'll just call in," he thought.

Fifteen minutes later he was being chauffeured by cameraman, B. J. Dean, toward NSP headquarters and some answers to questions that haunted his mind.

CHAPTER FIVE

Off in the distance the New York skyline was beginning to light up like the tiny shimmering pieces of a crystal chandelier as Peter emerged out of the transit station and stepped down on to the sidewalk. He paused momentarily to glance down at the escalator and at the station below that it led from. What a stark difference lay before him. The transit station so modern, so sterile and the street level so run down and shabby. It was a though someone had purposely left this section of town untouched when the city was rebuilt after the turn of the century. He wondered why.

Peter Alton stood six feet two inches though his thin build made him look taller. His dark, piercing eyes seemed often to look right through a person leaving one wondering what was going on behind them. Such was true today as he stared at the scene before him, past the occasional transit passenger who walked by him enroute to who knows where. A pair of dingy faced young boys running loudly by brought Peter out of his thoughts and again set his mind on his destination. The evening air came in cool wisps slowly erasing the mugginess of the hot September afternoon. There was something real and fresh about this run-down crumbling place. He breathed deep and the smell of some outdoor fire filled his nostrils. Somehow it touched a place deep down inside of him as if some primeval instinct was crying out. This place and its people made him feel good. He didn't know why but it was true.

Two blocks from the station he came to the old building which housed the free clinic. Though it wasn't much from the outside, this dilapidated old place was the only medical facility in the whole area. Since few of the locals could afford treatment at any of the corporate medical centers or hospitals, the free clinic meant life or death to its patrons. Staffed by a handful of volunteers, most from the area itself, it barely managed to stay open.

As Peter opened the door he was greeted hastily by the clinic's only doctor. Dr. Frank Rubens had once been a corporate doctor with ITEC, one of the largest textile corporations. When one day deep in thought, he got off of the transit at the wrong stop, he found himself in the middle of lower Manhattan. Overcoming his natural inclination to hastily turn around and head back to the safety of the transit, he decided to walk through the area. It wasn't long before he came upon the free clinic. One look around the place had him hooked. The cleanliness of the building showed signs of the hard work that kept it that way. An old rundown building such as this would resist the most thorough cleaning. But what grabbed him were the people, both staff and patients. Nowhere in all of the sterile coldness of the corporate hospitals had he seen the love and compassion that he witnessed here. Though desperately understaffed and without a doctor, this place unbelievably cared for the problems of a people steeped in poverty and squalor. He stayed the rest of that day and had been back every day since. Soon afterwards he announced that he'd be at the clinic full-time. No one had the nerve to ask him why or how. They were all just very thankful that they now had a full-time doctor.

"Hello Doc, how's the day shift been?" said Peter cheerfully.

"Oh, hi Pete. Not to bad, thank heaven. We're so low on supplies that we couldn't deal with too many." Peter noticed the fatigue in his eyes and haggard expression on his bearded face as the young doctor spoke.

"What can I do today?" asked Peter.

"I'm not sure kid, just go check with Jenny in the office. Say, how're classes going?" the doctor was trying hard to sound sincere.

"Not bad" he paused, "what's the use though Doc! They don't teach anything that fits in with what I want to do" he said revealing the deep frustration he felt within. "All my old man can think of is fitting his neat little family into neat little executive positions with his company. That's not for me! What I want is right here, right here with these people, right. . ."

The doctor broke in angrily, taking Peter by the arm. "Look Pete, don't get any stupid ideas about working down here very long. It's great while you're a kid. You get a chance to see how the outcast of the world live. But get it out of your head that this is some kind of a future for you. This place ruins people. . . before you know it you're one of them. . . look, the best thing you could ever do for these people is to make something of your life and then figure out a way to send supplies to them . . ." His eyes stared past Peter and his hand relaxed around the young man's arm and dropped to his side. "More supplies that's what we need. . . more supplies." He mumbled as he walked blankly away.

Peter stared speechless as he watched the doctor disappear into an examination room.

"Don't mind him Peter," a soft voice from behind him spoke. As he turned he was met by the smiling face of Jenny, a clinic volunteer. She wore a long sleeved shirt rolled up to the elbows and tight fitting jeans, hardly the attire to the average clinic employee. "He's been here for three straight days without rest, and he's right, we're almost out of supplies. Where are those goody two shoes elitists with their conscience offerings when you need 'em." As she spoke the strain showed on her face and her deep blue eyes filled with tears.

"How long have you been here Jenny?" Peter asked, concerned about the pretty young girl.

"Not long. It's just been a hard day. Three more cases of malnutrition and more cases of. . . who knows what. Dr. Rubens can't even figure out what it is. It just wastes people away. He says that without the proper equipment, it's impossible to treat these people effectively. Nothing we can do. This morning," her speech became broken, "a little baby. . . just died in my arms." Tears flowed down her face as she cradled empty arms. Peter stepped toward her, and she fell into his arms weeping bitterly.

"You need some rest Jen. C'mon, use room 4. I'll cover out here for you." The young girl just nodded through streams of tears and went sobbing along with Peter into room four. They entered the little room, which never really seemed clean no matter how hard one worked. Jenny sat on the bed, head in hands and sobbed for a good five minutes with Peter standing by and stroking her hair. After composing herself, she smiled up at him, embarrassed for her show of weakness and emotion. As he left the room she said, "Oh yeah, Peter, a little boy has been here all day waiting for you. He said his name is Nathaniel." she paused looking down at her feet. "And thanks. You're really sweet."

CHAPTER SIX

He stood at the door smiling down at the pretty young girl sitting on the bed. Her clear blue eyes seemed so beautiful to him that he had to force himself to continue on out the door, "Nathaniel, huh. I don't know anyone by that name. Wonder what this kid wants" he thought to himself as he made routine rounds through the clinic greeting weary, worn volunteers as he encountered them. The clinic was not very busy, but it obviously had been. As he looked into room after room, he saw signs that they had seen many patients over the past few days. Some of the rooms hadn't been cleaned up from use and others had cupboards wide open revealing the desperate depletion in supplies. Peter figured he'd best help by cleaning the rooms that the exhausted staff had not gotten to yet. Better start down the hall he thought. Off at the other end of the clinic he heard a baby crying and he remembered Jenny's story. Knowing that such a situation would be far too much for him to handle, he turned to walk toward the other end of the building. As he did, he nearly knocked a small boy off his feet.

"What're you doing, kid! You could get hurt around here standing in the middle of the hallway." He bent down and took the little boy by the arms and stared into his dirty little face. The little eyes stared back at him so frightened and helpless it made Peter's heart melt.

"What is it that you need little guy. How can I help you?"

"Are you Peter Alton?" a precocious little voice squeaked out.

"Why yes, I am. . . and you must be Nathaniel. I understand you've been looking for me." The little boy nodded. "What can I do for you?"

"My papa wantza see you. Follow me." The little man spoke as he turned and waved to Peter to follow. Before Peter could say a word, the little guy had disappeared through the front door.

Peter chuckled to himself and sprinted after the boy, half expecting to lose him. As he stepped outside he barely caught sight of Nathaniel disappearing through an old, broken-down, wooden fence. He arrived there just in time to catch a glimpse of him darting down an alley. The next fifteen minutes were spent in exactly this fashion. Peter getting to where he last saw the boy only to catch brief sight of him as he vanished again. On the verge of giving up the chase, Peter finally came upon the boy standing coolly on the steps of an old brownstone as if he had just finished a leisurely Saturday afternoon stroll through the park. The boy grinned up at Peter and simply pointed toward the door.

"Your Papa?" he said out of breath. The boy nodded. "Well, just let me catch my breath." the boy's smile became an angry scowl as he continued to point up at the door.

"Okay, okay. I'm goin. . ." he chuckled collecting himself. Peter stepped up to the door and turned a rusty old knob which rang a bell inside the house. He waited for a moment and just as he was about to ring a second time, he heard the peephole on the old door slide open. The eyes that peered at him through the rusting ironwork were followed by a voice. "Who is it please?" came the smooth voice of a woman behind the door.

"Uh, Peter Alton. This little boy here. . ."

"Yes" he was cut off. "We've been expecting you Mr. Alton." She slid the hole shut and opened the door.

"Please come in and sit down. Father will see you shortly." said a young dark haired woman with a short but polite air to her voice.

He was led into a surprisingly well-furnished living room. The room smelled of old leather and all of its walls were covered with bookshelves filled with old books of every size and shape. What an odd sight in the 21st century where books had long been relegated to museums and replaced by a wide variety of data storage and retrieval systems. The sight before him fascinated Peter. He found himself moving from shelf to shelf reading titles and authors. Why many of these were books he had read himself. How wonderful they looked in this form. So much more. . . personality.

" I see that you are an admirer of fine books, my dear young friend." Peter turned with a start to find he was in the presence of a very distinguished looking man in his middle ages. He wore a satin smoking jacket with a high collar, which came up to his white bearded face. A pipe protruded from his lips and filled the room with its sweet odor, adding to the wonderful atmosphere already there. Not knowing exactly what to say Peter just stood there until the man spoke again. "You're Peter Alton?"

"Yes, sir," Peter spoke timidly.

"Thank you very much for coming. I am Dr. Frederick Noah. You and I have many things to talk about. Please, follow me."

Peter hardly had time to react as the professorly figure disappeared through a hallway. He followed with a jerk, just arriving in the passage in time to see the old man sink through a doorway and down some basement stairs. He waited at the bottom for Peter to catch up.

"Somehow I get the feeling that you and Nathaniel are related." Peter chirped as he stumbled down the stairs.

"What's that?" Dr. Noah asked as he motioned Peter to follow him further.

"Nothing. . . uh nothing" an explanation would be too hard so Peter decided to shift full attention at his destination. This whole situation had him thrown for a loop and Peter was beginning to feel a little anxious. Did these people know that he was the son of James Alton. . ..probably not a cherished figure in lower Manhattan. A bead of sweat formed on his brow as he followed the Dr. down the hallway, quickly revealing itself to be too long for one house.

The Doctor reached what seemed to be the end of the passage, he looked back over his shoulder. An old bare light switch hung above him and before the young man knew it Dr. Noah had stretched a hand up to pull it. Peter gave a start as the wall to his left began to shift. In a brief moment he and the Dr. stepped into a large room lit dimly around the edges giving it an eerie ambiance. Three men looked up coldly from a large illuminated table at the center of the room spread with what looked like maps of some sort. Peter caught a glimpse of the pretty dark haired girl, standing just in the shadows. She stood silently, arms folded, steely stare focused upon Peter.

"Gentlemen, and lady, this is Peter Alton." Dr. Noah said to the group in the room who continued to gaze at Peter with not so much as a change in expression. "Peter, sit down for a moment, make yourself comfortable." He pointed to a worn couch at one end of the dim room. Peter nodded uncomfortably and timidly moved to the sofa. As he sat he noticed oldish looking maps filling the walls around his end of the room.

Dr Noah and the others conferred in whispers, occasionally glancing in his direction. A hard looking, soldierly-type seemed openly agitated at Peter's presence. Peter wondered if it was a mistake to wander out into the slums this far. He chided himself at how uncomfortable he was feeling.

Just as things seemed to be reaching a boil in the conversation the dark eyed beauty placed a calming hand on the general's shoulder, which seemed to subdue him considerably. She leaned in to the group, whispering something, causing the whole group to look in Peter's direction.

With a nod, obviously collecting himself, the tough looking character walked briskly toward Peter. Reaching out a hand to him he declared. "Welcome Mr. Alton. My name is Brice Fulton.

Before we share with you I hope you don't mind a few questions." He and the others pulled up chairs.

"How do you do" replied the nervous Peter, half standing. "Questions. . . yeah, I guess I don't mind. Only I don't honestly know of anything that I would know that would be of interest to you." He sat again but stayed on the edge of his seat as if ready to make a hasty exit if need be.

"Mr. Alton, you've been volunteering at the clinic for some time now?" asked a shy looking gentlemen.

"Yes". Peter replied

"Why, may I ask, would the son of James Alton, of Altrex, be spending his time here. . . in lower Manhattan? What are you trying to find out?" queried Fulton.

Peter was stunned that his motives would be questioned. "Hey Mr. . . I just happen to care about those people. And my father has nothing to do with what I do or don't do."

"Forgive us Peter," added the kindly, soft-spoken Dr. "You must admit that it is strange to find one such as you. . . here. If our questioning seems a bit harsh. . . please bear with it, you'll know soon enough why we must know."

With this the three men began a systematic process of questioning Peter, more like a gentle interrogation, which went on for some half hour. Then as suddenly as it started, the query ended. The group of men merely looked at one another, nodded and moved off to the other side of the room leaving Peter and the dark eyed girl.

"Peter, I'm Rachel. . . Dr. Noah's daughter. I'm really sorry that our welcome has been so cold. . . You must know that we've got to be very careful." He noticed that the look in her eye had softened considerably, which set him more at ease. Just then chairs squawking away from the center table told Peter that the foursome had finished another private conversation. Fulton stood, and with a dead seriousness in his eyes, beckoned Peter to come to join them at the table. Somehow Peter sensed that what he was about to hear would be of monumental proportions. His gut feeling was correct.

CHAPTER SEVEN

As Zack and B. J. Dean streaked along toward the NSP headquarters and the ensuing press conference, Zack let his questions about what he'd just witnessed rest. Riding in B.J.'s new DXR was a real experience. The latest in automobile technology, it was incredible. A product of space engineering, the car actually hovered using the same basic principle as would occur when one tries to put two magnets of the same polarity together. The technology was discovered by accident when scientists were dealing with trying to create artificial gravity in space vehicles. When Mercurite began to be experimented with, it was found that the substance contained tremendous magnetic power. It was a short step to paving roads with the substance and developing cars, which worked on an electromagnetic system. When the car is turned on, the powerful electromagnet created the same polarity as the paved road, thus forcing the vehicle upward. After its development three years earlier, the car manufacturers immediately began to standardize it in all vehicles. B.J.'s car was one of the premier models, and what a beauty! It had a sleek aerodynamically designed body, and it contained literally every new feature known to the industry. The excitement came, though, when the ride began. Gliding along three feet above the expressway in total silence, the experience was incredible. It was projected that within two years the solar powered ground models would be rendered obsolete.

A flood of ideas for his report flowed into Zack's mind as they sailed along nearing the National Security Police Headquarters. He gazed at the city below them in awe. What a beautiful place, so clean, so filled with the comforts of 21st century technology. Any doubts he might have had about the events he'd witnessed that morning had been totally quelled. He had always had faith in the NSP, and he trusted that their actions were justified.

It wasn't long before Zack realized they were pulling into the large parking complex of the NSP building. A guard in the familiar blue and white uniform greeted them, and after the customary wrist scan, the car was admitted. "There!" Zack thought. "Another incredible bit of 21st century technology." He'd totally overlooked small wrist implants that made life so safe and easy. It was one of those things that one gets so used to that it becomes second nature. The guard had simply touched each of their arms with a tiny probe. The implanted chips gave him all of the information that he needed to clear them for entry to the facility.

As B.J. parked, Zack dictated a few notes onto his pocket word processor. "The year 2003 brought many great advances in technology but none that equaled the importance of the Wrist Implanted Identification Chip, commonly known as WIIC. This incredible invention had changed the lives of literally every man, woman and child in the world. The little chip, implanted now in the wrist of babies as they are born serves many functions. It allows medical personnel to have a total readout on all bodily functions just by scanning the wrist. All personal financial transactions were simplified by the simple system of crediting and deducting from one's account, again by scanning the wrist. This replaced the antiquated system of credit cards, checks, and currency. It also provided a fail-safe method of identification."

Zack's concentration was interrupted by the sight of the magnificent NSP Headquarters building. Emerging from the parking garage into a glass tunnel it loomed before them. State of the art was the rule as this gigantus was erected. Covering a whole city block this 100 story multi-towered skyscraper looked more like a modern cathedral than a police headquarters. The sight of this majestic monstrosity filled Zack and B.J. with awe.

As the parking garage was situated across the street the pair found themselves gliding through the transparent tunnel on a moving sidewalk three stories above the busy road below. Included on their stationary journey were numerous unmanned security scan stations indicated by various signs warning the unwary of the consequences of bringing concealed weapons into the building, and an occasional beep or lazar scan.

"Makes ya feel as though you're on "Star Journey Theater" doesn't it" B.J. said somewhat nervously, obviously overwhelmed at the technology evident before them.

"As I understand it, you ain't seen nothin yet" chuckled Zack.

The duo entered the bowels of the huge NSP headquarters and was immediately greeted by the voice of a beautiful sounding young woman.

"Good afternoon Mr. Murphy, Mr. Dean. You're here for the press conference." spoke the voluptuous voice.

"Yes we are" replied Zack in an unattached tone.

"Very well Zack, please take transport three. Bye." replied the voice in a seductive timbre.

As they continued across the ramp presently Zack felt a small tug on his shirt. He realized that B.J. was trying to subtly get his attention. "Psst, Zack. . ."

"What is it B.J.?"

"Do you know that chick? She sounded pretty chummy." B.J. said, red faced.

"Well. . . you might say we're acquainted" Zack chuckled.

"Hey bud. . . what about getting me a date? That lady sounded like hot stuff!" he had a look of hopeful desperation in his eyes which quickly turned to anger as he realized the reporter was laughing at him. "Hey, what's with you! So keep her to yourself!" This caused Zack to laugh even harder.

B.J. slowly realized something wasn't what it seemed.

"B.J. Dean. . . let me introduce you to Miss Mable Microchip!" Zack laughed "Computer simulations are incredible, aren't they!" he was nearly rolling by this time.

Showing his basically good-natured self, B.J. quickly traded his scowl for broadening smile. "Oh man!" he pushed Zack as the comedy of the situation overtook him. The two slid into in a brief uproar of laughter, which was broken momentarily by the sweet voice.

"Gentlemen, please step into the chamber on your right. Zack, Bentley, have a good time!"

"Bentley!" laughed Zack "She loves you! And I didn't know your name was Bentley . . . They say people get far more formal at the beginning of a true romance!"

"Alright, you got me!" chortled B.J. "And hey, not a word to anyone about my uh. . . real name!"

Silent doors closed around them and both had the sensation of a gentle forward motion. As each stood, awaiting a short elevator type ride, a burst of light flooded the space they occupied revealing it to be a tiny craft of sorts, attached to who knows what, who knows how. Before them exploded a spectacular sight. The NSP headquarters was actually a gigantic mall-type structure, huge in expanse, a little city unto itself, with a myriad of blinking lights and activity.

"Wow! Gotta get this on tape." B.J. fumbled for his equipment and began shooting footage of their incredible flight. All too soon though, the trip was over and the two momentarily found themselves again in a darkish chamber until silent doors opened into a long curving hallway.

"Down the hall and to your right, gentlemen" came a familiar voice.

"Thanks sweetheart!" chuckled B.J. poking Zack in the ribs.

The two padded silently down the hall until they came to a door which, sensing their presence, swooshed open. Zack entered first and as B.J. began to pass through the door the voice returned.

"Have fun, sweetie!" B.J. tripped in the door backwards choking.

"What's the matter Beej!" Zack asked as he half caught his cameraman.

"You wouldn't believe me if I told you, bud!"

The pair found themselves in an expansive, plush auditorium, filled with what they took to be members of the press. They found a couple of seats toward the rear of the room just in time for the meeting to begin.

A uniformed officer approached the podium to greet the audience.

"Good afternoon ladies and gentlemen, thank you for attending our press conference." came the cold, nearly monotone voice. "I'd like to give you a report on an incident which occurred earlier this morning. At approximately nine a.m. this morning it was reported to agents of the NSP that an employee of the Altrex Corporation was attempting some technological espionage. The suspect was a known felon with numerous offenses on his record."

Remembering the small, frail, scholarly man he'd seen that morning somehow Zack had a hard time seeing him as some hardened criminal. "But, who knows", he thought.

"I am pleased to announce that a unit of patrolling NSP officers were able to locate and apprehend the individual in a fairly short period of time. Unfortunately he was killed in an armed struggle with our agents. His name will be withheld pending notification of next of kin. Now, if there are questions, I will be pleased to answer what I can." The officer's cold stare moved across the room.

Zack looked around absently waiting for the first question when out of the corner of his eye he noticed someone very familiar. Across the room, with his hand raised intently, sat the tall thin reporter he'd seen that morning. Zack was intrigued by what he might ask.

Finally recognized from the podium the man stood resolutely.

"Lieutenant. . . what do you know of the Utopia Project?"

A brief flurry of confusion behind the podium told Zack that the thin man had hit on something. Momentarily a tall, dignified man came to the podium. He calmly cleared his throat and spoke in a very controlled tone.

"Mr. uh. . . Wallace. I am captain Smithlin of the NSP. After careful consultation I'm afraid that none of us know anything about any such project . . . Further, ladies and gentlemen, we'd ask that you keep your questions pertinent to this case." He stared at Wallace who, after an intense moment, slowly and sullenly took his seat.

Questions again began to rise in Zack's curious mind and he determined to get to Wallace after the conference for a few answers. In the meantime he needed to use the restroom so he asked B.J. to catch the rest on camera. He'd be back in a jiff.

Out in the hallway Zack pondered on which direction to turn in search of a men's room. "Restroom. . . restroom," he mumbled to himself when that familiar voice again chimed.

"Take a right down the hall and you'll find our facilities on the left."

"Thanks," Zack spoke to the bodiless voice. He padded down the hall a few steps before pausing.

"You. . . a. . . won't be. . . uh. . . with me in there. . . will you?" he blushed.

"Oh no sir. . ." was the chuckled reply.

Zack could have sworn that this computerized pixie was laughing at him on some main frame somewhere in the building.

Moments later he was exiting the most amazingly modern bathroom he'd ever experienced. He wondered just how to delicately bring it all into his report. Then a commotion down the hall caught his eye. He looked up just in time to see a couple of police officers wrestle someone into a room. Too far to see much else. But, he thought, this is police headquarters . . .

He returned to the large room just as the conference was ending.

"Did ya get it all?" He whispered to B.J.

"Yeah, not very exciting stuff though." he said, shutting down his camera. Zack again let his vision sweep across the room. Something seemed missing. What was it? And then, just as the final words were being spoken to release the reporters he realized. Where was the thin man? Where was Wallace? His chair was conspicuously empty. What was going on? And then Zack remembered the incident in the hallway . . .

CHAPTER EIGHT

Forty minutes later Zack was in the newsroom ambling toward his office deep in thought.

"It doesn't make sense" he thought. "It doesn't add up. . . at all." Halfway into his office he was shaken out of his thoughts by a familiar bark.

"Kid! Hey kid, in here." Sam was beckoning him into his dingy office. Expecting a good chewing out Zack complied, feeling like a ten year old again.

"Yeah boss?" he said a little overconfidently.

"4th and Selmer. . . what'd you see there?" Sam groused.

"What do you mean?. . . I uh. . ." Zack gave in to the inevitable. "Alright. . . I did go there."

"Now listen here Zack, when I give you an order. . ."

"Wait a second before you ream me out Sam. . . there's something fishy going on. It was good that I was there. . ." Zack explained.

"What're you talking about!" the old editor wiped his brow, obviously steamed. "I told you the NSP didn't want anyone near the there and what did you do? You rush over there. I tell you

Zack, there's just enough of your dad in you to get you well in trouble!"

"Sam, please. Listen to me. . . I'm sorry about goin over there. But there's something not right with this situation. You gotta help me figure it out." Zack pleaded.

Sam sat on the edge of his desk, arms folded, still fuming but willing to listen. "Okay, settle down. . . tell me what great mystery you've uncovered. But make it quick. . . we've got work to do." The balding old newsman knew he couldn't stay mad at Zack long so he played it for all it was worth.

Zack recounted the whole story, from his arrival at 4th and Selmer to the odd disappearance of Wallace the thin man. Knowing Sam, he figured the old guy would begin to grab hold any moment. . . but instead he just sat there, staring at nothing in the direction of the floor. The only time Sam flinched at all was when Zack mentioned the Utopia Project. He seemed to flush a bit but quickly regained his surly posture.

"Look kid, it sounds to me like there are probably great and very simple explanations to everything. You don't know Wallace, you don't know that he was the man being hustled into the room, you don't know "if" there truly is any such thing as the "Utopia whatever". Zack. . . you've got much more important things to take care of. I trusted you, above the rest of the staff, to do a great job on 2030. If you go chasing around flimsy little stories like this you're not gonna meet the deadline . . . And furthermore you'll be of no use to this line of work if you loose your license because of run-ins with the police. Now, take my advice, take the weekend off, get away, and go visit your grandparents in the country. Just be ready on Monday to get your rear in gear on your story!"

Zack knew the old guy well enough to sense when the last word was spoken. It had been. Somehow he'd try to lay his questions to rest. Still, something wasn't right. . . even in his editor's response.

There are times in everyone's life that stress creeps up and takes hold of him or her. Zack realized that part of his obsession over these unanswered questions stemmed from a growing tightness in his gut and tension in his neck.

"Maybe a trip to the country would be good about now." He thought.

"Sorry Sam. . . I guess I just get wrapped up in things. I will take your advice. I haven't been out to see the folks in a while."

He got up sheepishly and moved toward the door. "See ya Monday."

"See ya, kid," Sam said, softening a bit. "Get some rest. . . and say hi to the old man for me." He patted his adopted son on the back kindly meeting him at the door.

CHAPTER NINE

The hot afternoon was slowly meandering toward a golden sunset as the stooped old man finally wiped the beads of sweat from his furrowed, brown brow and laid down the rusty old hoe. Viewing his day's progress in the small garden with some amount of pride he slowly turned and made his way to the lumbering old farmhouse that he and his wife had called home for so many years. The old man's wrinkled face showed his years as did the old barn with its peeling paint and broken boards. His back ached from the long hours in the garden but a smile rearranged the creases on his face as he felt the joy that hard work brought to him.

Richard Murphy was Zack's 76-year-old grandfather. His six-foot, stocky frame had long since given way to the effects of old age leaving him thin and stooped of back; but though he was lean of body the old man was still filled with the spunk of a teenager. He and Zack's grandmother Sarah lived on a small plot of land sixty miles west of New York City on what once was a huge farm. The three acres that remained served the couple well in their retirement years. They moved there at Zack's father's insistence some twenty years earlier after "Granddad", as Zack called him, had retired from 30 years as a public school teacher on the west coast. Their life was simple but full of gardening, books, arguments, and grandchildren, especially Zack.

Sarah was a tall woman with a firmness about her that kept Granddad in line, but with the wisdom to keep him feeling like he was the king of the house. Her deep blue eyes sparked when she talked, revealing the deeply loving nature she possessed. On the surface one would think that the two disliked each other the way they bantered back and forth so with words. At further examination though, one sensed the deep love that they had for one another. They'd seldom been apart in forty-four years of marriage and the moment they had to be separate even for a few hours they seemed like lost souls.

"Mr. Murphy!" came Sarah's voice from the back porch. "You come in and rest, you're too old to be out in that sun so long. What do you plan on doing, killing yourself!?" She stood like a general on the porch, hands on hips with furrowed brow.

"Old?!. . . Old?" he looked up with a mischievous grin. "I'll show you old!" With that he dropped his hoe and loped toward the house with surprising agility. "I'm comin to get you little girl," he growled in a playfully monstrous voice.

"Rich, now don't you hurt yourself," the old woman said as she backed toward the house girlishly. "Get away you old fiend!!" She giggled as she fumbled for the door all the while seeing the old man getting closer. The knob turned finally but too late. He was upon her tickling her wildly until she was no more than a giggling blob in his strong, loving arms. Time stood still as the two, locked in embrace, looked for a moment silently into each other's eyes. Forty-four years seemed only a short time as each remembered and relived precious moments of the past. He saw before him the same sweet determined young nurse that he'd met so long ago. He remembered their first meeting over an allergy shot in the backside. How she'd impressed him with her firm gentleness while she poked him with the huge needle. Somehow he believed her when she said that it wouldn't hurt much, even after it did! This woman had filled out his life so much through the years. How lucky he felt.

She remembered the idealistic young man that she'd married so full of dreams and plans. His life was filled with kids and music when they'd met and she remembered feeling lucky to find a place there for her also. A place she did find though, right above his students and below his God. The arrangement was more than satisfactory though the years, for their choice to place God first in each of their lives, though extremely unpopular in the age of the corporation, had cemented them together better than the strongest glue.

Silent minutes passed, filled with a warm, loving glow and each slowly moved toward the other kissing as one might think only young lovers might do.

The magic of the moment was shattered as each sensed the presence of someone staring at them. Then a voice.

"Excuse me Gramps, Gram. I don't mean to interrupt" smiled Zack through the back door.

Looking up the pair cried with glee. "Zack!" Their total lack of embarrassment didn't surprise Zack in the least as they had always been very affectionate, passing the trait downward to children and grandchildren.

"Good to see you son!" exclaimed Granddad shaking Zack's hand heartily.

"Oh Zack, you look just wonderful", came Grams voice as she buried him in a big, loving hug. "How are you dear?"

"Just fine Gram. You two look great as usual. I thought folks your age were supposed to start looking old." Zack teased as he walked, an arm around each into the house.

Smiling broadly Gramps spoke up, "Now see Sarah, what'd I tell you about that gettin old business. Son, I must tell you that your grandma is gettin pretty feeble. . . don't know what she'd do without me around. Poor, tired old woman."

With that Grams gave her husband a swat on the backside with the oven mitten she'd picked up. "And I suppose you'd like to fix dinner for this poor, tired old woman?"

"No, that's quite alright, old gal. You go right on ahead." joking to Zack. "Keeps the old woman busy! Me and the boy'll be in the living room." He put his arm around his grandson and the two scooted toward the living room just avoiding a snap of Gram's dishtowel.

The kindly old woman called after the two escapees, "Zack, I hope you don't mind. These are real vegetables. We don't use Rhetta foods very often. Your grandpa just doesn't like them." she said, wiping her hands on a towel.

"No problem Gram. Why don't you like Rhetta foods, Gramps? Don't tell me you can tell the difference!" Zack said as he continued into the living room with his grandfather. They each sat down in big overstuffed chairs facing each other at one end of the room. Between the chairs was a large picture window, revealing a view of the whole valley below the small farm. The panorama was spectacular. Green, rolling hills dotted with trees surrounding small houses off in the distance. Scenes like this were hard to find in the year 2030.

Zack sat and looked out the window thoughtfully for a moment. "Gramps, I'm curious why you avoid Rhetta foods."

"They just don't seem natural, Zack. Never have liked em. Plus, I don't really know too much about the stuff. Never took the time I suppose," the gray haired old man spoke, looking out the window also.

"I've done some research on Rhetta foods for the story I'm doing, Gramps. Would you like me to read some of it to you?" Zack asked reaching for a small pad in his shirt pocket.

"I suppose so son, but I'm sure you didn't come out here to lecture me on the wonders of fake food!" Gramps chuckled.

"Okay, I get the picture. I'll make it short, and, just for the record. Rhetta food is much more healthy for you, so pay attention!" He flipped open his pad and searched through his notes for a second. "Here it is. Now let's see. Okay, "A dramatic new discovery in the last decade has forever changed the nutrition of the world. Dr. Charles A. Montague of the Nutritional Technologies Group announced on May 14, 2024 that he had discovered a new substance, which could literally replace every food source in existence.

"Rhetiplasmic Endorfolin, or Rhetta for short is actually a plant similar to the algae that grows in the ocean but which contains enormously high quantities of vitamins, minerals, protein, and other elements essential to humans. The amazing thing about Rhetta though is its incredibly nutritional match to the human body. Six years of research after its discovery has proved it to be a nearly perfect food for human beings.

"The problem remained though; how to make it desirable for human consumption. Almost immediately the solution arose through the work of the Hosaka Research Company. They found that the molecular structure of Rhetta could be altered through bombardment by Scitic particle waves. With varying amounts of bombardment literally any texture, consistency, and color could be achieved. One only need add artificial flavors and aromas, which also had reached a high level of development, to replicate any food known to man. When computer optics were used even the most minute differences could be achieved with total accuracy. A breathtaking example was demonstrated as a whole, cooked turkey, with stuffing was replicated, down to the bones (which were edible too). Now the family could stuff itself on Thanksgiving without the worry of too much fat, cholesterol, or any other undesirable food by-product."

Zack looked up from his notes surprised to see that his grandfather actually seemed engrossed in what he was saying. Encouraged, he continued.

"This spectacular breakthrough meant an end to world hunger and a drastic improvement in the nutrition of the whole world. A gigantic new problem arose though, threatening the world economy. Rhetta production meant an end to traditional farming procedures and a total annihilation of the system as it stood. Facing this challenge head on the World Council of Corporations came up with a solution, which would be a big first step in drastically altering the free enterprise system. Corporations all over the world began buying up struggling farms and ranches, converting them to Rhetta farms and hiring the original owners to run them. They trained the farmers in Rhetta production and processing. Tapping into the farmer's knowledge of the products that they once raised or produced, they used that knowledge to perfect the processing goods until one could scarcely ever tell the difference between Rhetta foods and their predecessors.

"What we have here in the 21st century is a nearly perfect food source which can be made to order to suit even the most discriminating of palate." Half expecting his grandfather to be dozing by then Zack glanced up at the old man. He seemed to be deep in thought, looking again out the large picture window.

"Well, what'd you think?" Zack queried.

Gramps looked at him through softened eyes as though close to emotion. "Very well done son. It all sounds really good. I don't know why it's difficult for me to accept these new things. I don't know why."

"It's hard for anyone to accept change, Gramps. Especially if you've had so many good years behind you as you have. You really should eat more Rhetta though. Lot's more healthy for ya." Zack said with concern in his voice.

"I know Zack, I guess the hard part for me is that it doesn't seem right. The Lord put food on the earth for us and here we go changin it all around. It just doesn't seem right." His voice trailed off as he looked out the window. "Hey, what're we doin jabberin on about this stuff for anyway! Shoot, we haven't seen you for a month of Sundays. Whatcha been up to lately?" he said reaching out and patting his grandson lovingly on the knee.

Zack mused to himself, "What do ya think I've just been talking about!" But he said "Oh, I've been real busy writing this story for the station on the wonders of the 21st century."

"Oh, I know, you just came out here to interview me, cause I know so much about it. I understand. Well what d'ya want to know?" Gramps chuckled.

"No Gramps! You're the original 20th century man!" Zack smiled. "None of this new fangled technology for you!. . .. No Gramps, I'm here purely on a social visit. I got to missing you two. It has been a long time since I was here, and even longer since YOU came to New York! In fact last time you came was our trip up to the space station nearly six months ago." Zack chided his grandfather.

Gramps leaned in "That trip did it for me. You can keep New York, and that space station for that matter. I just don't like big cities. Guess I'm gettin a bit claustrophobic in my old age."

The two were interrupted by Grams, "You two ready for dinner? come on in here while it's hot."

Soon the trio sat around the old kitchen table laughing and eating, reliving old memories and at times just sitting quietly enjoying one another's company.

As they finished dinner Grams looked thoughtfully toward her grandson. "Zack."Her words seemed to come hard as she cleared her throat, glancing tentatively up at her husband. "Zack, what do you know about the retirement colonies?" Gramps looked hard at her as she spoke.

"Now, Sarah, don't be wasting the boy's time with foolish questions such as that. I told you once and for all that I'm not going to any retirement colony. I like it here."

"I can't say that I'm an expert on the subject but I'll tell you what I can. Let's see. As I recall they were founded in the early years of the century by the WCC to relieve the plight of retired people in the world. Just where they are is top-secret information. That's to keep people from breaking their strict quarantine regulation. You see, each person who goes to the colonies goes through a sterilization process to rid the body of any harmful bacteria or viruses. The only problem is that this leaves the body very defenseless against disease, so the price for a long, healthy life is strict quarantine. I heard though that the colonies are wonderful places. People have every luxury that one could ask for. They've even come up with a new process, which slows the aging cycle down immensely so that people live longer. The isolation from families and friends is bridged by the use of the holophone, so it's not all that bad. A buddy of mine talks to his parents every day."

"Zack. . . should we consider the colonies?" asked Gram hesitantly.

Zack became thoughtful for a moment. He never really thought of his grandparents going away. But, he knew that he'd much rather see them live long, happy lives, than not. "I have mixed feelings Gram, but if I was to have to choose the best for you I'd have to recommend. . . going."

"Thanks for the advice son, hope you don't mind if we don't take it." Gramps got up from his chair and left the room.

"He feels pretty strongly, doesn't he, Grams." Zack asked sheepishly.

"Yes, but don't worry. He'll come around. When he realizes that we'd just become burdens on you or some other relative. . . he'll see. Anyway, let's go join him in the other room and talk about something else." The two walked arm in arm toward the living room and the old man they both loved.

CHAPTER TEN

Five minutes from his grandparents house Zack found himself gliding down an expressway that would take him directly into the heart of the city. Hardly noticing the time, he'd been deep in thought from the moment he left their house. A smile crossed his face as he relived the warm hours he'd spent with the dear couple. He didn't even mind their usual talk about religion. It was a part of who they were, even if it did keep them from enjoying much of the very wonders he would tell about in his story. He knew that if they changed he'd be more than a little disappointed.

The thought of his grandparent's Christianity brought to his mind the section on religion in the 21st century that he'd begun some days before. He decided that now would be as good a time as any to work on it while the topic was fresh in his mind. Looking for the nearest vehicle monitoring station he pressed the button on his dashboard marked "M.O.", for "Monitored Operation", and was immediately greeted by a voice. Good evening Mr. Murphy. Will you be traveling all the way into the city tonight?"

"Yes", replied Zack. "I'll be getting off at the 47th street runoff and meeting some people at Barney's Place."

"May I suggest the 40th street exit instead? 47th street has been slightly congested this evening and you should find much less traffic on the new suggested route," spoke the smooth, computerized voice.

"Fine, may I plug in now?" Zack replied.

"Yes sir, if you will move to the far right lane I will engage guidance. I will signal you five miles prior to your destination, which will give you approximately three minutes to resume control of your vehicle. If you do not resume control I will pull you into our 65th street station until you choose to do so."

"Thank you very much." He spoke to the voice as he pulled the car into the right lane.

Moments later Zack had his word processor out, working on "Religion in the 21st century." As he typed away on his antique word processor he thought of the many times he'd been ribbed by his fellow reporters for using his father's ancient machine. He'd kept the old thing, and actually preferred it over his new, voice activated equipment. He guessed it was for sentimental reasons also. . . he missed his dad.

Settling back in the comfortable seat Zack began to organize his thoughts on "Religion in the 21st Century". As the machine before him began to display his notes on its screen Zack thought back to his interview with Alistair Blakely, the minister of human affairs for the WCC. He remembered the cool, calmness that possessed the white-haired, smiling clergyman.

"Religion in the 21st century has finally come of age" spoke the dignified old gentleman. "Finally religion has caught up with the development of man, breaking free of the old, primitive superstitions of the past. Up until the last twenty years ancient religions were the greatest factor in the separation of mankind, bringing on tremendous social problems and plunging us headlong toward world destruction. Old myths such as the legend of Jesus Christ did little more than keep people from truly achieving true peace and harmony with fellow human beings. Eastern religions kept people hopelessly steeped in superstition, which did little more than chain them to artificial social stratas. It's amazing to think that people could have been so gullible to have been blindly led for thousands of years by such disorganized travesties in the name of God. The bloody wars of Israel in claiming the land it finally settled in, the barbaric spread of Islam and, in response, the Crusades. More recently were great exterminations of Indians and others in the guise of spreading Christianity in North and South America, as well as the war in Ireland between the Catholics and Protestants. No other issue has brought so much bloodshed and violence and yet, isn't it odd, religion should bring peace and harmony to mankind.

"The World Council of Corporations has, oddly enough, brought about the possibility for true religion to be spread throughout the world. An organization devoted solely to peace, peace with the world, with each other, and an inner tranquility. . . peace of heart and mind."

"Mr. Murphy. Mr. Murphy." It took several repetitions of his name for Zack to snap out of the trance he was in as he wrote. He realized that the Monitored operation tower was signaling him.

"Yes. . ." he replied haltingly.

"We are now approaching the 40th street runoff. Would you care to reengage?"

"Yes. . . yes of course . . . Just give me a second to get situated," he said, fumbling to ready himself to take the wheel.

"There. . .disengage anytime." His car made a slight dip as the tower disconnected control. Zack could see the lights of the city before him like a huge Christmas tree . . . "Beautiful night" he thought as he neared his exit.

Turning off at 40th street he made his way in the general direction of Barney's, a local hangout frequented by upwardly mobile young professionals from all over the area. The atmosphere was great, the food exceptional, and just occasionally one would meet. . . someone special. That hope always lingered in the back of Zack's mind. He really wasn't much of a ladies man. He tended to be shy, and pretty picky.

Tonight he was meeting a couple of friends, Pat Erwert and Stu Smith, old buddies from high school, the only friends he'd stayed close to. He looked forward to an evening of relaxation sharing glory stories from their youth, as they always seemed to do. Seldom did the trio discuss their current lives and situations even though all three had very successful careers. Pat was a world traveler and had made his modest fortune in investments while Stu took over his dad's distributorship in town and was very comfortably situated.

Within a few moments Zack found himself gliding into a parking garage near Barney's. He leisurely strolled the couple of blocks to their hangout enjoying the warm evening. The soft glow of multi-hued fluorescent lights tinged the street in front of Barney's and told Zack he was at his destination. As usual the place was packed and it took some time for Zack to locate his friends.

"Zack!" exclaimed Pat as his lifelong friend arrived at the table, slapping him on the back. "You're late, as usual man . . . We've just been debating the condition of this years "Jets", and Stu is showing his ignorance as usual!" he beckoned across the table to a distracted Stu. "Oh, hey man. . . good to see ya Zack." The three began to chatter immediately about the state of their favorite football team, which, as usual, led them to reliving their own glorious football careers in high school. All the while they buzzed Stu kept looking over his shoulder every little bit.

"What's so interesting bud", Pat teased, punching Stu in the arm.

"Ya guys see, way over there across the room?" Stu said, pointing just enough for his partners to get a bead. "There. . . are some classy looking ladies."

Zack smelled a rat with a capital "R". These guys were always trying to fix him up with someone or another.

"Yeah. . . didn't I see you with the tall blonde last week." he punched Stu's other arm. "You guys don't need to fix me up! I'll meet someone. . . in my own time."

"And. . . in the mean-time we'll all be old and gray!" chided Pat. "Come on Zack. Me and Stu went to a lot of trouble to find a girl just to your taste. Look. The one on the left."

Zack could see that a similar conversation was taking place at the other table. A tall, ravishing blonde woman and an equally attractive redhead seemed to be urging their friend to acknowledge the three guys. The girl obviously wanted nothing to do with the situation and just stubbornly sat, her back to Zack and his friends. All Zack could see from the back was short, dark hair.

"Guys, look. . . she's gettin pigeonholed into this also. Look at her, she's less interested than I am." He could tell his words were falling on deaf ears.

"Zack, just meet the girl. You'll like her!" Stu urged.

It was inevitable. Zack knew these two well enough to know that he'd just as soon give in now. They'd never quit.

"Alright! But it'll be your fault if I end up in ten years with six kids, a beer belly, and a pear-shaped woman harping at me day and night!"

"Man, when you put it that way. . ." Stu began playfully. They all looked at each other and burst out, "NAH!"

It took, what seemed to Zack, an eternity to get across the room. With every step he felt more uncomfortable. He could see his prospective friend turn slightly every few moments, roll her eyes in total embarrassment, and turn away covering her eyes and shaking her head.

"You guys are real friends," Zack said sarcastically just before they reached the three girls.

"Don't mention it pal. . . don't mention it!" Pat replied in an Eddie Haskell tone of voice. "Hello ladies. . ." he kissed the redhead's hand.

"Hi Pat, Stu," both she and the blonde replied.

"Uh. . . hi. . ." the third girl said, barely looking up at them.

"This is Zack Murphy. . . Sandy and Linda," Stu interjected. "You've probably seen him on the holovision."

"Yes we have. Nice to meet you Zack," spoke the beautiful blonde admiringly as she shook his hand. The redhead just smiled and nodded his direction, obviously anxious for moments with Stu.

"This is Andy Wilford, Zack." said Pat in a more gentlemanly tone. "Zack's been anxious to meet you, Andy." Zack stepped on Pat's toe hard.

"Nice to meet you Andy. . ." he said finally making eye contact with her.

He was surprised. Pleasantly surprised. She wasn't the typical blind date arranged by his so-called pals. He could tell instantly that this was a girl with class. For one thing. . . she didn't seem too impressed with him. That actually set him at ease. Andy Wilford had a simple beauty. . . not exotic or ravishing, like her friends. She had short, dark hair, which outlined a pretty, unmade-up face. Her eyes were deep and dark, with a sparkle that even showed itself in this uncomfortable situation.

"Hi," she said, looking up for just a moment and then concentrating on the rim of her drink.

Everyone else was seated by this time, leaving one chair, wedged in beside Andy. Zack uncomfortably climbed onto the chair, nearly tripping. Finally settled in, the two sat silently as Pat, Stu, and their dates chattered non-stop for the next twenty minutes, only occasionally acknowledging Zack and Andy's presence. From his perspective Zack could only see Andy out of the corner of his eye without actually turning to face her.

"Andy Wilford huh!" he thought. She looked like an Andy. She wasn't masculine at all, but on the other hand she had a different look than the two girls seated across from him. They were both beautiful, and very sexy, but their femininity came out in a way that almost demeaned them. Definitely not Zack's type. Andy was feminine. . . but in a strong kind of way. She had an intelligent look about her, and even from his sideways perspective, Zack could see that she had a deep, serious side. He found himself longing to have the opportunity to talk with her, alone, away from his idiotic buddies and their air headed dates.

As Pat began to recount his third or fourth high school football story Zack knew he had to do something. Sandra and Linda sat transfixed like a couple of cheerleaders at the big game while Andy tried hard to hide her fourth or fifth yawn.

Breaking in all at once Zack blurted out, "Oh man, I left my word processor on in the car. If I don't get out and turn it off the batteries with loose their charge and I'll loose the work I've been doing today. You want to come along?" he said to Andy, who looked up with a start. Zack noticed relief in her eyes as she said, "Yeah, sure. Uh, you guys don't mind do you. I could use some air anyway."

"Oooooh, Nooooo" the others teased. Both Zack and Andy knew what they were thinking, but, better than being tortured with another football fable they went along with it. Zack helped Andy with her chair, which surprised, and then rather flattered her. They made their way through the maze of tables and chattering bodies, finally reaching the door. A gentle, cooling, breeze blanketed them as they stepped into the sparkling night air.

Two steps out the door, they turned, looked seriously into each other's eyes, and then burst into fits of uproarious laughter lasting long moments, only interrupted by an occasional reference to the idiotic scene inside of Barneys.

Finally, exhausted, they plopped down on a bench and found themselves gazing upwards at the same twinkling, star-filled sky.

Long, silent moments passed as each drank in the beauty of the warm fall night.

"Wanna walk?" he said still looking up at the sky.

"Sure, I'd love too." Zack noticed a warmth to her voice.

As the pair casually strolled down the quaintly lit boulevard, specially designed by city planners for evenings such as this, the evening air seemed bright and sweet. They walked silently for some time in this simulated park setting, drinking in the magic atmosphere created by manicured grass, an occasional fountain, and tiny glittering lights in perfectly shaped trees.

"Andy. . . is that short for something?" asked Zack finally breaking the silence.

"Yes. . . Andrea. . . Andrea Wilhelmina Wilford, my dad calls me Andy" she smiled. "And what about you? Is Zack your only name?"

"No . . . I've got middle names. . ." he said, a little embarrassed.

"Names? You mean you have more than one?" She asked, trying to be as delicate as possible.

"Yes. . . I come from a very traditional clan. They feel that middle names connect family. So, having three uncles. . ."

"Three middle names. Ah hah." She waited. "Well?"

"Zachariah Jeremiah Joshua Joseph Murphy," he confessed with an embarrassed grin. "Quite a mouthful!"

"I like it. The names sound old fashioned. . . biblical," Andy showed her sincere interest.

"My ancestors were pretty. . . religious people. I guess I like the names too," he said, relieved that Andy appreciated that generally secret part of his life. "Tell me about yourself. What do you do?"

"I'm a free-lance photographer. With primarily old type film medium. I fell in love sometime in high school with the old two-dimensional black and white and color photography. There wasn't much of a market for it until the last five years or so. First couple years out of college it was more like a hobby. . . I nearly starved. And then almost overnight there was a renaissance of older photo styles and voila, I've had more work that I've known what to do with." Zack seemed sincerely interested so she continued.

"Well, during the lean years I got used to living with my folks . . ." she drew inward a bit. "Then, five years ago. . . my mom died."

"I'm sorry." Zack put a gentle hand on her shoulder.

"Oh, it's okay. I'm pretty much over it by now. But my dad!" she shook her head with a giggle. "He's the original absent-minded professor. In fact, he was a professor for years at Bradford College. He's like a big overgrown puppy. After mom died there was no way that I could have left him alone . . . So, I still live at home." She was prepared for the usual response to her statement. More than one guy had been turned off by her living situation. Actually that had been just fine with her because most of them were jerks anyway, but Zack. . . she hoped she wouldn't catch that familiar look in HIS eyes. He was different. She liked him.

Searching his face for some negative response Andy thought she saw a little shine in Zack's eyes.

"You must really love him," he said, not looking at her.

"Yes I do. . ." she replied incredulously. "What about you?" she pried. "What about your parents?" There was a long pause. Andy understood his reaction now. "I'm sorry, Zack. . . I. . ."

"No." he said with a slight tremor to his voice. "Don't be sorry. . . I don't mind. I just get a little touched when I hear about someone with such a loving relationship with their folks. It seems a rarity these days. Anyway, about my folks. . ." the long pause told Andy that this was a hard topic for Zack to talk about.

"I had a really great upbringing . . . My mom and I were really close, but my dad and I were clones. We loved the same thing as far back as I can remember, the same sports, the same hobbies, the same everything. He was a reporter in the early days of the WCC when holovision was new. I guess that's where I got my love for the news." he got thoughtfully quieter. "It was just like we could read each others minds."

"What happened?" Andy asked tenderly. There was a long silence.

"About fifteen years ago. . . I was sixteen at the time. I'd just made the varsity football team at school. . . quarterback, my dad's old position. I remember rushing home from school to tell my dad. I figured he'd go through the roof. But when I got home to tell him, he hardly responded to the news. I knew something was wrong. He was real troubled. He took me aside and told me that he and mom were going on an overseas assignment. They'd be back in a month or so. Something told me though, that they'd never come back. I remember clinging to them and crying like a baby as they left." he was clearly shaken and sniffed a bit, holding back tears.

"My Uncle Sam tells me that their plane when down over the Alps. No one ever found the wreckage. They just disappeared."

"Oh Zack." It was all she could do not to take him into her arms to comfort him. She found herself patting his muscular shoulder as one would comfort a child.

"Hey. . . I'm sorry. I don't ever talk about this. I didn't mean to bring you down," he said collecting himself and putting on a cheerful face.

"No. . . no, you didn't bring me down, not at all." Andy knew that this was going to be a special friendship. Zack Murphy. . . she'd never met a guy quite like him.

The two strolled on into the evening softly sharing as they walked, each totally engrossed in the other's words, and each secretly cherishing the other more and more.

A majestic harvest moon was sinking deep in the west when the pair realized just how long they'd been talking.

"Oh no!" Andy burst out, looking at her watch. "It's nearly 2:30 in the morning. We've gotta get back. Sandy's gonna be mad. She's gotta work at six!" The pair made a beeline for Barney's only to arrive, out of breath, to find the building long since locked up and dark.

"Oh great! Sandy's gonna have my head!" she said plopping down on the bench outside of the hangout.

"Ya know, Andy. . . I don't think any of our friends were at all disappointed when we didn't get back in time." he smiled down at his pretty new friend.

She looked up knowingly, "You know. . . you're probably right, only. . . what they must think! They've all got dirty minds!" they simultaneously began to giggle at the realization of what their "match-makers" were thinking right at that moment.

"I don't think we ought to tell them anything. . . keep em guessing." Zack laughed. "That'll teach em to assume anything about our virtue. . .."

Andy added "Or lack thereof!"

At that point in the evening everything seemed funny and the pair found themselves alternating between fits of laughter and giggling attempts to control themselves. Soon they were staggering from uncontrollable glee.

"Better. . . be. . . careful," Andy barely spit the words out. "We could end up. . . in the drunk tank!" At that she became weak at the knees and fell, a giggling mass into Zack's strong arms. Their laughter gently diminished leaving them looking softly into each other's eyes.

"This is incredible." Andy thought as they just stood there gently, ever so gently holding one another.

Zack studied her lovely face intently; every minute feature blending together to form the portrait of an angel. Her dark eyes seemed to unlock a hidden place in his heart. He wanted to kiss her. And yet, holding her sweetly and tenderly in his arms, he knew that a kiss would taint the moment. "No," he thought, "she's too. . . too. . . precious."

"Thanks Andy. . . thanks for the best evening I've had . . . in a long time."

"Thank you Zack" she replied tenderly.

After a moment each gently released the other from their tender embrace. "I'll drop you home," he said quietly.

"Sure. . . thanks."

As they fell into place side by side for the walk to Zack's car Andy slipped her hand into his. They walked along silently for some time savoring the precious moments left of their evening.

"Say, have you ever been into space?" Zack burst out all at once.

"What?" she asked with a puzzled expression.

"I've got to go up to Aurora Station in a couple of days to do some work on my story. I'd love it if you came along . . . that is, if you don't think it's too forward of me to ask. We would be there overnight. . . separate quarters, of course. I mean. . ." he began to fumble embarrassingly for the right words.

"Zack, I'd love to go."

CHAPTER ELEVEN

DR. NOAH

Peter listened intently to the men in the room under Dr. Noah's house. Brice Fulton, the military man spoke first. He'd been employed by the WCC as a security man, a lower level position at a rhetta plant in Buffalo. Years before that he'd been a Green Beret in the old defunct Army, fighting in the Middle East and in various conflicts in Europe. His specialty was intelligence and he was an extremely well trained observer. He noticed things . . .

For twenty years after the military had been dismantled he'd worked various places for the WCC, always in security and, frustratingly, never at a level that really challenged the skills he'd learned in the service. Finally, two years earlier he'd been transferred to the Buffalo Rhetta Plant. Working the night shift he'd been checking out the main offices when he'd stumbled onto some documents relating to the former residents of a slum area in Chicago.

"They were non-corporates. . . like the people here." spoke Fulton with dead earnestness. "I didn't get the chance to see the whole document before I was interrupted by one of the bosses, but what I saw left me feeling sick. Somehow. . . someone in the WCC was involved in the mass extermination of these folks, hundreds of thousands of them. I was nearly caught reading the stuff. If I had been. . . I wouldn't be here today."

"You mean that some official in the World Council of Corporations? Involved in mass murder?" Peter asked in disbelief. "I can't believe it. . ." He distrusted the corporations for their focus on materialism but. . . murder . . .

"Peter," spoke the gray haired Dr. putting his hand on the young man's shoulder. "There's more. . . your father's corporation, it seems, is the origin of the whole affair. All the signs indicate that Altrex is the Corporation at the top of the stack, so to speak, and that someone from there is involved in this sinister business."

"My dad?!" Peter lashed out. "No way man. . . you guys must be loony! My dad may be a selfish old skinflint but he's not. . ."

"No one is accusing your father of anything, kid!" said Fulton harshly. "All we're saying is that someone at Altrex was involved in the killing. Your dad may or may not know anything about it."

"Peter, forgive us." said Noah reassuringly, "We think that our area may be the next target. It is possible that we already are.

We have some terrible diseases running rampant through this area, you've seen that already. Well we've discovered that a similar situation occurred in Chicago."

"Oh God. . ." Peter though out loud. He had seen the toll being taken by these unknown maladies. Now it all started to come clear. "But why bring me in on this? What can I do?"

"You're our only current link to the corporate world. The rest of us have long ago discarded our wrist implants. We can't get close to the places." Noah looked at Peter earnestly "Peter.. we have very little information, just sketchy details from here and there. And, our people are dying . . . We need your help." Peter shook his head, deep in thought. He looked at the small group gathered there, sensing a level of integrity amongst them he'd seldom sensed in corporate employees. "Sure," he said. "I'll do what I can."

"Thank you Peter," Noah said kindly. "There's more . . ." He took an old leather bound book from a nearby shelf. The cover was worn with use and the yellowing pages showed signs of many readings. He turned to a spot, marked with a slip of ribbon, and began to read. His voice had a deep, dark tone to it, and the words that he spoke from that leather backed book seemed somehow alive to Peter. . . in a way he'd never known.

CHAPTER TWELVE

Aurora Station:

The sun was just peeking over the horizon cutting silver streaks in the early morning darkness as Zack pulled his Merc up to Andy's door. He was eager to see her again after their meeting two days earlier and hoped she'd feel the same.

Off on a distant hill Zack noted a gigantic air-purifying plant, looking like a huge lighthouse as it continually worked at sucking in city air to purify it. Similar structures around the world had twenty years earlier nearly eliminated all pollution. As he pulled into a space directly in front of the Wilford's quaint brownstone he immediately saw motion through the small glass panes in the door.

"Well, at least she's interested enough to be ready on time," Zack reassured himself.

He stepped out of the car into the crisp morning mist and breathed deeply, drinking in the delicious sweetness of the morning air. He leaned against his car as Andy appeared through the front door followed by a kindly looking old man in pajamas. She gave his bald head a kiss and shushed him back into the house before turning to wave at Zack.

"What a girl," he thought admiring everything from her cute figure accentuated by the sharp looking outfit she wore to the bounce in her step as she came down the walk toward him.

"G'morning Zack." she whispered cheerfully so as not to disturb the neighbors. "All set!"

"Yes ma'am your chariot awaits!" he clicked a button on his watch and both side hatch doors noiselessly swung open revealing the plush interior of Zack's Mercury. Andy placed her overnight bag behind the seat and slid into the passenger side with a shiver of delight.

"I am very excited!" she announced with a girlish giggle. "I'm going to space today!"

"You'd never know", Zack chuckled. He pressed his watch again and both hatches swung shut with a whoosh. "Beautiful morning isn't it?" Andy just nodded happily and snuggled down in her seat to enjoy the ride to the spaceport.

Fifteen minutes later the pair found themselves being swooshed through the parking garage at JFK International Spaceport as the automated parking system moved them into a parking stall. As they got out of the car Andy was overwhelmed by the incredible technology displayed there. . . and they were still in the parking area. Escalators swiftly moved people along toward flights to who-knows-where, robot porters glided past them, luggage neatly stowed, and the two went through no less than three wrist scans before they could even enter the main terminal.

A clear tunnel bridge connected the parking area with the main terminal as Andy and Zack were whisked along a moving sidewalk. Emerging into the massive central space complex, Andy was astounded at its immensity. The Spaceport had been in operation for nearly three years but she'd never had the opportunity to see it up to that point.

"This is unbelievable. . ." she said with a stunned expression. "I had no idea how immense this place was. You get the feeling you've stepped into some futuristic sci-fi movie". She grabbed Zack's arm in excitement. As she gazed out at the nearly three acre, five story building, hover crafts were all around moving passengers from floor to floor and area to area with an ease and grace that no elevator could come close to. For such an immense building there was practically no sound except the slight hint of soft classical music mixed with. . . with whale sounds. For such an incredibly busy place there was an air of total relaxation and calm.

"Good morning Mr. Murphy, Zack. . . we've been expecting you," came a sexy voice from out of nowhere that Andy could see. "Please follow the yellow uniformed⸱ guides to your departure gate." Andy had the sense that this young lady knew Zack very well. An old flame? She sensed a touch of jealousy, quickly chiding herself and pushing the feelings aside.

"Thanks," responded Zack coolly. "Oh, there we are, Andy. . . the yellow guide." As Andy looked up ahead she saw a beautiful young lady dressed in a stylish yellow uniform greeting and directing passengers. Relieved at the sight of another female she determined to ask her where the ladies room might be.

"Excuse me Zack. . .. I need to ask the lady a question." Andy said stepping on ahead of him on the moving sidewalk. She didn't catch the mischievous look on his face as she passed him. As she neared the pleasant smiling young woman Andy stepped from the sidewalk, desiring to pull her aside to ask her the sensitive question, but as she did her shoe caught on something sending her sprawling toward the yellow-clad guide. Expecting to fall into the girl's arms Andy was surprised when she hit the soft carpeted floor with a quiet thud. Unhurt but totally puzzled she looked back only to realize that she had passed right through the girl in yellow and, in fact, was. . . sitting directly inside of where she should have been standing.

In moments Zack was at her side helping her up.

"I'm so sorry Andy. . . I should have told you. . . I didn't think that. . ." he looked at her for an agonizing moment, afraid he'd embarrassed her, afraid she'd hate him. . . afraid. . . and then all at once she began to snicker.

"Oh my," she thought, "I must have looked pretty stupid. . . trying to talk to a hologram!" Zack wanted to nod but just sat there not knowing what to say. "All I wanted to do was find the bathroom!" At once they both burst into laughter.

"I can tell you where it is. . . if its not too embarrassing for you," Zack said with a grin, composing himself.

"Thanks, will you? Do we have enough time?" she said sheepishly.

"Oh yeah, we're early. . ."

Minutes later the pair were continuing down endless corridors, Andy nodding as they passed the same girl in yellow at every junction. Finally they were greeted by the now familiar sexy voice as they approached their departure area.

"Hello again Zack. Please proceed down ramp 10. Your shuttle is boarding now. Have a nice flight," she said in a provocative tone.

"Don't I exist?" demanded Andy, a little miffed at not being acknowledged. "And if you two want to be alone before our flight, be my guest!" she immediately regretted her emotional outburst.

Zack, thinking she was kidding, said, "Do I detect a hint of jealousy?" he immediately knew these were the wrong words to say. For the second time he'd embarrassed her! She'd hate him for real now. "Andy. . . um. . . you are aware. . . the voice is a simulation."

She hadn't been but he'd never know it. "Of course Zack, just a little joke," she said playfully tapping his cheek as she past by him a little down the ramp. Her face out of Zack's sight she rolled her eyes, disgusted and embarrassed at her naiveté. "I'm just a 21st century gal!" she chuckled to herself continuing on down the ramp faster than the conveyance. Zack smiled knowingly and trotted along behind her.

Another yellow-clad stewardess type stood behind a monitor at the entrance to the shuttle. Andy recognized the by then familiar wrist scanner as she approached and readily bared her forearm to it.

"Good morning Ms. Wilford. Welcome aboard Galaxy air," chimed the genial young woman in yellow.

"Thank you." Andy smiled purposely brushing her arm a bit as she passed, just to make sure she was really there. Pausing just outside the shuttle entrance she waited for Zack to catch up. Before his arrival though, the young stewardess was called into the cabin momentarily, leaving her monitor fully exposed to Andy. She casually glanced at the screen, wondering what information her little wrist implant might have provided the airline. To her horror she found a screen full of personal data including her height, weight, and the date of her last menstruation. She stood there, cheeks flushing bright red as Zack caught up to her.

"Is everything okay?" he asked meekly.

"Yeah. . . I just never realized how much info was on one of these," she pointed to her wrist, "or why in heaven's name they'd need it!"

"Well, space travel is much more complicated than normal airline flights . . . What's on the screen?" he leaned in.

"Nothing. . . nothing," she pulled him toward the wrist scanner. "I think you'd better get scanned so we can board." Zack complied with a shrug. Just then the stewardess reappeared at the shuttle passageway.

"Thank you Mr. Murphy, Ms. Wilford. Your seats are waiting for you. Please enter to your right. . . here," she indicated holding out her arm.

The two entered the shuttle and found their way to their seats. The inside of the craft looked like a large passenger airplane with fewer seats and no windows. The seats were large, and very comfortable with numerous buttons on the inside of each arm rest. They were scattered a pair every five to six feet. The front of the cabin was entirely occupied by a holographic viewing screen, which alternately showed the outside of the shuttle and its destination, Aurora Station.

As they were getting comfortably situated Zack reached over to Andy's seat, pressing the button marked "Privacy." All at once she was plunged into darkness.

Andy let out a shriek, "What's going on!" and then the lights came on again. She glared over at Zack playfully. . . "How'd you do that!"

"It's the latest thing Andy . . . I wanted to show you before the stewardess got a chance. It's a photon light field. Scientists have discovered that by projecting harmless photon rays in a blanket pattern it actually reflects all light creating a perfectly dark little chamber. Perfect for napping." Engrossed in his narrative Zack was unaware of Andy's hand upon his privacy button.

"Hey! What gives!" Zack screeched. Popping out of his dark cocoon he found Andy smiling sweetly, head tilted mischievously.

"Shhh!, the stewardess is about to. say something." she said with mock seriousness.

The trip to Aurora took nearly three hours all of which was chronicled on the screen to the front of the cabin. Passengers were well strapped into their seats to compensate for the partial weightlessness of space. 'Mercurite's magnetic properties allowed for a partially weighted atmosphere but making the trip to the restroom was still quite interesting. Stewardesses would fasten passengers into a weighted, magnetic vest, which would keep them from bouncing too high as they walked. Toilets in the spacious bathrooms were actually much like vacuum cleaners, activated as the user sat down. It was an experience that Andy wouldn't soon forget.

Two and a half hours into the flight Aurora Station appeared on the viewing screen, first as a tiny dot, then growing ever larger until its immensity filled the monitor before them. It was the size of a small city and branched out in seemingly all directions looking like a huge tinker toy with its endless modules and passageways. Small maintenance crafts buzzed around the perimeter like bees around a hive keeping careful watch over this massive behemoth.

"Something else, isn't it?" Zack leaned in to Andy who sat, mouth agape drinking in the spectacle before her eyes. She could only nod agreement.

Within minutes the shuttle craft had docked and the passengers were being ushered into an immense landing bay. From there they were directed into a small passageway and onto another moving sidewalk, which seemingly burst out into space as it passed through a transparent connecting tube. The tube emptied into a large central terminal where another wrist scan awaited the pair. Just beyond the scan station Andy noticed a rather gangly android, looking about with jerky motions resembling an earth bird. To her surprise it walked directly up to Zack and Andy and gave a slight bow.

"Welcome, welcome," it said rather over-enthusiastically in a squeaky, almost human sounding voice. "Welcome Mr. Murphy and Ms. Wilford to Aurora Station. I am Sydney. I will be your guide for the duration of your stay here. I am at your service." as it finished it smiled a quirky, mechanical smile, which hit Andy in the funny bone.

"Why, hello Sydney. And thank you," she replied in a playful tone.

"Hello," added Zack with a chuckle.

"We've been expecting you. Your rooms have been reserved at Aurora Hilton. On the way I'll show you some of the sights," he chirped with an odd tilt to his head. "A full tour has been arranged for you later this afternoon, after you have a chance to freshen up. Oh, please, let me take that for you," Sydney offered to Andy, reaching out for her bag. She liked him more and more.

The trio moved to a nearby car, no bigger than a golf cart but with comfortable seats and a car-like feel. Andy climbed into the rear seat while Zack joined Sydney in the front.

"All set?" Sydney looked around jerkily. At once they sped off through a nearby two-laned tunnel. Again their journey took them through a transparent tube leaving the passengers with the eerie sensation of traveling through open space for a hundred yards or so. Halfway through they passed a "T" in the road with tunnels on each side branching out to unknown areas of the station. Emerging into another huge module Andy was delighted to see a slightly miniaturized shopping mall bustling with people moving in and out of quaint shops and restaurants. Sydney slowed his breakneck pace considerably, looking back toward Andy with a mechanical smirk.

"Thought this area might interest you Ms. Wilford. Your bio indicates in intense love for shopping."

"Thanks Sydney!" she said blushing.

Through another tunnel, and another huge section filled with offices of some kind, and then halfway through another, the trio took a right, leading them to an immense module which housed three plush hotels and a couple of nice restaurants. Within moments their little buggy was parked and the three were being whisked upward to their 5th floor suites.

"Here you are," said Sydney opening Andy's room door. "I hope you will be very comfortable. Your room is right next door, Mr. Murphy." He placed Andy's bag on the dressing table, fluffed the bed pillows and turned with a quirk of his head. "I'll be back to pick you and Mr. Murphy up at 2pm. Is there anything I can get you?"

"Oh no, Sydney. . . and thank you." She hesitated a moment and then gave the gangly android a peck on his synthetic cheek.

"Why. . . thank you madame." he said with an odd twist of his head. Andy could have sworn she saw a little twinkle in his eye.

As Sydney scooted out the door Andy saw Zack leaning against the door post. "Hungry?" he said.

CHAPTER THIRTEEN

The Call

The old oaken grandfather clock chimed ten as James Alton Sr. sat at his massive mahogany desk, slumped in his huge leather chair. He felt sick and wrung his hands incessantly, worrying about Peter. . . much more. . . worrying about the trouble his youngest son was causing him at work.

Earlier that day he'd been called into the conference chamber for a little chat with the executive board of Altrex. He remembered feeling like a child in the principal's office as he sat a long table length away from the trio of high level bosses waiting for, he didn't know what.

They conferred together for some time before addressing the Sr. Alton.

"Mr. Alton. . . Jim," a pasty looking gray haired gentleman finally spoke. "We've been informed by certain sources about a situation involving your son. . . Peter is it? It seems that he's been spending a great deal of time in lower Manhattan."

"Yes. . . I'm afraid that's true." Alton spoke in as controlled a tone as possible.

"Then you've been aware of his visits there?" asked another, equally unhealthy looking elderly man.

"Yes. I've tried to stop him. . . but he's very headstrong and. . ."

He was cut off. "Mr. Alton. . . it would be in your best interest to find a way of keeping your son out of such areas. Our corporation, the WCC, does not need the son of one of its top executives associating with. . . such people. For one thing, there are terrible diseases rampant in such places which do not need to be spread." He looked at the others, "And. . . well let us just suffice it to say that. . . certain elements need not have access to the sort of sensitive information that you possess. Do we make ourselves clear?"

"Yes. . ." he remembered feeling three sets of beady eyes boring into his forehead as he spoke.

And now. . . what were they going to say? Didn't Peter realized that all of their lives were apt to fall down around their shoulders.

It was a moment before Alton realized that his phone was ringing and another long moment before he mustered the courage to answer it. Beads of sweat began to form on his forehead and his stomach hurt. Slowly he moved his hand over and pushed the answer button. On the screen before him appeared the shadowed face of Mr. Sinclair. . . CEO of Altrex. He was not often seen, and almost never did anyone receive a call from him directly. He nearly always worked through his executive committee. . . who themselves rarely had direct contact from him.

The seriousness of the situation engulfed Alton. For Sinclair to call him personally. . .

"Mr. Alton. . . good evening." The voice came from the shadows.

"Good evening, sir. . . uh. . . what can I do for you?" Alton inquired, swallowing hard.

"You were spoken to today by the executive committee? Of course you were," answering himself. "Well Mr. Alton . . . we have a great problem. You see your son, Peter, has been seen again entering the lower Manhattan area. I'm afraid this will not do." The voice came like cold steel.

"I tried, sir." he tried to explain.

"Tried. . . tried! How hard will you try when classified information is jeopardized? Shall WE deal with your children, Mr. Alton?"

"Now wait just a darn minute. You leave my children out of this." Alton's anger overtook his judgment. "I'll have you know that If my children are so much as touched I'll go to the press with your precious classified information!" he regretted his outburst immediately.

"That would be highly unadvisable my friend!" snarled Sinclair. Then, calming himself, "I'm sure that you understand our concerns about security. I had hoped a personal call from myself would bring that home to you. I trust you . . . Now please, please speak to your son. And Jim, I'm sure you were not serious about the press. Anyway, you should know. . . they work for us. Now. . . . get some rest."

The shadowy figure disappeared leaving Alton a wreck. He collapsed, head in hands, sobbing uncontrollably. The pressure was just too much. It wasn't the threats from his bosses, or the work. It was what he knew. . . those classified secrets. For years they had been eating away at him, and now. . . now he didn't know what to do. Soon the normally dignified executive sat a silent, numb, lump of a man.

Nearly an hour passed when he heard the front door close. Exhausted, the senior Alton looked up weakly.

"James? Is that you? Sondra? Peter? Who's there!" but there was only silence.

CHAPTER FOURTEEN

James in lower Manhattan

Parking his car, James made his way to the subway station. Anger built inside of him with every step. His little brother had always been a rebel. He'd caused one problem after another in the family. Why couldn't he just try to fit into father's world? It wasn't so bad. In fact he'd found corporate work to be very satisfying, in most ways.

Stepping out of the train James felt a shiver run down his back. He'd never been to lower Manhattan but he'd heard a tremendous amount about it. The stories came just short of painting the people of the area as animals. He honestly didn't know what to expect.

Stepping up to street level James was greeted by the pungent smell of wood smoke. The area was almost entirely blanketed in darkness broken only by an occasional reflected flicker from some outside fire. The whole scene left James cold.

He made his way down litter filled streets occasionally passing a shabbily clad individual and realizing how conspicuous he was here in this section of town. Finally he noticed a red cross on the outside of a dilapidated looking building. He cautiously stepped inside looking around. The interior of the clinic was surprisingly neat and tidy, if a little run down.

James made his way to what seemed to be the front desk. Finding it empty he was deciding where to look next when he was greeted by the chipper young voice of a girl.

"Hello, can I help you?" she said.

"Uh, yes. . . I'm looking for someone." he said turning to find he was talking to a young girl in her early twenties with a bright cute face.

"You must be looking for Peter. . . and that means you're James. You two look so much alike, you couldn't be anyone else," she replied with a grin, holding her hand out to him. "Hi, I'm Jenny."

"Why yes. . . you're right. Very pleased to meet you Jenny. Have you seen Peter?" he said a little taken aback.

Just then a door shut from somewhere behind him.

"James! What're you doing here?" came a familiar voice.

He turned to find Peter standing at the end of the hallway accompanied by two men and a dark haired young woman.

"Looking for you, little brother,." he said approaching the group. "Do you think we could find someplace to talk?"

"Ah. . . James, this is Dr. Noah. . . Mr. Fulton, and Rachel Noah. My brother James," Peter said.

James politely shook hands with each. When he came to Rachel their eyes met for a brief moment. He was struck by her stunning beauty. She had a deep seriousness in her dark, alluring eyes canvassed on a pure, delicately featured face, long black hair, and a dainty and statuesque figure. He found himself momentarily forgetting why he was there.

"James." Peter said, bringing his older brother back into focus. "We can talk over here," he pointed to an examination room.

James was struck by his brother's unaccustomed good nature. The two had been fairly close up until the last few months or so. Since then Peter saw his older brother as too much like his father whom he had begun to loathe.

As the door shut behind them James at once began to lecture his little brother.

"Peter, do you realize the position you're putting father into?"

"No, James. But do you realize the position that father is in by himself?" Peter said defensively.

"What do you mean?" replied James a little angrily.

Peter recounted the information that he'd been given earlier while his brother listened intently. James didn't believe a word of it but wanted his brother to be able to talk. Maybe some open communication would be the first step in bringing him around.

"Look, Peter. I know father. I think we ought to go home, talk to him. If any of what you say has any basis in fact father will tell me. Let's at least give him the opportunity to present the other side," he said, with a kinder tone to his voice. "Peter, he really loves you. He loves all of us. You two may not see eye to eye on everything but. . . believe me you have more in common than you know. I think that he's got a lot of the same struggles that you do, or at least he did. You and he are a lot alike. That's why you clash so much. Pete. . . dad could be in real trouble. Come home with me. Please."

"OK James, but I want you to know that I'm gonna pin father down about Altrex's involvement in the Chicago massacre!" Peter said stomping toward the door. "Oh, I hope ya don't mind. Jenny's comin along. She's a friend. We were gonna go do something later."

As they reentered the hallway James noticed the two men talking with Rachel. She seemed to be arguing with them, as though they were urging her to do something she objected to.

Finally she nodded her head and walked toward James and Peter.

"Would you two mind if I came along? Jenny said you'd be going out somewhere. I uh. . . I'd like to ask you a few questions James," Rachel said a little sheepishly.

"You mean, your father wants you to ask some questions," replied James.

"Yes. . . do you mind?" she said.

"No. . . Peter and I have to stop at home for a bit to talk to our father. Then I'm all yours. You can ask what you will."

Soon the four were zooming beneath the city toward the suburban subway station where James' car and Peter's motorcycle were parked. It was a short five minute drive through well lit, immaculately paved country roads to the Alton Estate. Peter, with Jenny riding behind him on his French racing cycle, dreaded the confrontation assuredly waiting for him at home.

The blue lights of an NSP car were plainly visible even down the mile long driveway that led up to the Alton home. James arrived at the door first and was greeted by an hysterical Sondra followed by her latest boyfriend.

"Daddy's. . . dead!" she said falling into her older brother's arms. Just then Peter arrived. "You! You! It was you that drove him to it! I hate you!" she said, pulling away from James and flailing weak blows at Peter.

"What happened?" said Peter, finally freeing himself from a sobbing Sondra who immediately left with her friend.

"I don't know. . . I don't know." James said as he rushed into the house.

The foyer was full of police who spilled into the study. There on the floor James found his father, dead. He had a glass still gripped in his fingers.

"Are you his son?" asked a uniformed policeman.

"Yes", James said. "What happened?"

"Looks like suicide." said the officer coldly. "He left a note," he said, pointing to his father's desk.

James recognized his father's handwriting as he sank down into the senior Alton's chair. He was in shock as he read the simple note. It said merely. "The pressure is too great. Sorry children. I love you."

CHAPTER FIFTEEN

Two o'clock came all too slowly for Andy. She felt like a child on Christmas Eve as the pair awaited the return of their charming guide and the tour of Aurora Station. All through a delicious lunch at the hotel restaurant she found herself watching for his little buggy to pull into view. She had so many questions to ask. What a wondrous place this. . . Aurora was. She couldn't remember feeling so excited.

Zack found himself sitting back and observing Andy. She was full of exuberance and life. He loved her positive approach to everything. It seemed that everything she did carved a deeper niche within his heart for her. He was steadily, ever steadily, falling deeply in love with his new friend.

"Excuse me Sir, Madame," Sydney's voice. "Are you ready for your tour? Mr. Murphy, your appointment with the station commander is arranged for this evening. He'll meet you here for dinner. . . if that is acceptable."

"Yes, wonderful Sydney. Let's go. Andy, you're gonna love this."

"I already do!" she chirped eagerly.

Within minutes the three were zipping again through clear, two lane tunnels. A short trip brought them to a massive module with a sign labeled "Horticultural Annex." Sydney slowed as they entered a lush green building.

"Here we have the Aurora Gardens." Sydney explained. "All the food for the station is raised here, most consisting of Rhetta but also various other fruits and vegetables. In an atmosphere where gravity is less than on earth's it has been found that most plant species do exceptionally well. In addition to food production an abundance of all kinds of flora are experimentally produced." He pointed toward a section of the building teeming with beautiful and exotic flora. A right turn swung them into the heart of the tropical garden.

"Shall we take a moment to enjoy the area?" asked Sydney, looking back with a mechanical grin.

"It's beautiful." Andy said stepping out of the car into the park-like setting. She and Zack walked through smooth paths occasionally encountering a technician in overalls.

"I had no idea Zack. All of this. . . up in space." she said looking around in wonder.

"It is beautiful, isn't it?" Zack agreed. "We'd better get back to our tour though. There's a lot more to see."

The next two hours were spent in visiting one incredible sight after another; an industrial module where all types of manufacturing was done, a clinical module containing the station health clinic plus numerous research buildings. There was even a recreational module containing a station health club, movie theaters, and numerous other types of entertainment. Zack took notes for his story, often stopping to quietly consider each detail before typing them into his word processor. Seeing him at his work Andy admired the seriousness with which he pondered each word that he wrote.

Andy was struck with just how tame. . . outer space could be. Everything seemed totally. . . under control. Suddenly a major question began to eat at her. Under control . . . She realized that, though she felt a bit lighter than normal, there was almost normal gravity.

"Zack, do you mind if I ask a technical question?" she said, not wanting to step on his work.

"By all means. . ." said Zack, curious at what she might be wondering about.

"Gravity! There's almost normal gravity here on Aurora. I know about Mercurite but its magnetic power is nowhere near strong enough to create a total gravity atmosphere." Zack was impressed by the intelligence of her question.

"Momentarily we will be entering the core of the station," replied Sydney. "Enroute to the Colonies Processing Station we will be passing the Central Atmospheric and Gravitational Plant. There the total atmosphere for Aurora is produced. When we get to it I'll explain the whole process."

Suddenly the road ahead seemed to dip sharply and before them loomed a gigantic sphere a mile in diameter. The tunnel took them around the huge ball for probably half a mile before it gently sank within it. All at once the little car and its passengers were plunged into the major high-tech area of Aurora Station. Zack recognized the name "Altrex" on numbers of the inner translucent buildings of this central matrix, which was alive with a myriad of flashing, pulsating lights of all shapes and colors. Deep within six to eight clear floors, obviously at the very heart of the station core glowed what seemed to be a giant gyro which was a blur as it spun, giving off a reddish light which permeated the whole area.

"Down there is the Central Atmospheric and Gravitational Plant. The gyroscope, constructed of irradiated mercurite, actually produces a strong gravitation pull, which reaches nearly five miles out from the core. This allows for nearly normal gravity throughout the station and beyond. Amazingly, it is mercurite itself which shields the station from the radiation of the core and yet allows the gravitation to pass through." He paused waiting for questions.

"Is this technology able to be used in space travel?" asked Zack.

"Very soon miniature replicas of the station core will be used in space craft of all kinds." replied Sydney.

"Amazing!" Andy said with awe written all over her face.

"Shall we proceed to the Colonies Processing Station?" asked Sydney with a smile.

"Certainly," Zack replied.

Within minutes they approached a large building marked "Colonies Processing." The trio parked outside and entered the stylish structure finding the waiting area posh and comfortable with pleasant music lilting through the air. Around the walls of the waiting room were attractive pictures of, what Andy assumed, the different colonies. She went from one to another with great interest, examining each one intently. There was a colony for the physically handicapped which featured an atmosphere, lower in gravity, allowing for its inhabitants to get around much easier, and mechanical devices which corresponded to endless infirmities and allowed the wearer to live a near normal life. The picture showed the handicapped, even severely handicapped and paralyzed with great smiles on their faces enjoying normal daily activities. There was a colony for the mentally ill which showed beautiful, verdant meadows and forests teeming with cuddly little animals. The ad spoke of a place where even the most deeply ill could live, peace-filled, full lives, unmedicated, and free.

She found a beautifully illustrated poster of what must've been the retirement colonies with a smattering of three dimensional photos showing the smiling faces of ecstatically happy older people. Some played golf, while others swam or played tennis, and yet others seemed involved in some sort of business, obviously for the retired workaholic. Two graceful grandmothers strolled leisurely through a garden teeming with tropical flowers of all types.

Something about the last picture caught Andy's trained eye.

"Hmm, I'll have to ask about that one," she thought to herself just as the trio was greeted by the superintendent of the Colonies Processing Station.

"Good afternoon Mr. Murphy." crooned the dignified gentleman. Andy guessed he was around fifty as streaks of gray highlighted the sides of his perfectly styled hair. "I'm Kenneth Lockburn, Superintendent of the CPS, the Colonies Processing Station."

"How do you do, sir," responded Zack politely, shaking the older gentleman's hand. "I'm Zack Murphy of the Corporate Broadcasting Company. I believe you've been expecting me."

"Yes I have. Would you step this way please. We're very pleased at the timing of your report Mr. Murphy. . . you see we've been desiring to publicize our work here to a greater number of people for some time. Your story will help us a good deal to spread the word about the services that we offer mankind."

"This is Ms. Andy Wilford. I hope you don't mind if she accompanies us," asked Zack sincerely.

"Not in the least, Mr. Murphy. I am very pleased to make the acquaintance of such a lovely and charming young lady." he said bowing to kiss Andy's hand. Andy smirked at Zack as if to say "now here's a gentleman." He chuckled and gave her a wink.

Leaving Sydney in the waiting room Zack and Andy were first led to a perfectly decorated, plush office where Lockburn had them sit in two overstuffed chairs. He handed both a brochure on each of the colonies.

"As you can see, we offer a wide variety of services. Recent space exploration has enabled us to locate and to colonize a large, unpopulated planet some distance from earth. On the planet we've been able to create colonies suited perfectly to people in each of these categories. It has been an incredible advancement for civilized mankind. Massive domed structures have been built in order to totally control the environment of each colony. All harmful bacteria have been removed from each, along with any harmful solar rays, virtually bringing the process of aging to a halt. Especially for our retirees this has been a wonderful thing. Our people live decades longer than they would on earth and can maintain productive, meaningful lives."

"Fascinating!" said Zack, jotting notes on his word processor. "But how do you eliminate bacteria in your incoming residents?"

A pleasant smile graced Lockburn's dignified face. "Very simply Zack, we have developed a computerized process which, similar to the anti-cancer machines developed a decade ago, thoroughly scour the body for harmful bacteria, zapping it with harmless delta rays. Once a person has been scanned, literally all unwanted microbes cease to exist, allowing us to keep our

atmosphere in the colonies sterile. One slight inconvenience. . .
once one has been scanned and lived in the pure atmosphere
for a period of time that person looses the ability to fight off
disease, and thus, is never allowed to leave the colony. " He said
with compassion.

"We were aware of that situation." Zack replied. "I uh. . . sure
would like an opportunity to visit your facility here.

"Certainly. But before I show you around. . . do you have any
further questions?" Lockburn asked kindly. Zack shook his head
but Andy, holding up one of the brochures, remembered her
previous question.

"You scc this picture?" she said pointing to the pair of
grandmas walking through a park.

"Why yes. As a matter of fact I know both of those ladies very
well, you see this one is my mother, and this one is my aunt." he
said proudly. "They both reside in the retirement colony at
present."

"Where was this photo taken?" asked Andy.

"Why in the retirement colony, of course. Isn't it lovely?" he
smiled at Andy. "Any other questions. . .?"

"No. . .no. . . it really is lovely," Zack could tell there was a
strain in her voice.

"If there are no further questions, would you both care to follow me. There's not much to see but I'll show you what there is."

Soon they were walking down a long carpeted hall, which opened, into a circular, windowed atrium. Out the windows, Mr. Lockburn explained, were the different stages of processing for the colonies.

Zack and Andy saw before them a large, well decorated warehouse-type building, separated into high walled cubicles. As they stood, in what seemed now more like a raised control tower, they could easily distinguish most of the different classifications of people.

In one area crisp uniformed nurses tended to obviously retarded children and adults, leading one by one into an adjoining room. Another area housed inmates being processed for prison colonies. Zack recalled how prison sentences had been increased drastically some years earlier in the WCC's attempt to get crime under control. Lawbreakers could expect life sentences in most cases above a misdemeanor. The upside was that prison colonies were the most humane penal institutions in history, allowing prisoners to lead productive lives for the duration of their sentences. The prison systems of the world, cruel and ineffective from the dawn of civilization, were largely unneeded in 2030. Most had been torn down while others had been scaled back and renovated to be used as minimum security facilities.

Continuing their observation they saw a room full of wheelchair bound and bedridden people, some obviously quadriplegics, unable to move at all. "How merciful," Andy thought, "it'll be for these people to finally live in a world where near weightlessness will allow them to lift their normally heavy limbs and to feel in control again."

Finally Mr. Lockburn pointed out the largest and most plush of the processing areas, the retirement colony section. There they witnessed happy seniors waiting for processing and a new life at the colonies.

"Please follow me", Lockburn said kindly. "Next we have stage two in processing for the colonies."

They moved down another hall and into an adjoining, similar atrium. There they witnessed people, one by one, laying on a table, undergoing what seemed to be some sort of X-ray scan. The equipment, operated by technicians in protective suits, passed over their bodies a number of times before they were cheerfully ushered through another door.

"This is the biostatic purification area". stated Mr. Lockburn. "All who go to any of our colonies must undergo it. You've heard already that we strictly control outside bacteria. Our colonies are free of harmful microbes, thus allowing residents the best possible quality of life. No more sickness, a much longer life-span, and a quality of life only dreamed of on earth. . . even in this age of high technology." He waited for questions. Assured there were none he continued. "We'll now proceed to an area overlooking our personal shuttle bays. There we can see the actual shuttles that go to various colonies."

Zack noticed an exit door cut into the dark blue wall. He allowed Lockburn and Andy to continue down the hall and around the corner before he gently pushed on the door, opening it just a crack. He took the chewing gum that he'd been working on for some minutes and put it over the electronic locking device, and then allowed the door to gently swing shut. He tried opening it without the handle and was assured that it would open from the outside. Sprinting on down the hall he momentarily caught up with Lockburn and Andy.

Realizing they had noticed his absence Zack blurted out, "Sorry, I was just tying my shoe." Lockburn smiled, nodded his head, and continued down the long dimly lit hallway, leaving

Zack in an unnoticeable panic. He realized that he was wearing slip-ons!

Soon, in another glassed in portico, they were overlooking a large shuttle bay. Below them were two shuttles, hooked up to closed landing ramps.

"We have our own flight tunnel out of the station." explained Lockburn. "This keeps us free from encountering traffic. We send a shuttle out every half hour. We never have delays. This allows for a very smooth operation. Each of our clients arrive by appointment, are processed on schedule, and. . . depart on schedule to their respective colony. The only problem we encounter is that occasionally the shuttle from earth is late. Every afternoon this month that's been the case. Fortunately, we planned for this eventuality in setting our itinerary and are able to make up the time and keep our clients on schedule."

As they watched, a third shuttle appeared through what must have been their two-laned flight tunnel. It all seemed very smooth, very professional. As they stood, looking over the departure bay, Zack wondered why the loading ramp to the shuttles wasn't clear as most other tunnels seemed to be. In fact, the only windows in the place seemed to be the ones that they looked out of. Why wouldn't they allow departing passengers or their relatives to observe flights? "Oh well, not a big deal", he thought.

"Well, there you have it folks. This is the end of the tour. I really need to get back to my desk." Lockburn smiled and indicated an exit door close to where they stood. "You'll find the parking lot is just out this door and around the corner. Thank you folks for your interest and. . . oh. . . I nearly forgot." He pulled a disk from his pocket. "Mr. Murphy, this disk will give you all the footage you'll need for your story. Now, if you will excuse me." he smiled pointing to the door.

Moments later Zack and Andy had joined Sydney and were whisking through transparent tunnels back to their plush hotel. Not a word was spoken on the return trip, in stark contrast to the chatter that filled their earlier drive. Once back at the Hilton Zack asked Andy to join him in the lounge about an hour before their scheduled dinner. She nodded and the two separated with a silent smile.

Back in his room Zack sat for a long time, looking out his window at the garden patio below and the clear space wall beyond it. The fascinating sight before him should have dominated his attention. He was preoccupied though. Something bothered him about the Colonies Processing Station. He didn't know exactly what, but he planned to go back there later that night.

After a shower and a change of clothes Zack headed for the hotel lobby. He found his way to the lounge and ordered a tonic and water. Soon, lost in thought, he was startled by a tap on his shoulder. Andy stood before him adorned in a stunning, black dress.

"What's on your mind? You look a million miles away." She asked taking a seat across from him.

"I don't know exactly. . . something about our little tour today. . . bothered me."

Andy looked at him thoughtfully for a moment and then said, "I'm glad to hear you say that . . . I felt the same thing right from the start. And ya know something else?" She pulled one of the brochures she'd picked up earlier from her purse. "Look at this picture Zack. You're gonna think I'm crazy. . . but I've been there before."

"But you couldn't have been. . .. I heard Mr. Lockburn specifically say that this picture was taken in the colonies." He looked at Andy expecting her to recant her last statement, but she only looked more certain of herself.

"Two years ago my father and I took a vacation up into the Allegheny mountains. We stopped in a little town overnight. There were so many quaint little things about the town that I decided to take some pictures. This is a garden right outside the town hall. I know! I've got an identical picture at home. Only without the little old ladies." She looked earnestly at Zack.

"Why would Lockburn want to deceive us? He really did seem certain, in fact adamant about it. It just doesn't add up." Zack said puzzling over the already troublesome situation. "Well, there's only one thing to do," he finally declared. "I'll just have to go back later tonight and do some sleuthing."

"But how'll you get in? And what if you're caught?" Andy asked showing her deep concern for Zack.

"Well, I rigged one of the exit doors to stay open, and. . ." he held up Andy's purse. "If I'm not mistaken, the lady left her purse behind on our tour." He gave a wink.

Andy smiled a mischievous smile. "Uh, Zack. . . my purse and I are never separated. . . so I guess that means I go along," she chirped with a tone to her voice that told Zack he'd better not argue the point. He smiled, indicating he'd been convinced.

"What about Sydney?" she said all at once.

"Oh, I've got a plan for our dear friend Sydney." Zack replied with a grin.

CHAPTER SIXTEEN

All through the incredibly boring dinner meeting with Col. Horace Moore, the Aurora Station Commander, Zack could hardly keep his mind in the present. He could tell that Andy was itching to get sleuthing also. Occasionally they would catch each other's eyes, understanding what the other was thinking. Finally, mercifully, Col. Moore signaled the end of their meeting by producing a disk from his pocket, explaining that it contained great footage of the station. Zack showed a burst of charm and enthusiasm in thanking the Col. for his time and in assuring him of the great coverage his station would receive when his story aired. As soon as the Col. was out of sight they looked at each other and then sprinted to the elevator, a change of clothes and. . . adventure.

Ten minutes later both were clad in jeans and t-shirts, ready to go. Sydney greeted them in the lobby.

"May I drive you somewhere?" he said politely.

"Well, I was hoping you'd let me drive a bit. . . by myself." Zack replied.

"Oh, sir, I'm afraid that wouldn't be possible. You see. . . I've been instructed to accompany you everywhere you go," replied Sydney with a polite smile.

"No problem Syd. . . but I forgot my briefcase upstairs. Would you mind getting it for me?" Zack said winking to Andy.

"Certainly sir. . . just one moment." and he was off jerkily toward the elevator. Soon he had entered Zack's hotel room not noticing that the door had been slightly ajar. As the door slammed shut behind him Sydney heard a metallic click. With briefcase in hand he tried to leave the room. The door was jammed solidly. After a moment's attempt at the door he went to the phone.

"Hello, hello," he said tapping at the disconnect button. "Oh dear . . . oh my." and he sat quietly on the bed waiting for someone to come along.

The clear tunnels were far more complicated than Zack remembered. Soon he found himself in an area of the station that he knew he'd never seen before.

"Uh. . . Zack." Andy said gently. "I think we should take a left up ahead."

"I don't think so," he replied overly polite.

"I'm sure, Zack," she insisted. Zack smiled smugly. "Ok. . ." he said placating her.

Immediately as they made a left the road began to slowly curve downward. Zack turned to Andy, meekly smiled, and continued on silently to their destination. She made a weak attempt at modesty, though her grin gave her away.

The front office at the CPS was dark and seemingly empty, which was exactly what Zack had hoped for. He wanted to see the operation up close. Parking down the block from the office the pair silently slipped back to the rear of the building and to the door that Zack had rigged. Sure enough, though there was no handle on the outside of the door, it easily swung open with the help of Zack's penknife.

Once inside they quietly made their way back to the first viewing portico. Keeping in the shadows they could easily see that the station was as busy as it had been earlier that day.

"Good," Zack whispered. "We'll be able to see everything in full operation."

They made their way back through the series of hallways until they found themselves overlooking the loading bay. Examining the only door leading to a stairway and down into the bay itself Zack found that it opened by an I.D. card.

"I've got to get down there to those shuttles." Zack said, half to himself.

Andy took his hand and whispered, "Zack, that's too dangerous. Anyway, how are you going to get down there? And what if you get caught?"

Just then they heard the faint sound of footsteps from down the hallway accompanied by a roughly whistled tune. Just in time not to be seen the pair crouched in a dark corner of the atrium. They held their breath as a loading bay technician paused, surveying the bay before him at length before taking the card off of his overalls, slipped it in the slot and waited for the door to swing open with a swish of air. He ambled on through the door and down the stairs. As it swung shut Zack leapt from his hiding place with a silent pounce just wedging a hand in the door before it shut completely.

"Auugh!" he whispered in pain just able to pull the door back open. He quietly slipped through, opening it only enough for his body to fit through. Then he took a pen from his pocket, laying it where the door would shut so as to keep it slightly ajar.

"You stay here Andy, I'll be back in a couple of minutes." he said with a wink of his eye.

"Be careful," she replied reaching her hand through the doorway to touch his face gently.

The dozen or so technicians in the shuttle bay were busy tending to a flight about to depart. They didn't notice a figure in jeans and black T-shirt slipping down the stairs. Zack quickly found a pair of overalls and a hard hat, which he donned, slipping into a small locker area. Keeping hat low over his eyes he casually strolled toward the loading ramp where two shuttles were being boarded for the colonies.

"Hey!" Zack looked up, panic-stricken into the face of the shift supervisor. "You must be the new guy. I thought you weren't coming till next week! Oh well, go on over there by shuttle four and stand by." He pointed to one of the shuttles being loaded.

Zack gulped and obediently jogged over to shuttle four. No one else seemed interested in his presence in the least so when the supervisor turned his back Zack moved up close to the vessel as though checking some equipment. He found a small window, which he had to stand on a nearby tool chest to peer into. He saw rows of seats. . . all empty. He could also see the loading tunnel. . .. dark and devoid of activity. Stepping down from his perch he moved to the front of the craft. He could clearly see the face of the pilot who turned, smiled, and gave a friendly, somewhat detached wave to Zack.

"Shuttle four loaded and ready for departure," came a voice over the loudspeaker. Zack couldn't believe what he'd heard. There were no passengers! Even still the ramp was pulled away from the triangle shaped spacecraft. It gave a nuclear whine, lifted off and gently maneuvered out of the shuttle bay.

Zack walked around discretely for nearly half an hour taking mental notes. Having seen enough and concerned about getting caught, he formulated a plan. He approached the supervisor without looking up and, getting his attention, mumbled.

"Uh, sir. . . I was supposed to be assigned to the scanning station. . . I'm sorry. . . I uh. . ." acting as ignorant as possible.

"What!" the older man growled. "Well. . . get up those stairs. The scanner rooms are down the hall to the left! Why didn't ya tell me!"

"Sorry sir. . . I uh. . ." Zack said meekly.

"Well. . . hurry up!" Zack heard the man mumble something about incompetent techs as he quickly shed his overalls and scooted up the stairs. Andy had panic in her eyes as Zack slipped in the door and then allowed it to shut silently behind him.

"What happened? I saw you talking to that man and. . ."

"Shh. . ." he said, slipping his hand gently over her mouth. There were footsteps coming, far to close for them to dive to safety.

"Oh, I'm so glad it was still here," he said a little loudly as he signaled her to play along.

"Yeah. . . I don't know what I would have done. . . oh. . . Mr. Lockburn." she said.

Lockburn turned the corner, obviously shocked to see the pair.

"Why. . . what are you doing here. . . uh. . . how did you get in?" he sputtered.

"Andy lost her purse. . . and. . . well. . . I'm a little embarrassed. I saw an exit slightly ajar earlier today and. . . well, she was sure that her purse was here in this room. So. . . after noticing your office closed. . . I. . . uh. . . took the liberty of coming on in. You don't mind do you. We're very sorry." he acted sheepish.

It was obvious that Lockburn wished to avoid a scene. "Oh, no problem." he sighed. "I'm glad you found your purse. Now. . . may I see you out the door that you entered. I'd like to make sure it's well locked." he smiled curtly.

Looking back Zack noticed a shuttle arriving. It had a number ten attached to the side of the vessel.

"Would you mind if we watched this shuttle come in." Zack asked. "I find it fascinating."

"Very well. . . we can take a few minutes, but then I really must insist that you leave.

There was nothing noteworthy about the landing. The craft smoothly glided into place where shuttle four had departed earlier.

Then Zack caught sight of the pilot. . . it was the same pilot. The one that left in shuttle four!

"We can go now. Thank you." Zack said to Lockburn. As they reached the door Andy realized that Zack's gum was still stuck in the door. She blurted out, "Oh no. . . my wallet!"

Zack took the cue. As Lockburn turned toward Andy he quickly removed his double bubble.

"Here it is. . . sorry," she said seeing that the coast was clear. They left a rather irritated Lockburn behind them as they made their way toward the little car.

Once safely out of the central complex they finally let out a collective sigh.

"Good thinking Andy. I'd totally forgotten about the gum in the door. That would have been hard to explain!"

"No problem. . . but tell me what you saw," she said earnestly.

"I can't figure it out," he said. "There were no passengers on the shuttle. . . but they announced that it was full . . . Then, I could have sworn that the shuttle that came in a few minutes ago had the same pilot as the one that just left. Something is wrong here. . . I can't put my finger on it exactly, but something is very wrong."

Part II: The Discovery

CHAPTER SEVENTEEN

Zack rubbed his eyes, trying to bring the room into focus. He must have dozed off when he laid down to rest a moment between chapters of his story. His eye was caught by a dimly flashing light and a gentle beeping sound coming across the room. It took him some seconds before he realized that some persistent caller was awaiting the answer of his pictophone.

Still half dazed he stumbled across the room, banging his shin hard on a low table. He noticed that the image-receive button was flashing so with one hand clutching his throbbing shinbone he responded with the other, pressing the button marked image-send. Instantly the pretty face of Andy appeared on the screen before him. She frowned and turned her head sideways quizzically.

"Zack, are you alright?"

"Yeah, I mean. . . " he tried to explain, "well. . . I'm fine . . . I just woke up, that's all. What time is it anyway?"

"I'm sorry Zack, I didn't mean to wake you. It's seven thirty." She paused, worry obviously showing on her face.

"What's the matter Andy? Is everything alright?"

"I'm just. . . worried. . . about my father. Zack do you suppose you could come over? I mean right now?" her soft voice broke slightly as she spoke.

"I'll be right there," Zack answered collecting himself. "It should take me ten to fifteen minutes. That okay?"

"Yeah, sure. . . see you when you get here." She smiled as the phone went dormant.

Moments later on the road Zack puzzled over what might be the cause of Andy's worry. She looked and sounded pretty scared. He didn't have long to ponder as the sparsely trafficked streets put him in front of her house in less time than he figured. Andy met him at the door wearing jeans and a sweatshirt. As she showed him in he chided himself on noticing just how nice she looked in such casual attire. Her petite figure framed perfectly in her "grubbies.'

"What's up?" he asked, genuinely concerned.

"It's my dad. Zack, I'm really worried about him and. . . I didn't have anyone else to turn to. . ." Andy leaned into him sobbing gently. Zack put his arms around her and held her silently until she could gather herself again.

"I'm sorry. . ." she said, wiping her eyes with a hanky. "It's just that Daddy has been acting so strangely the last three days. It all started the day we met. . . he didn't go into work that day. . ." she looked into his eyes, "Zack, Daddy hasn't missed a day of work in thirty years!"

"Well, was he sick?" Zack queried. "I mean everyone gets sick once in awhile."

"No. . . that's not it. Not it at all. I've never seen my father like this . . . Even when my mother died. He has a look in his eyes like. . . like. . . he's panicking on the inside and doing everything that he can not to show it on the outside. Mostly he stays in his office pacing the floor, mumbling and reading. . . an old bible of my mother's. I don't think he's slept for three days. Zack, something dreadful must be wrong."

"What does he say when you ask him about it?" Zack said with growing concern in his voice.

"He won't say anything. And that's strange too. My dad and I can talk about anything. It's not like him to keep something to himself like this. Do you see why I'm so worried?" Andy said, desperation showing in her voice.

"Would he talk to me?" Zack asked.

"I don't know, it's worth a shot," Andy said, grasping for hope.

The pair ascended the long staircase that led to her father's study on the second floor of the old elegant house. They cautiously approached the large double doors which were slightly ajar revealing the old man hunched over his desk, pouring over an old leather covered book. The room was illuminated by a single light, which cast its single golden shaft upon Dr. Wilford and his studies.

"Hm mm." Andy cleared her throat as she and Zack quietly padded into the office. Zack was taken aback by this wonderful room, every inch neatly cluttered with old books and mementos of a life spent in academia. The smell of old leather richly filled the place adding to the aura created by shadow and light.

"Wha. . . what?" Dr. Wilford said, half looking up. "Oh, Andy, I'm busy dear. . . please come back later."

"Uh, daddy. . . this is my friend I was telling you about. Zack Murphy. . . he'd like to talk to you." Andy said sweetly.

"I'm sorry children. . . I just don't have time. . . please see me later. . . I. . . just don't have time!" he yelled turning his swivel chair to block out their presence.

"DADDY, I WON'T STAND FOR THIS ANY LONGER, YOU'VE GOT TO SNAP OUT OF THIS AND TALK TO US! NOW!" Andy screamed, startling both men.

Dr. Wilford looked at his daughter in shock for a long moment and then, as though crumbling before their eyes he sank to his desk, head buried in his hands. "I can't tell you . . . I just can't," he sobbed. "It's already cost one life. Please children."

"Dr. Wilford," Zack said after a long silence. "You've got to tell someone. It's obviously eating you alive . . . Please, you can trust us."

Dr. Wilford composed himself and then looked intently at his beloved daughter and her friend. Reading the insistence on their faces he finally gave in. "You don't understand how serious this is. I can tell you only this . . . I blundered onto something one night late at the lab. It was information on a project called, "Utopia". The information was. . . horrifying. I had to tell someone, so I called an old friend, Milt Hammerstone. He works the morning shift at Altrex computer labs. Or I should say. . . he did work there. I should never have told him. . . he was always a bit of a hot-head. He went right to the authorities of the company and when he got nowhere he threatened to go to the press. . ." the old man paused sadly. "The next thing I knew. . . he was dead, and accused of stealing corporate secrets . . . I just thank God that he didn't mention my name. . ."

It all came together in Zack's mind. Hammerstone was the old man that Zack had seen killed by the NSP at 4th and Selmer!

"I was there. . . when Hammerstone was killed." Zack went on to relate the events of that day including the reporter "Wallace" who had used the very words "Utopia Project" before disappearing.

"I'll bet it was Wallace being dragged into that back room. Wonder what his fate was," Zack said resolutely.

"Well I guess you're already involved, Zack. . . I cannot relate the horrible details of "Utopia". I didn't see that much, and what I did see left me in shock, so my description wouldn't be that accurate. . . but I'll give you a copy of the Alpha program. You can go to the main city library. The basement has a lot of computer terminals . . . I believe they're hooked into the global system so you should be able to access the program. Better yet, I'll go with you." Andy hugged him, sensing the relief at being finally able to talk to someone.

CHAPTER EIGHTEEN

Soon Zack, Andy, and Dr. Wilford were making their way through the city to the public library. It stayed open until nine, so that gave them only forty-five minutes to get there, access the program, and copy any data they might need. No one spoke a word as they drove. They anticipated something bad, but neither Zack or Andy had a clue just how bad.

Fifteen minutes later the trio were huddled around a small computer terminal in the basement of the massive downtown public library. Zack and Andy watched intently as Dr. Wilford laboriously reconstructed the Alpha program, this time from a sheet before him on the computer table.

Andy felt dazed as the information and events of the past three days went round and round in her head. It had a dream-like quality to it. She prayed that she would wake up soon.

Zack's reporter's curiosity had been switched on high as he awaited the final pieces to this huge, insidious puzzle. He had no idea that what he was to witness would strike a blow very close to home.

Finally a flash and a surge of numbers and letters upon the screen before them told the small band that they had accessed the "Utopia Project" program. A few more seconds and they found themselves reading the opening credits and title to a professionally produced video-program from the early part of the century.

CHAPTER NINETEEN

"The Utopia Project"

"TOP SECRET: Any unauthorized viewing or dissemination of the following information is an international felony and is a capitol offense. You now have five seconds to turn this program off to be free from prosecution."

The screen went blank for five seconds after which time it sprang into life with words, music, pictures, and narration by a smooth, dark, male voice.

"The world was in chaos after the conflict of 1998. Governments, in their petty attempts to gain power and control over other lands, had placed the whole world on the brink of destruction. Religious ferment only added fuel to the fire with radical Islamic groups throughout the world hell bent on destroying all others not of their particular slant, and most especially Christians. Terrorist bombings were at an all-time high, and other acts of terrorism were commonplace in all nations of the world.

"The newly formed World Council of Corporations felt compelled to do something before the world was annihilated.

They found, within its ranks a young computer technician who had, innocently, and unknowingly created the technological framework upon which a whole new world order was to be created. He had developed a system of ties with the four large computer centers of the world. When activated and brought under a central control this system enabled the WCC to bring the nations of the world to their knees by freezing factories and other workplaces all over the world. This further turned people against their governments in support of the council.

"During this time a crack security force of men and women from around the world, later named the National Security Police, began to be assembled. They set out to systematically assassinate leader after leader in the world, leaving behind false evidence that the murders had been committed by local workers, angry at the system. It was a very short time before the WCC had total control of the world and all of the people in it. They gladly welcomed the peace, security, and prosperity that the WCC offered.

"To further strengthen their hold on the people of the world the WCC decided to implement the use of the Wrist Implanted Identity Chip across the globe. This wonderful piece of technology totally eliminated the need for currency, another source of division amongst people, by the use of a tiny computer chip each individual in the world was able to be monitored by one of the main WCC computers. All trade was linked to the WIIC through the use of wrist scanners. After working so many hours an employee would be scanned and given so many credits in his computer account. Then when he or she wished to purchase anything a simple scan of the wrist automatically subtracted credits from their account.

"Another advantage of the WIIC was its aid to doctors in allowing them to diagnose illnesses in bearers of the chip. All vital systems could be monitored through another scanner, thus simplifying the diagnosis and treatment of disease and illness.

"By far the greatest advantage of WIIC though was that it was a built in listening device. Anyone suspected of disloyalty or treason toward the WCC could be carefully monitored by the central computer. The computer could literally "tail" millions of individuals at the same time, monitoring them for signs of trouble.

"The mastermind of this project, Mr. Pierre DuMonde, rose from the ranks of anonymity as a junior executive in a small textile firm in France. Through the connections that he made in the newly formed World Council and his smooth, persuasive manner of speech he soon rose to the top position in the WCC.

His brilliance came into full view as he proposed the early installments of the "Utopia Project", a plan to systematically rid the world of such major problems as poverty, disease, unemployment, ignorance, and superstition. A man of great hope and vision he dreamed of utopia, a nearly perfect world."

The narrators smooth speech made everything that had been presented seem good and right, and it took all that Zack and Andy could do to keep in perspective the implications of this insidious "project".

He went on to speak of religion as a number one enemy to the new order. Religion kept man in the dark ages, unable to fully unite and unable to ever reach his full potential. Religion was also systematically eliminated, or nearly so, by replacing it with a secular philosophy wrapped in a religious garb.

"Secular humanism had been introduced to the world many centuries before but had always met strong opposition from radical religious groups. Then in the late twentieth century its proponents became aware that nominally religious people could be drawn into their way of thinking if it had the guise of a religion itself. Instead of claiming that man was merely a biological part of the universe, here for a while and then gone, they began to put forth the idea that each and every individual had a part of "God" in him. This especially drew those who did not fit into the narrow, orthodox religions of the world to that point. People were urged to "find themselves" as a part of the family of man, all equal, all part of the great entity. . . God.

"Soon these teachings began to infiltrate the public school systems throughout the world through school counselors and teachers until it was officially adopted as the religion of the World. Young people were taught to bear with their superstitious parents if they were of any of the "old" religions. Time would show the truth of the "new" way. People all over the world began to be unified under the new "Corporate Religion."

"Of course, it was necessary to eliminate certain religious leaders and again the NSP were called upon to take them out neatly, leaving only false evidence to fuel the fires of discontentment with the old line religious.

"Certain groups posed greater problems to convert to the new world system. Radical Christians, Jews, and Moslems refused to become a part of the "New World Order" and at times threatened to turn things around in their zeal, attempting to convert the masses back to primitive religion. It became necessary to develop ways to eliminate whole groups of people without causing a lot of chaos.

"Again the idea came from the brilliant mind of Pierre DuMonde. In 2020 he proposed, as the next step in his "Utopia Project", that the WCC should begin advertising special colonies where those who could not share the new "Corporate Religion", could go, and practice their religions in peace. These colonies would be on newly discovered planets and were being set up for these different groups specially. The advertisements would portray these colonies as little utopias, or, in their terminology, lands of milk and honey. In reality, no colonies would exist at all.

"Technology had reached the point where a computer scanner could record nearly everything about a person in a manner of minutes right down to patterns of speech and thought, and then reproduce a lifelike hologram which could actually seem to converse with anyone who would want to get in touch with the person. After the subject was scanned, he would be shown visions of the imaginary colony, filling him with peace. Moments later a powerful laser would simply disintegrate him, leaving his image in the computer, happily ready to extol the virtues of colony life to any who wished to speak to him.

"At first the advertisements brought few takers, but when the WCC began a systematic persecution of those involved in radical religions, the small trickle of customers began to grow until all around the globe "Space Colony Substations," as they were called, were packed with a steady stream of patrons.

"Soon the program moved so efficiently that WCC officials, under the advisement of Mr. DuMonde, initiated phase three of the Utopia project.

"Since the dawn of man the world had been shackled with the care of the aged, the incurably insane, ill and diseased, the crippled, and the criminally irreformable. Corporations for quite some time had given much to all of these causes out of a false sense of humanitarianism. It was the opinion of Mr. DuMonde and many of his associates that these too should be allowed to be "put out of their miseries", and at the same time relieve the world of the great burdens that it bore in caring for them. Therefore the recommendation was made that other colonies be advertised. The ads would speak of perfect environments that would allow the infirmed fuller, happier lives in a special colony geared just for their brand of disability. The aged would be offered the opportunity to live longer, healthier lives in "retirement colonies", which promised every amenity right down to golf and tennis all year round. Prison colonies allowed criminals a greater amount of freedom and tremendous opportunities for rehabilitation totally unheard of on Earth.

153

"In the year 2023 these special "Space Colony Stations" opened. That year the hospitals and prisons were cleared, nursing homes closed their doors, and a huge number of senior citizens just. . . ceased to be."

This was all that Zack and Andy could bear. . . both feeling as though the wonderful world that they had lived so happily in up to now had come crashing in. The three embraced in the dark corner of the basement, and sobbed uncontrollably, grieving for a world that had died. . . or more rightly, that had never lived.

After some time they glanced again at the computer terminal, that one eyed monster that had blown their lives apart with a truth too terrible to know.

"Doc," Zack asked, trying to pull himself together. "Can the main computer sense when this program is being accessed?"

The Doctor was startled by the thought and immediately responded, "Oh my Lord. . . I believe so!"

CHAPTER TWENTY

The sound of heavy footsteps scurrying quickly down the stairs of the library filled the basement. A contingent of fifteen NSP troopers swiftly made its way through rows of ceiling high bookshelves, honing in on the corner of the room where Zack, Andy, and Dr. Wilford had spent most of the evening. When they arrived they found the computer terminal flashing incoherent symbols and three chairs neatly arranged around its table. The officer in command gave silent instructions for the others to fan out around the building in search of whoever had just finished there.

"That was close," Zack sighed as he wove his car up and down back streets quickly leaving the library far behind. "Are you two Okay?"

Silent nods were all the answer he got from his passengers as they stared blankly out into the night. Zack just continued to drive every back street that he knew leading out of the city and to safely, at least temporary safety. He found himself on a road that led out in the direction of his grandparent's farm. He refused to think about how it might have been if they'd followed his wishes to go to the so-called retirement colonies. He felt an urge to dash out to them, to warn them, but more to just fall into their safe embrace as he did as a child. . . and to be comforted. To make the horror of all he'd just learned go away . . .

Just then the car phone buzzed. Everyone sat bolt-upright. "Could they have known who we were? Were they calling to tell us to give ourselves up. . . to face. . ."

Zack collected himself and slowly picked up the receiver. "He. . . hello," he stammered.

"Zack, Zack, is that you?" spoke a familiar voice on the other end of the phone.

"Yes, this is Zack. Who's this?" he said, already somewhat relieved.

"Zack, this is James Alton . . . I haven't seen you in awhile but. . . I need your help. Can you meet me?" James sounded very troubled.

"Hello James. . . uh, yeah, sure. . ." Zack replied, sensing an opportunity, "as a matter of fact I've got some things to talk to you about too. . . you name the place, old friend."

Soon the trio was headed toward Barney's for a meeting with James Alton Jr.. Zack hadn't seen his old friend in nearly a year, but somehow he sensed that James was a person he could talk to about. . . "The Utopia Project."

I've got to stop by the station," Zack said to the somber group riding in his car. "I've got some notes there on my desk. . . it all makes sense now."

"What're you talking about?" asked Andy, still half dazed by their discovery of the "Utopia Project." "Are you sure that it'll be safe?"

"Yeah, I think so. Most everyone has gone home by now and I've go to get my file on the WCC. Ya know, I always had a feeling in the pit of my stomach that something was just not right. The file, plus what we know now should prove to be even more enlightening." He said somberly.

It took longer to get to the WBC building than usual as Zack took back streets all the way just to be sure. He parked behind the building and, using the manual entry code so as not to use his own card code, he secured entry into the door marked, "Deliveries". There was an old man slumped over in his seat sawing logs as Zack slipped past the rear security office. The elevator had only manual controls, which allowed him to continue in his anonymity all the way to the newsroom.

The normally bustling, reporter-filled room was silent and devoid of activity as Zack slipped across the area toward his glass walled cubicle. He reached his office and was thumbing through a file on his desk when he sensed another presence in the room. A shot of fear-induced adrenaline coursed though his body as he slowly turned, expecting to be confronted by a blue uniform. He searched the room for something to help him get away and immediately his eyes fell upon his antique baseball bat signed by the legendary Ken Griffey Jr. Without a word he reached for the old yellowed hunk of hickory at the corner of his desk. As his fingers closed around it he gently eased it toward him and then, all at once turned with a jerk, bat raised above his head.

"Hey!" came a familiar cry. "What're you doing Zack?! It's me, Sam!"

The figure, now crouched over, arms above his head for protection, carefully peeked out.

With a sigh of relief Zack recognized the round form of his boss, Sam McDermott. "Sam!. . . I'm sorry! I. . . I."

"What's goin on, son? You're awful edgy." Sam spoke, finally out from behind his hands.

"Oh, Sam! Am I glad to see you . . . I've stumbled onto something that you won't believe!" Zack said, relieved to see his surrogate Dad.

Sam was cautious, "It must be something serious for you to almost bean me in the head!"

"Sam, things aren't as they seem! The WCC. . . it's not the benevolent organization that we all think it is. . . and the colonies. . . they. . ."

"Zack!" Sam snapped, cutting him off. "You've got to leave this alone! Forget anything that you've learned."

"What?" Zack responded with confusion.

"Just please do as I say, son . . . I can't explain further. . . please, just trust me," Sam pleaded, grabbing onto Zack's broad shoulders.

Zack looked at him in disbelief for a moment unable to comprehend why he was so adamant.

"Sam. . . I don't know why you are saying this. I trust you . . . but. . . this is too big." He searched the old, balding man's face, "Unless you can give me a good reason. . . I can't let this alone." He paused a moment waiting for a response. Sam let go of Zack and turned away sadly.

"Zack, I didn't want to tell you this. . . I can't say as I fully understand it all. . . but. . . you leave me no choice."

He turned again toward Zack. As he searched for words, Zack could see the pain that filled Sam's heart.

"It's about your mother and dad, Zack. You've been led to believe that they died in a plane crash." He paused. "That's not exactly right. You see. . . they didn't just die. We don't really know what happened to them."

"What? What do you mean?" Zack exclaimed in disbelief.

"You two are so doggone much alike . . . It's no wonder you're into the same trouble! Zack, your dad was on to the same thing that you are. He wouldn't leave well enough alone when he started putting it all together, whatever it was, and. . . well one day. . . he just announced that he and your mom were going to Europe. He said he was on to something. And then, they just disappeared. I told him to cool it, but he was as stubborn as you are! Zack. . . that's why you've got to let it go! Just forget about all of this, whatever you've found, and let well enough alone!" Sam looked broken as he finished.

"Sam, do you know how deep this thing goes?" Zack had a seriousness in his voice.

"No, and I don't want to know!" Sam snarled back. "I don't want to know. . . and I want you to get away from all of this nonsense!"

Again Zack just looked at his adopted father. He felt pity and contempt for him. How could he be so weak? How could he have kept this news about his parents a secret for so long? Why, they might still be alive somewhere! After a silent moment Zack turned with a disgusted shake of his head and with long determined strides, made his way toward the service elevator.

"Wait, Zack!" Sam pleaded, knowing that his words fell on deaf ears. "Wait. . ." His voice broke as he fell into a nearby chair holding his head in his hands. "Zack . . ."

Moments later Zack was lifting the hatch of his Merc. The look on his face concerned Andy as he silently started the car and began to drive.

"You look as though you've seen a ghost," she said touching his arm gently.

"Just one more. . . horrible discovery," he said with a slightly disgusted tone. "I'm sorry Dr. Wilford. I broke my promise to you. I told someone what we've learned. I just hope it wasn't the wrong somebody." He related his conversation with Sam McDermott as they cruised along toward their rendezvous with James Alton. Afterward the trio sat in stunned silence as they wondered what would be their next discovery, little knowing that it would be the most important that any of them would make in their lives to date.

CHAPTER TWENTY-ONE

James glanced at his watch, nervously wondering what might be keeping Zack. He and the others seated at the table had been waiting for nearly half an hour. Barney's was packed as usual, but the five felt less than inconspicuous as they stared at the front door.

"James?" came a voice from behind them. The junior Alton turned to see Zack and two others, obviously having slipped in through the rear door.

"Zack!" James exclaimed with a hushed enthusiasm. The two shook hands warmly. Zack surveyed the group seated at the table with some guarded curiosity.

"Let me introduce you to my friends Zack," James spoke with a hushed tone. "This is my younger brother Peter, you might not remember but you met him when he was around twelve. This is Jennifer Morrel, Dr Benjamin Noah and his daughter Rachel." Zack smiled politely at each and then in turn pulled up chairs and sat down, huddled around the small table as a young waitress approached them.

"What can I get you," she said, tired after a busy night's work.

"Uh. . . coffee?" James said, half asking the others. They all nodded their approval more to get rid of the waitress than anything.

"I hope you don't mind me bringing Andy and the Doc along James. We have some things to talk to you about, too," said Zack quietly.

"Can you trust them?" Zack noticed that his friend looked rather gray. "I have some rather sensitive information for you."

"You can trust them," he whispered, dreading what he felt would be more startling news.

James addressed the whole group somberly. "Tonight, my father, James Alton Sr. . . died." He quickly continued through the silent shocked responses of those around the table. "It was made to look like a suicide. . . but I don't believe it for a minute. My father would never . . ." His voice broke slightly as he continued. "Anyway. . . even though I've been groomed to be an executive for the WCC, I honestly think that they had something to do with this. Peter and I have met with Dr. Noah and. . . well we think that something is really wrong. Zack, I called you because I found your name on some kind of report on my father's office computer. Most of it was erased but. . . I figured you might know something. . ."

Why would Zack's name be mentioned on such a report? Did they know already. . . or was it something else? Maybe his father's situation had made them suspicious of Zack, or maybe it was the space station? One thing was certain, he'd have to be extremely careful now.

Look, I have some things to share with you that you won't believe. The World Council of Corporations is totally corrupt. I don't think that we're safe here," Zack said, looking around. "Does anyone know of a secure place where we can go to talk?"

"I do," said Dr. Noah. "There's a warehouse somewhat near the clinic that should be very safe. The authorities stay out of that area altogether."

Just then the waitress arrived with steaming cups of coffee. As she served each she held out a wrist scanner to collect for it. When she got to Dr. Noah, he seemed slightly panic stricken, looking around anxiously. It took James a moment to catch on before he quickly blurted out. "Uh. . . I'm getting theirs," he said, motioning toward Dr. Noah and his daughter. The waitress shrugged and finished placing the cups around the table before she adjusted her scanner and passed it over James' forearm. She got to Zack who calmly held out his wrist. After three attempts to scan his arm Zack heard a low beeping sound.

James got a look over her shoulder at the readout on her scanner before she hurried off.

A couple of sips later she was out of sight across the room and the band quietly slipped out the rear door, leaving the bustle of the restaurant behind them. It was as they grabbed their coats that Zack saw the reason for Dr. Noah's nervous reaction, for on the wrist of the kindly looking old gentleman there was a noticeably crude scar across the area where his wrist implant had at one time been planted. Zack wondered who else in the group might have a similar mark of nonconformity, and this led him to ponder his own situation. Should he too have a scar? If not, would he endanger all of their lives?

Parking their cars in different areas of the city the group agreed to meet at the subway station at lower Manhattan, each taking a different series of trains to get there. Andy and her father grabbed a train, which swung them by their house and allowed them to get freshened up, and for Andy to pick up a few things. It would be a long night ahead.

James, Peter, Zack, and Dr. Noah rode together for part of the trip while Zack shared sketchy details about what they'd learned about the "Utopia Project." The Doctor just listened intently without saying a word. As Zack finished, the four men sat quietly for some moments before James spoke up.

"We'd better split up at the next station. We'll see you all at the warehouse in an hour or so."

Three of the four stepped off of the train at the next stop and immediately disappeared without a word in different directions.

CHAPTER TWENTY TWO

Some time after midnight the group began to straggle into the old warehouse in the slums of lower Manhattan. As each arrived they found Dr. Noah seated in front of a table with an old set of surgical instruments neatly laid out before him. One by one they took seats around the cloth covered table and silently waited for the rest to arrive.

Zack arrived last and found the whole group seated and staring at him with a strange seriousness.

"What's going on? What're you all staring at?" Zack asked somewhat defensively.

"Zack," James spoke up quietly, "I read the waitress's wrist scanner at Barney's. I'm afraid that you're a wanted man. The only hope for you is to have your wrist implant removed. Otherwise it'll be easy for the police to find you. . . and us."

Zack looked at the instruments and cringed a bit. His head was spinning as he remembered the events of the evening. It all seemed like a dream. How could he have gone from being on top of the world, a celebrity. . . to being a common criminal, a fugitive! It wasn't fair.

"Do you think that the others are in danger too?" he asked.

167

James spoke up, "Technically we're all in danger. From what you've told us about the surveillance capabilities of the WCC I would recommend that most of us have our chips removed. Of course a few of us. . . myself and Dr. Wilford might want to keep ours for awhile. We have an inside track into the main computer center at Altrex. It may prove helpful in getting more information."

The operation was simple enough. Andy, Zack, Jennifer, and Peter all bore their arms. Dr. Noah injected each with an old form of anesthetic and then made a small incision in their wrists. With a pair of tweezers and a magnifying glass he probed gently beneath the skin until he produced a tiny silver square. The incision was then treated with an antiseptic and sprayed with an adhesive solution, which allowed the skin to be bonded together without sutures.

"What will you do with the chips?" Andy asked, finally assuring everyone that she had a voice.

"Watch and you'll see." said Dr. Noah with a kind smile.

At that moment a couple of young men appeared leading four scroungy looking mongrels on leashes. The Doctor carefully placed each chip on the skin side of a leather collar, placed a drop of silicone cement over it, and then put the collar around one of the dogs. When all four of the mutts had a collar securely fastened around their neck they were led away to be released somewhere in the city.

Amidst the dread seriousness of the situation they all had a good laugh over the thought of the Corporate Police chasing all over the city after. . . a somewhat hairier version of Zack.

Andy noticed that, of all those gathered in the room, Dr. Noah seemed most at peace. Somehow he didn't seem as troubled over everything as the rest. She watched him as he stood to speak.

"Now ladies and gentlemen, will you all please take a seat. I want to talk to you." He waited while everyone got situated around the large table.

"What we've learned tonight, as all of the pieces have fit together in this great puzzle, is truly shocking and sinister. For many years I have suspected that such things might be going on, and frankly, they don't surprise me. You see, not long ago I discovered something in an old book . . . I found this all predicted in a sort of general way.

"You see, beneath the shell of the idyllic world that the WCC has created, man is still as corrupt as ever. No amount of shining up the outside can change the inside of man. The WCC's way of dealing with this is to eliminate anyone who doesn't fit smoothly into the neat little system that they have created." He held up an old leather covered book and then opened it, and carefully and painstakingly turned the pages before him.

"Far too late in life I realized that there was more to our existence, so much more, than most people ever realize. Listen to these words . . . They were written by a very special man." He reverently smoothed the pages, as though stroking a cherished friend, "I have come that you might have life, and life more abundantly." You see, I was a product of the 21st century. As a medical doctor I was thrilled with the wonderful advances in science and technology that the "new world order" brought with it. I was so enamored by the wonders of the 21st century that I couldn't see the forest for the trees. My wife was different though. While I focused upon helping to create a perfect world from without she had me beat already. . . her perfection came from within . . . She had found the only `real' perfection that exists." He saw that Dr. Wilford was with him all the way, understanding everything that he was saying.

"What I failed to realize was that while my world on the outside was becoming smoother and shinier, my heart was becoming colder, and more and more filled with turmoil. I had an easy existence, a solid practice and great esteem within my profession and, I might add, in the corporate world. Yet with all of this I felt more and more isolated. I got to where I didn't want to see my patients. . . they were the imperfect part of my practice. My machines were the perfect. I began to plunge more and more in the sterile world of technology, I suppose to hide the emptiness that I felt within.

"On the other hand, I watched my dear wife. . . her life never seemed smooth. She was prone to every disease and infirmity still known to man. She grew weaker and weaker with every year that went by. . . and yet there was such tranquility, such peace. She claimed it was from her closeness to Jesus. Of course I thought that was pure nonsense. According to all that I knew, this Jesus was just some historical figure that tried to get the barbarians of his time to be nicer to each other and was killed for it by his own people. I took her for granted." His eyes began to mist as he spoke. "Her sicknesses drove me away from her. . . you see, it showed that medical science was not perfect. I was not willing to hear that. It was people who were imperfect, not science! It wasn't until she was on her deathbed that I finally had my eyes opened. There she lay, wreaked with pain, and yet she had more peace in her heart than I did. Me, who had all the answers, who was a perfect specimen of health. . . in that brief time I saw the blackness of my soul. . . the emptiness of my life. . . the hollowness of my obsession with technology." By this time Zack too was taken by the gripping sincerity of Dr. Noah's narrative.

"As my wife slipped away from me she said something that will burn in my memory forever. She said, "Ben, Jesus is alive. . . and I'm going to be with Him very soon. Please, darling. . . don't let any more of your life go by without knowing Him. If you do. . . I'll never see you again. He alone can fill the emptiness in your heart. I see it, and so do you . . . I'll be waiting for you Ben. . . I love you. . ." and then she was gone. I found myself kneeling beside her weeping, not for her, but for the emptiness of my own life. I knew, somehow in my heart, that she was somewhere better, that her words. . . were true, but that I. . . was lost!

After kneeling for some time beside my dead wife, examining the dark chasm that was my soul, I found myself doing something that was totally unlike me. I was reaching out to. . . to someone . . . to God. I asked Him to show me. . . if He was real somehow . . . and if He was. . . if He could fill the cavernous void of my heart.

"Immediately it was before me, the wreck that my life had been. I knew that none of my accomplishments really meant anything, and I also knew. . . don't ask me how. . . that Jesus, this same Jesus that my wife claimed to know. . . was real . . . He was REAL! I found myself asking Him to forgive me for everything . . . What's amazing is that He did. All at once the darkness of my soul lifted and I was filled with what seemed to be a glorious light. The heaviness of my life disappeared. . . I felt lighter than air and filled with a deep, abiding peace. . .

"You know, I opened my eyes to look at my dear wife's face. She had the most beautiful smile, even in her death. Finally I understood just where it had come from. Jesus filled my heart now too!"

As Dr. Noah looked around he saw that tears flowed freely down the faces of Zack, Andy, and Dr. Wilford. Obviously his words had hit home.

Zack walked away from the group embarrassed by his show of emotions. He knew it was true. He'd watched his grandparents go through a similar experience many years earlier. They'd gone from nominally religious people to zealous, life-filled, followers of Christ. He had quietly ignored their talk of this change in their lives and had written it off to the eccentricity of old age. Now though, he knew. . . it was not some fad or fanaticism, it was real. Before he'd been blinded, like Dr. Noah, by technology. He couldn't reconcile the two . . . If the one was faithful and true the other had to be just a wives tale. How could he have been such a fool!

Andy and Dr. Wilford wept openly as they embraced each other. Andy's mother, too, had been a strong Christian. She'd shared openly about Jesus with her daughter as she was growing up, and Andy even remembered praying as a little girl, asking Him to come into her heart. The influence of the corporate schools had obscured these "superstitions," as they called them, to the point that she totally tuned her mother out. So strong was the programming of her school that when her own mother had died she and her father had given her, against her willed wishes, a corporate funeral. She remembered leaving the service with a hollow feeling, a bit remorseful that she'd not respected her mother's wishes more.

"She was right, princess. . ." Dr. Wilford said through the tears. "Mother was right all along."

James watched the spectacle before him with detachment. It hadn't hit him at all. Why was everyone so emotional. It just didn't make sense to him. All he felt was anger. . . anger toward the WCC for its corruption and lies. . . and most of all, for his father's death. The reality of the latter had hardly hit him yet.

His thoughts were interrupted by a gentle touch on his arm. He turned to see Rachel Noah standing beside him, her dark eyes shining gently.

"James, I'm so sorry about your father. . . I haven't had the opportunity to tell you before. If there's anything I can do. . ." Her compassion reached into James' heart, tugging at a place untouched for a long time.

"I'm fine. . ." he said, beginning to feel his emotions churn within him. He turned slightly away to try to get control again.

"I want you to know. . ." said the dark haired beauty, "that it's really alright for you to grieve. I mean, you've been so strong through all of this, I certainly wouldn't think badly of you."

James was a young man of deep character. He had no need to be phony and he wasn't prone to playing "macho" games. He sensed deep within him a need to mourn his father, and in this young woman someone who would share his loss. Somehow it seemed right. Right to feel. Right to let the controls go.

He looked up to see Peter standing a ways off, watching him. As their eyes met the two brothers spontaneously moved toward one another. All of the grief that they shared burst forth as they fell into each other's arms, unashamedly weeping bitter tears. Soon they were joined by Rachel and Jennifer, and with the two gentle spirited young women, the four became one in sharing the loss of James Alton Sr.

"If you don't mind, I'd like for all of us to join a small meeting a couple of blocks away," spoke Dr. Noah gently. "What we've begun here will best be finished in this group of friends."

The group fell in behind the Dr. as he and Rachel led the way out of the building and down the street. A short five minute walk left them standing in front of a crumbling old storefront. The windows were boarded up but shafts of golden light streaked the sidewalk in front of the building, revealing that someone was indeed at home there. The tiny band quietly entered through the creaking front door and found themselves at the rear of a small chapel inhabited by twenty to thirty people of all ages. The group was engrossed in the gentle words of an old, weathered looking lady who stood at the front, gesturing as she spoke. Her words were of Christ. . . of his love. . . and of his faithfulness.

The sweet old grandmother paused as Dr. Noah and the others entered. "Benjamin, so good to see you. We've awaited your arrival and prayed for you. Come, sit down."

Dr. Noah moved toward the front of the room gesturing for the others to follow. "Folks, I'd like you to meet some new friends, some who have become more than friends tonight. He introduced Zack, Andy, Dr. Wilford, and James to the group seated at the front of the church and then said, "Now I'd like you to meet our little fellowship."

CHAPTER TWENTY THREE

As they sat discussing the horrifying situation, Andy noticed that Zack was preoccupied. As soon as she could get his attention, she motioned him away from the group huddled in the Wilford living room.

"There's something else bothering you, isn't there?" Andy asked as they reached the kitchen. She noticed a hint of a tear forming in Zack's eye as she waited for his answer.

"I've just been thinking. . . about my grandparents. I tried to call them, but there was no answer. I've been trying to talk them into going to the retirement colonies, and I'm afraid. . ." his voice broke.

"Look Zack, you told me you've been trying to talk them into going for years now," Andy said trying to console him. "Why, after all these years, would they change their minds, especially now? They're probably working out in the yard. Let's drive out to their house."

"I know an unmonitored road that leads right by the place. I did a story on a farm out there last year." Zack seemed relieved.

"We'll be back in a couple of hours. We've got some business to attend to," Andy announced to the group as she and Zack grabbed their coats and hurried out the door.

Within moments the twosome were glidingdown a back road to the Murphy farm. Neither spoke a word through the whole trip but shared a growing anxiety over what they would find when they arrived.

Andy sat for some time looking at Zack, his bronze skin and dark eyes gave him the appearance of a noble warrior. There was a new gentleness about him, and a peace, which exuded from his innermost being. Her heart seemed to reach out and to share the pain of his uncertainty. She reflected on the short few days that they had known each other. How much they both had changed and yet as they changed, they seemed to grow closer together. "Thank you Lord," she prayed.

The tension in the car was thick as they pulled into his grandparent's driveway. As they passed the tiny garden plot, it's rows neatly manicured and tools meticulously stored, Zack knew the answer to his question. The winding driveway that led around to the back of the house brought them to the old screened porch which normally carried with it a pair of smiling faces and warm hugs. Today it was empty and devoid of that treasure. A note tacked to the door was clearly visible from the car.

The pair sat in silence for a long time, Zack gripping the steering wheel as though to crush it. Finally, with a sigh, he mustered enough courage to leave the car. The note simply read, "Zack, just too hard to say good-bye in person. Will call you from the Retirement Colonies. Took afternoon shuttle. Love, Gram and Gramps." The note scribbled in grandpa's handwriting crumpled easily in Zack's strong hand. Tears flowed freely as he mumbled a bitter prayer. "Why God. . . why them?" He was angry at God and at himself at the same time. He slowly turned to survey the quaint little farm that his grandpa had built. A flood of memories surged through his mind. Everywhere he looked the place cried out of the love that he had known from his grandparents.

Zack sat pale and speechless, the note crumpled in his hand for what seemed an eternity to Andy.

"They've gone already. . ." Andy knew it before Zack said the words. "They took the afternoon shuttle. . ." He slumped onto the steering console.

"The afternoon shuttle! Zack, we may have time to catch them. Don't you remember that Lockburn, the guy from the

Retirement processing station, said that the afternoon shuttle has been late every day this month."

All at once Zack's despair burst with a hopeful thought. "Let's go!" he said with urgency in his voice.

The road seemed strangely longer than before as Zack pushed his new Merc to the limit, passing trees and occasionally farm houses in a blur.

"Careful, all we need is a police escort," Andy said, putting her hand on his shoulder.

"We'll just have to take our chances, there's no time to lose," Zack said, not looking at her.

Sure enough, on the outskirts of the city, the speeding car tripped a radar trap. Within seconds Zack recognized a quick flash from behind him indicating they had just had their picture taken.

"It won't be long now," Andy said nervously, now gripping Zack's whole arm tightly.

Zack spoke confidently, "I know a few back streets of my own." Quickly turning left, then right, then left again, Zack wove his way swiftly toward the spaceport.

Within moments they were parked in the pick-up zone of JFK. None of the automatic doors seemed to open fast enough as

Zack and Andy hurried through the spaceport. The escalators that so pleasantly moved them toward their shuttle just days earlier seemed to creep along at a snail's pace. Finally Zack grabbed Andy by the hand and began to jog through the thick crowd dodging right and left.

What seemed very far in distance Andy saw the departure station for the retirement colonies. She saw the desperation in Zack's eyes as they sped along.

"I need to check on a couple of people who might have left for the retirement colonies," Zack blurted out as they arrived at the check-in counter.

"Names?," asked a blurry eyed attendant.

"Richard and Sarah Murphy. . . and please hurry," Zack spoke as his voice shook.

"Hmm . . . let's see . . . ah yes, they were seated on flight 58, which departed half an hour ago."

Without a word Zack turned, his eyes filling with tears, unable to hear the rest of what the attendant was saying. Andy hurried along behind him, searching her mind for words to comfort him. She reached his side just as Zack's car became visible across the huge building and outside a glass window.

With a jolt Zack realized that a pair of blue uniformed NSP officers were peering through the windows in his car.

He grabbed Andy by the arm and with a jerk, pulled her to a hiding place behind a nearby counter. No sooner had they disappeared from sight than the two uniformed officers briskly entered the sliding doors. Their path took them directly past where Zack and Andy crouched, and not ten feet from their hiding place they stepped off the moving sidewalk. Each second that passed seemed an eternity as the pair approached the service counter. Zack held Andy's hand tightly and looked into her eyes one last time as he prepared to stand and make a break for it, leading the officers away from her.

"You! Come over here!" barked one of the policemen. Zack steadied himself to make a run for it when he noticed an elderly spaceport attendant out of the corner of his eye. He seemed to be responding to the policeman's command. As he passed the counter the porter gave Zack a wink and motioned subtly with his hand for he and Andy to keep down. They couldn't quite make out the conversation but it was clear that the old man was sending the officers off in another direction.

Moments later the NSP troopers hurried off away from them, leaving the old porter and the terrified pair behind the counter. A huge grin spread across the old man's face as he motioned Zack and Andy out of their hiding place. "I figured you two was in trouble the moment I saw ya." He spoke with a deep southern drawl. "I had a few scrapes with the law myself."

"Thanks, Mister, you see. . ." Zack said, trying to explain.

"Shhhh, I don't need to know nothin," the porter said. "Just get on outta here before those cops come back."

Zack shook his knarled hand while Andy planted a thankful kiss on the old man's face. Within seconds the pair were out the door and climbing into Zack's Merc.

Blocks away they finally breathed a collective sigh of relief. It was clear that the reality of Zack's grandparent's situation weighed heavily on him. He silently stared at the road ahead. There was nothing for Andy to say. She leaned over, kissed his cheek softly, and gently squeezed his hand. They drove silently, steadily on, out of the city, down a familiar country road, past a deserted old farm house, and on into a crimson sunset.

CHAPTER TWENTY FOUR

The Plan

Gathered around the table were a somber band of determined faces. Dr. Benjamin Noah had assembled everyone in the basement headquarters. As he looked around, he wondered at the miraculous way that this group had been weaved together. Just days earlier many of the group had not even known of the existence of the others, much less the incredible task that lay before them.

"Ladies and gentlemen, the work before us is clear. We must strike a death blow to the heart of this evil computer. At the same time a carefully prepared message must be broadcast to the whole world."

Zack swallowed hard as he looked around at the faces of his comrades before him. There was Peter, full of fire and zeal. Where once a rebellious streak overshadowed his nature, Zack noticed a new, focused peace. Beside him sat Jennifer, still tired from her work. Through her weariness a sweet spirit shone from her eyes.

James showed the strain of his father's death on his face, yet through his grief, a quiet determination prevailed. Zack had known James most of their lives. He was always serious, always dedicated to what he felt he needed to do in life but there was never an over abundance of self confidence in him. Now though, James seemed strong, full of purpose.

At the corner, deep in thought, sat Dr. Benjamin Wilford, his furrowed brow exposing the depths of his thoughts and concern for the upcoming mission.

Behind her dark eyes, Rachel Noah remained totally calm, her confidence in her father's leadership very clear. Her gaze shifted alternately between Zack, Dr. Wilford, and her father, who seemed strangely confident in the midst of the turmoil that lay ahead.

"I will lead a group of the following individuals to our first objective. James, you and Dr. Wilford will enable us to enter the Altrex complex. We'll pose as a group of technicians on a tour of the plant. They shouldn't be aware that you're with us yet so you should have no trouble getting us into the gate. We'll make our way to the main computer room, set charges, and then try to get out somehow. Peter, you, Jenny, and Rachel wait down the block in James' car. Give us twenty minutes . . . Then leave, with or without us. Here's a map to a cabin in the mountains where you should be safe, for awhile. Now, Mr. Fulton has some things to brief you on."

Fulton stood, solemnly. His hand trembled as he reached into a bag on the table. Carefully, oh so carefully, his hand emerged with a plastic, putty-like substance. "For those of you that don't recognize this ancient material, this is C-4, an extremely powerful plastic explosive. One advantage of having such old materials is that there is no current technology to detect it. Placed at the proper points on the main-frame, we should be able to totally incapacitate it. . . and the Utopia program."

Dr. Noah looked intently at Zack. "Son, you're prepared to get into the World Holographic Corporation Broadcast Studio?" Zack nodded. "Have you made the recording?"

"Yes, I made it last night. It should do the trick."

"Will you need anyone else?"

"No. Once I get into the building I can do everything myself."

"I'm planning to help," Andy chimed in. "I'll go along."

"No, Andy, I don't need any help . . . You just stay with Rachel and Jenny. . . get to safety."

Andy looked at him with steely eyes. "There's no discussion. I'm going with you." Once again Zack knew that there was no

187

dissuading her. She'd made up her mind and he'd better concentrate on keeping her safe rather than fight her going at all.

He sighed deeply, "Alright. . . Andy'll go with me. We won't need anyone else."

"How will you get out afterward?" but the Dr. knew the answer to his question before he'd asked it. There probably wouldn't be any afterward. . . for any of them.

CHAPTER TWENTY FIVE

Joe, the guard at the gate of the Altrex Corporation was overweight, red-cheeked, and well into his fifties. He sat, half dozing in the tall stool which nearly filled the tiny security shack.

As the group of white coated, dignified individuals approached his post he was in the middle of a dream of turkey and mashed potatoes. A tiny stream of drool crept from the corner of his mouth. Sensing a bit of gravy escaping his lips he awoke with a snort.

There in front of him, slowly coming into focus as he rubbed his eyes, came an official looking entourage. In the lead were the familiar faces of James Alton Jr., and Dr. Wilford. They were followed by Dr. Noah and Brice Fulton.

"How are you doing, Joe?" James spoke cheerfully, hiding his intense anxiety with a broad smile.

"Good evening Mr. Alton, and hey, Dr. Wilford, I haven't seen you around here in a couple of days. You been sick?"

"I've, uh. . . been working on a presentation," Wilford said, clearly shaken by the guard's extra interest.

James broke in, "Yes. . . you see Dr. Wilford has been helping me prepare for this group of technicians from Bradford College. We plan to show them around the computer center."

Joe sleepily glanced at a computer clipboard on the tiny desk in front of him. "Hmmm. . ." he yawned as his fingers scanned the list of names before him. "Don't see your name down here, sir. Must be a mistake. I'll just give the security chief a call."

His plump hand reached for the phone switch on the wall. Thinking fast James blurted, "Uhh, wait a minute Joe, don't bother Frank. He has enough on his hands. My dad just forgot to send the clearance through. We'll drop by the security office on our way."

The chubby guard scratched his head. "Well, I. . . guess. Whatever you say, sir. But make sure you talk to Frank. He'd have my head if he thought I let someone through without clearance."

The small group breathed a sigh of relief as they moved past the guard station, appearing as though they were heading toward the security office. Dr. Wilford, beads of sweat forming on his brow, exclaimed, "That was a close one."

"And I'm afraid that we have only a few minutes," James said, worry showing on his face.

"Just get me to the computer center," replied Fulton. "It won't take long."

Once around a nearby corner the group changed directions, heading for the main building and the computer center. Once inside the sleek, modern Altrex headquarters building the group fell in behind Dr. Wilford, who made his way, as was his usual custom, through a series of security doors. Finally they arrived at the main computer room.

"I normally work in the next room. . . where the individual monitors are operated. I only hope my scan with allow us entrance. I didn't find out until yesterday that the main unit was next door all the time."

"Well, if we have problems. . . we can just begin a little ahead of time. We'll get through the door." Fulton said, patting the bag hanging at his side.

Fortunately as Wilford passed his wrist across the scanner at the door's entrance there was a click and a swish, leaving the immense room before them open for entrance. The small group slipped through the opening, making their way around a high railing. Thirty feet below two or three technicians checked unseen instruments on a massive main-frame computer, hardly noticing as the four, white-coated men moved through the room.

Reaching into his bag Fulton produced three bricks of plastic explosive, each fitted with a crude timer. Wilford led the group down the stairs and into the heart of the computer room. He made his way as nonchalantly as possible through the large area as though leading a tour, while each of the remaining three men split off every few yards and silently crept toward his pre-arranged place on the gigantic machine. After placing his smooth glob of plastic each returned to the group. Moments later, all charges laid, Wilford led the group toward the stairs and to the safety of the outside hall. Just as his foot hit the bottom step a familiar voice chimed from behind them.

"Dr. Wilford! Doc!" a dark haired, young technician chirped, jogging toward the group. Wilford recognized him as Stan Lewis, a former student from Bradford College who'd graduated and gotten hired at Altrex the same time that Wilford had been hired on.

"Hi Doc! What're you up to?" the young Lewis asked inquisitively. He looked at the three other men with Wilford innocently.

"Just a quick tour of the facilities. Uh. . . these are some technicians from. . . uh. . . our Alma Mater, Bradford College." Wilford stammered. This complicated things immediately. All of the technicians would be killed surely when the explosives went off. Now one of them had a name. . . a face . . .

"Let's go Doc!" whispered Fulton coarsely.

Wilford took a step up the stairway and then paused. . . "We just can't let them die!" he looked up at Stan, who'd stopped short of the group of men at the bottom of the stairs with a puzzled look on his face.

It was too much for the old doctor. Reaching the top of the stairs he turned and yelled, "All of you. . . get out while you can . . . The computer is rigged to explode within two minutes. Get out!" he shouted as he made his way along the ramp that led to the outside door.

"Wilford!" yelled Fulton. "Shut up and get going!" The four men reached the door just in time as one of the unstable explosives went off, sending smoke and debris in all directions and setting off the other two charges in quick succession. There was no sign of Stan Lewis or any of his co-workers.

"I had no idea. . . that we'd be murdering people! This makes us no better than. . . them." Wilford wept, leaning against a wall. The others just stood for a long moment, speechless. Then the lights all went out. The computer had shut down. Their mission had been successful. Even emergency lights failed to come on, leaving the whole building blanketed in total darkness.

"It worked. . . we've shut it down," came the beleaguered voice of James. All had the same question running through their minds.

"Now what?"

"This way," said James after a long moment, "The back way out, through the loading area." The four followed James as he felt his way along the hallway. "The loading bay should be just around this corner. We can use one of the trucks." They cautiously moved around the corner finding the outline of a door some ten yards down the hall.

As he pushed and prodded the door to get it open there was a loud clicking noise followed by light coming on all over the building.

"What!" Fulton growled. "What's going on! I thought the power was controlled by the computer!"

"It is!" James barked. "Forget it. . . let's just get out of here!" With the power on he could get the door open by a wrist scan. He quickly found the scan panel and passed his wrist over it. The door immediately opened with a swish. The four men moved to scurry through the door but froze in their tracks. The loading bay was full of NSP troops, weapons leveled at four bewildered men in white coats.

An NSP officer stepped forward. "Don't move gentlemen. You're under arrest." He moved closer to James. "Tell me. . . why would you want to blow up the climate control system?"

James turned to Wilford who had a shocked look on his face. "The climate control system?" He realized at that moment that they had blown up a decoy. . . a decoy.

CHAPTER TWENTY SIX

The WBC building bustled with life late into the evening most days. Tonight was no exception.

Luckily, after the ten o'clock news the main broadcast booth was shut down and all operations shifted to an alternate booth, which required fewer hands to operate. This left Zack the opportunity to quietly get to the main booth, lock himself in, and override programming world wide, at least for a brief period of time . . . Hopefully long enough, he thought, to get the message out. The only catch was, that he'd have to take an elevator from the main lobby. If he was seen. . . it would be all over.

That was where Andy would come in. She'd have to make enough of a scene to draw attention away from him as he slipped through the lobby to the control elevator. He silently prayed for her. . . that she'd somehow get away. . . get to safety. He knew that he'd be arrested before it was all said and done. But she. . . had to get away. Even if he were never to see her again, it would be worth it.

In the shadows outside of the WBC building the pair held each other tenderly, knowing all too well that this may be the last time. In their silence they spoke. . . of all that they had come to mean to each other.

"Zack, I want you to know. . . that I love you," Andy said, softly caressing his cheek and looking into his deep brown eyes. "No matter what happens. . . I'll always love you."

It had always been hard for Zack to express his feelings. And yet, here, and now. . . it seemed to come easy. His eyes flooded with thankful tears. "I. . . I love you. . . more than anything." In a different time and place he knew that this woman was the one he could share the rest of his life with. Now though, he dismissed thoughts of what might have been for what they must do now. . . for others, for the whole of mankind.

"Ready?" he asked her gently.

"Sure. Let's go."

The receptionist greeted Andy with a polite nod as she walked past her, reaching for a brochure from a rack just on the far side of the front desk. As she reached the display she let out a loud gasp, grabbing her stomach as though in great pain. She fell to the floor in a heap bringing attendants from all over the lobby to her side and. . . leaving the front door unwatched for a few, precious moments.

Once inside the main control elevator Zack hugged the corner until the door shut with a swoosh.

"Main control room," he spoke, just loud enough for the computer to understand him. Moments later the lights of the city burst before him like the stars in the sky.

"So many millions. . . totally unaware," he thought shaking his head sadly. "I only hope they'll believe me. Dear God. . . let them believe me."

There was a faint swish behind him as the elevator door gave way to the hallway outside of the main control room. With a deep swallow Zack made his way quietly down the hall, making sure that it was empty. It had never seemed such a long distance from the elevator to the control room door but when he finally arrived he breathed a sigh of relief. Thankfully the door was voice activated as he, all too obviously, was missing his wrist implant.

"Zack Murphy," he spoke into a condenser type microphone on the wall. He was more than a little surprised that it opened immediately revealing a darkened control room.

He crept in quickly, reaching for the small metallic disk he had secured in his pocket. As he came to the main panel he switched on a small light, revealing a myriad of controls. Locating the slot marked Holographic Control Room Broadcast he slipped the disk in. Setting for global broadcast he paused, whispering a silent prayer over the button marked, "play".

As he braced himself to proceed something caught his attention. There was someone in the master control booth above him . . . It was Sam McDermott. The pair stared at one another for some time before Zack noticed his long time boss reaching for the panel before him. Instantly Zack pressed the play button, but even as he did he realized that his own panel had gone dead. It had been shut down.

Glancing up again Zack saw Sam sadly shake his head. Then all at once there was a sharp click as the door came open and Zack was surrounded by NSP troopers. He could see past them in the hallway. There was Andy, escorted by two blue uniformed men.

"How could you do it, Sam!" Zack growled as he was being roughly escorted out of the booth. "You didn't just sell me out . . . You sold the whole world out!" Sam shook his head sadly and disappeared into the darkness of the master control booth.

CHAPTER TWENTY SEVEN

In the stillness of the hallway two shadowy figures made their way toward Zack's apartment. Reaching the door the lead figure knocked several times. After a moment with no response, a knarled hand slid a security card into the slot by the door, causing it to swish open.

The pair silently made their way into the darkened living quarters, illuminated dimly only by a message board above the holophone. The simple message read "Watch the disk in the HCR".

A quivery steel-like voice spoke "H.C.R. On", and immediately a holographic image of Zack appeared in the room.

"This is Zack Murphy reporting on September Eight, Two Thousand Thirty for the World Holovision Corporation. The news I have will shock you, but please understand. . . it is true."

An old man cautiously slipped his way through the lobby of the World Holovision Corporation, made his way past the receptionist, and with a hard swallow entered the elevator, speaking the words "Main Broadcast studio, please." He prayed a silent prayer as the elevator whisked him towards his destination.

With trembling hands he moved through the strangely open door to the broadcast booth, eyeing the myriad of flashing lights scattered across the room. Without hesitating he moved swiftly to the control panel, slipping the disk, which he held in his hand into a slot marked H.C.D. He quickly located the button marked "Play." With his finger poised above it, he again prayed a silent prayer.

As he stood contemplating the global effects, which would result from pushing the button, he had the sensation that he was being watched. His feelings were confirmed when he looked above him in the control booth. There stood the imposing figure of Sam McDermott.

As their eyes met, a flood of memories filled the mind of each. Sam remembered with fondness, the warm summer spent with his best friend Josiah Murphy and how the old man before him, then young and vibrant, had come to mean so much to him. He could see Zack in him.

This reminded Gramps of Zack and of the message he'd found on his grandson's HCR. He was thankful now that he'd changed his mind just before boarding the flight to the colonies. He only wished that he would have come to find Zack right away . . . He'd felt ashamed and embarrassed, and now. . . Zack had probably been arrested. He'd said so at the end of his message. Now it was time for Gramps to come through.

The tension mounted as the two stared at each other. All at once Grandpa Murphy saw Sam reach down and press a button on the console before him. Expecting to see the power cut he was shocked when he heard the click of the automatic locking system securing the doors to the broadcast booth. Again he looked at Sam McDermott. This time he saw a sad smile on his face and a tear rolling down his cheek. Sam turned and left without a sound. Grandpa noticed that in his hand he carried the original copy of Zack's disk.

Swallowing hard Gramps reached a shaking hand toward the button before him. Immediately the darkness was interrupted as Zack appeared as he did in millions of homes around the globe.

"This is Zack Murphy reporting on September Eighth, Two Thousand Thirty for the World Holovision Corporation. . .

PART III: God's Way

CHAPTER TWENTY EIGHT

Thirty minutes seemed an eternity to the trio waiting nervously in James' car. The morning sun began to swiftly drive away the chill of the fall night. No one said a word as they awaited what secretly each dreaded. Peter sat at the wheel of the large vehicle while Rachel and Jenny sat in the back nervously clinging to each other's hand.

Finally Peter spoke. "It's been half an hour . . . We'll give them another fifteen minutes. . . no matter what they told us." But as he spoke, sirens could be heard from all over the city, obviously heading in their direction. . . toward the Altrex building.

Rachel Noah let out a shocked gasp. "Oh God. . . no!"

"Give em just a couple more minutes. . . don't panic yet. They still could have gotten out." Peter said trying to reassure the two girls with him, but they all realized the truth. No one would be coming.

Minutes later, when it became obvious that remaining any longer would be dangerous, Peter silently started the car and pulled into the street, and drove away from Altrex; from James, Dr. Noah, Dr. Wilford, and Fulton, and on to safety.

As they gently made their way to the expressway and on out of town Peter could hear Rachel in the back seat, tears streaming down her face, whispering a prayer as Jenny comforted her.

"Oh dear Jesus. Hold them in the palm of your hand."

Zack was just able to glance at Andy as the NSP led him from the control room and into a waiting elevator. His heart ached as he beheld her tear stained face and soft eyes, which seemed even then to be saying, "it'll be alright." He prayed for her constantly, hoping against hope that she might be spared.

He was hustled out of the WBC building through the main lobby and past Susan James. She watched silently, mouth agape, as the NSP troopers roughly hustled him through the front sliding doors and on into a waiting patrol car.

It seemed a very short time before he found himself looking at a very different side of the National Security Police Headquarters. After a brief booking ritual where he was searched and electronically scanned, he was placed in a small, stark cell with a toilet protruding from one wall and a small, uncomfortable cot built into another.

Remembering the other side of the bars and the incredible sight he and B.J. had witnessed, Zack marveled at the stark coldness of the cell block. The one amenity that the cells had was an industrial grade of holovision built into the wall opposite each cubicle's bed.

Sitting on the cot, Zack shook his head as the midnight news program ambled on before him as usual. . . as though nothing had happened. . . as though one of the network's top reporters hadn't just been arrested. As he figured, nothing was mentioned of his and Andy's apprehension, or the other team's success or failure out at Altrex. He guessed that they too, had failed.

What was going to happen? Would the world ever come to know what hideous things lay beneath the surface of their wonderful utopic society? He wondered if the WCC would be able to snuff out all knowledge of the "Utopia Project" by eliminating all who had information about it.

"Dear God, let the truth come to light," he prayed. Zack got to his knees, heart full and heavy, crying out to the creator of the universe, crying out for the world, for his companions: James, Peter, Dr. Noah, and Rachel, Dr. Wilford. . . and most of all for Andy. He prayed that somehow God would spare her. He also prayed, knowing that his probable end was the Aurora processing station, that he'd be able to stand to the end against this tyrannical system and FOR God.

Some twenty minutes later. . . still deep in communion with God, Zack noticed the familiar sounds of Larry Taylor, Network weather man. His broadcast had been taped earlier, as had most of the rest of the news program. All was usual until all at once there was an interruption in the broadcast. Zack rubbed his eyes in disbelief as his torso appeared in the set before him. Somehow, someone had succeeded in broadcasting his story. A surge of hope shot through his heart.

Then from down the hallway he heard the voices of several men. They were cheering! Zack couldn't believe his ears. He was sure that he heard the voices of James, Dr. Noah. . . and yes, Dr. Wilford!

"Hey! . . . It's me, Zack!" he yelled, hoping they could hear him above their screams.

CHAPTER TWENTY NINE

"Mr. Murphy?" Gramps looked up to see a figure standing in a small passageway, silhouetted in light from behind him. He had been standing in the control room for some time watching his grandson's image as he broadcast his shocking news to the world.

"Mr. Murphy. . . uh Gramps?" the man spoke again. Gramps thought he'd heard that voice before but he couldn't see the face, only the outline of a large man. "It's me. . . Sam. You'd better let me get you out of here. The NSP will be coming through that door any minute."

"Sam! Am I ever glad to see you! Sure thing, son. . . you just lead the way," spoke the old man with obvious relief in his voice. He patted Sam on the back as he followed him out the small hatch-type opening in the wall. The pair silently padded down a back hallway until they reached a service elevator.

"There's no time to talk, Gramps. You take this to the bottom floor. I've slipped the guard a strong sedative. He should be out like a light by now. Just get on out the back entrance. My car is waiting in the alley. Get as far from here as you possibly can," Sam spoke resolutely.

"But Sam. . . what about you, son? They're sure to figure out that you helped me."

"Don't worry. . . I have it all figured out." Gramps stepped into the now open elevator as Sam finished his goodbye. "And Gramps. . . tell Zack, if you see him. . . that I'm sorry, so very sorry. He'll understand." The door closed leaving Sam alone in the darkened hallway. He stood silently for a moment, strangely at peace and then turned with a jerk walking resolutely, every so resolutely back toward the broadcast booth.

It was a full twenty minutes before the NSP troopers were able to short circuit the system, allowing the door to the broadcast booth to be able to be forced open. Once inside they found the body of Sam McDermott slumped over the control panel, an empty bottle of sleeping pills still clutched in his strong right hand.

Andy found herself in a plush room, alone for what seemed hours. She didn't know how the police had known to arrest her, but as she exited the lobby of the Corporate Broadcasting Company they were there waiting for her. She'd been hustled back into the building and up one of the main elevators and then forced to watch in horror as the broadcast booth door was opened and Zack arrested. Before she'd had the opportunity to say a word to him, he was led away. . . to who knows where. Moments later she too had been hustled down the elevator and into a waiting car which sped her to NSP headquarters.

A feeling of total defeat came over her as she paced back and forth in the small room. Not only had they failed. . . but she felt that she'd never see Zack or her father again. The weight of the situation bore in on her, pressing her down. Andy sank to the carpeted floor in a heap, sobbing deeply.

Moments later, as if on cue, she heard the door behind her swish open. She expected to see a uniformed officer and was more than a little shocked to be looking into the face of a well dressed, dignified man with dark, deep set eyes, and a thin smile.

He moved to her side, helping her to her feet. "Hello Miss Wilford. . . Andy. I'm Mr. Sinclair. I'd like to talk to you for a few moments if I may." His voice was companionate, and his demeanor kind. . . just what Andy needed at that moment.

"Zack! Is that you?" came James' voice from down the hall.

"Yeah! I'm here . . . I got caught. . . but someone must have. . ." Zack realized the improbability of what must surely have happened.

"What happened with you guys?" he inquired, just loud enough to be heard down the hall.

"Not a good place to chat, friend . . . Let's just say. . . things didn't go that well," came James' voice, obviously down.

"Everyone's okay though. . . for now."

"How is Andy?" spoke Dr. Wilford anxiously.

"She's caught. . . though where she is I don't know. . . I just know that she's in custody somewhere." There was a bittersweet silence. All were gratified by the broadcast taking place, they hoped, around the world, and yet. . . the cost had been high. They were all certain that it had meant their lives, and most difficult. . . Andy's life.

Moments later a metallic clash told Zack that someone was entering the cell block. Steady footsteps down the concrete hall soon produced three men at the door of Zack's cell. One NSP trooper accompanied two men in dark suits.

"Mr. Murphy," spoke a dignified man with dark eyes. Zack knew who he was. He'd seen his picture somewhere . . . This was Andrew Sinclair. . . head of Altrex. "May I sit down?" came his smooth steely voice.

Zack just nodded. Sinclair sat on the opposite end of the bed from him and looked silently at him for some moments.

"It's amazing. . . the resemblance. You look so much like your father," spoke the dark eyed Sinclair.

"You knew my dad?"

"Yes, I did. . . we went to college together. I can't say that we were great friends, but. . . we knew each other. I think that our priorities were a bit different." He paused. "I wondered if the day would come when his famous son might step into the same role that his father occupied. I see by this presentation that you've picked up the banner that your dad, unfortunately carried. I'm sad for you."

"Sad for me! Sad for me! If you're aware of what's going on with the Utopia Project and are in favor of it, I'm sad for you. Are the goals of the WCC so sacred that it doesn't matter how they are reached?" Zack burst out angrily.

"It is obvious that you don't understand. Your mind has not grasped the incredible significance of the Utopia Project. Individuals are not important. . . society as a whole must not be burdened and dragged down by those unable or unwilling to be a part of the new world order." Sinclair spoke with passion as though delivering a sermon. "We are all a part of something much bigger than ourselves."

"You're sick! The whole `New World Order' is sick! It's all very clear to me now. Sinclair. . . you've got it all backwards. The individual IS important. Not the institution. God loves us each. . . individually. . ."

"GOD! You speak to me of GOD! You have no idea what you're talking about. I was sick to death decades ago with you narrow minded bigots. You speak as though you actually KNOW this God of yours!" Sinclair was loosing his calm demeanor. "Well there is a god in this world. . . and it's not that gray haired old myth from the middle ages! It's the corporation! You and your friends should have learned that before you tried to sabotage things! Now you'll all pay. . . with your lives!"

Zack stood resolutely. "Mr. Sinclair. . . you say that there is no God apart from the corporation . . . Well, I'm here to tell you, sir, that. . . just because you haven't met someone, it doesn't mean that they don't exist. I'll pray for you. . . I'll pray that God has mercy on your soul."

"Mercy! You and your friends should be praying to ME for mercy! You're all going to. . . the prison colony!" his eyes now revealed what lay in the heart of this man. There was a hellish, insanity buried deep within the front of sophistication. Zack shook his head and sat down, crying out to God for this man's soul, and yet knowing that he was probably too far gone.

The cell door shut with a click as Sinclair made his way toward the other prisoners. Zack prayed for each, that their resolve would hold. . . that they too would have the opportunity to proclaim the living God to this demon of a man!

The sun was just rising over the hills behind them as Peter and the two girls finally found the little rut filled road that led to the old cabin, which was to be their hideout for who knows how long. This place, deep in the Allegheny Mountains, was so far off the beaten track that the trio was lucky to find it at all, even with a very detailed map.

"Rachel, Jenny. . . we're here!" Peter said, rousing the two from a deep slumber. "This is the place. . . but. . . there's someone here already." He pointed out the smoke coming from the stone chimney. As they crept into the driveway. . . such as it was, a man stepped out onto the porch. He was tall, stocky, with graying temples, and had a serious look about him. There was something very familiar in his appearance. Peter couldn't quite make out where he'd met this man before. . . but he felt somehow that he knew him.

"Miss Wilford, I'm so very sorry to have inconvenienced you so, keeping you here so long. I was unavoidably detained in another part of the building. Shall we sit down?" spoke the smooth voiced Sinclair.

"Now suppose you fill me in on your involvement in this attempt to send out Mr. Murphy's. . . broadcast. I want you to know that his attempt failed. Therefore. . . if you will cooperate with us in our investigation, things could go easy with you." He studied her pretty face for signs of weakness. "Now what do you say?"

"So. . . what I hear you asking is whether I'll give you information about Zack. . . and. . . anyone else who might allegedly be involved?" she smiled at him sweetly. "And. . . in exchange you'll reduce my. . . punishment?"

"Exactly. . . I think that we understand each other," crooned Sinclair happily.

"Well, may I ask you a question first?"

"Certainly, my dear. . . certainly. Anything. Anything at all."

Andy thought for a moment, searching for the right words. "The Utopia Project. Are you familiar with it?" she finally asked with an innocent tone of voice.

"Yes, dear. . . the corporation's finest hour if I might be so candid," he answered proudly.

"Then you're very familiar with all aspects of it? I mean, it's such a complex program. It would take someone of great intellect to understand it all!"

"I sense that you've been an unwilling participant in Mr. Murphy's diabolical scheme, Miss Wilford . . . Ah, yes I am aware of every aspect of the project. It is a masterpiece. . . is it not? Finally, after so many centuries of living in the dark ages, man is free, free to be all that he was meant to be. . . unencumbered by the social problems which have held him down all along!"

Andy could play the part no longer. "Then, Mr. Sinclair, you are nothing more than an animal! No one with half a conscience could knowingly take part in this horrible project! NO, I will not cooperate with you in the least! The only thing that I WILL do is pray for you!" Andy blasted the unsuspecting Sinclair.

Momentarily taken aback, the dark eyed executive flashed an angry scowl toward Andy. "Why you little. . . I could have saved you! You fool. . . no one talks to me that way! You will rot in hell with the others!"

"No Mr. Sinclair." Andy replied with steel calmness. "I will not see hell . . . You on the other hand. . . have already purchased your ticket! May God have mercy on your soul!"

Sinclair was speechless. He merely rose, smoothed his rumpled hair, and left the room, turning at the door. "Have fun at the prison colony, Miss Wilford." With that he let out an evil chuckle and disappeared through the automatic door.

CHAPTER THIRTY

The five men were each fitted with a black helmet, which covered their face completely and allowed them to see only straight ahead. It was explained to them that if they did anything but follow their assigned guard, their helmets would subject them to excruciating pain. None desired to challenge this statement. Zack was in the lead, followed by James, Fulton, Dr. Noah, and last, Dr. Wilford. They were led out through a long hallway and into a waiting van, fitted with seats on each side of the rear interior.

Zack guessed that they were on their way to JFK and then on to Aurora Station. There had to be some way of escape. There just had to be.

The five men sat facing one another, two on one side and three on the other so that their feet touched. Immediately upon being seated Zack felt an almost imperceptible tapping on his big toe. He finally realized that it was Brice Fulton trying to get his attention. He must have been using Morse Code. Unfortunately Zack didn't understand it.

It was obvious, though, that the other three did. He could see out of the corner of his eye that the man to his right, whom he took to be James, was nodding his head, as were Dr. Wilford, and Noah, who were seated across from them. Zack figured that it must be some kind of escape plan. He only hoped it was a good one and that it didn't get them all killed.

Soon the sleek NSP van screeched to a halt at a side entrance to JFK. As they were shuttled out of the vehicle, Zack realized that they were at the JFK NSP entrance. This would be no place to try to make a break for it. He prayed that the others would wait.

Thankfully the five were led through the area to the very fringe of the NSP section. There were hundreds of busy travelers just a few yards ahead of them, travelers who would provide cover for their escape attempt.

All at once Dr. Wilford collapsed in a heap on the floor sending the attending NSP officers rushing to his aid. Seizing the moment, Fulton made his break. He pushed an off-balance trooper onto two others who were crouched over the Doctor. As he ran, the others could hear a blood curdling scream as his helmet kicked in. He continued to run, finally able to rip the black bubble from his head. Two large streams of blood coursed down Fulton's cheeks as he tossed the large helmet to the side. When he was nearly in the clear, a loud crack split the air. Brice Fulton was sent sprawling headlong onto a group of Japanese tourists. He lay there, lifeless.

Momentarily Dr. Wilford arose, limping his way along with his captors as NSP troops from the section behind him saw to the body of Brice Fulton. The others, who'd been paralyzed with fear, now continued on obediently down the ramp toward the space shuttle, toward Aurora. . . toward eternity.

Sinclair paced nervously back and forth across the imported rug, which covered dark mahogany floors in his spaciously plush office atop Altrex. Every few moments an angry snarl crossed his lips as he recalled the conversations he'd had earlier with Zack Murphy. . . and his little troll of a girlfriend, Andy Wilford. Each time he eased the anger spewing from his gut with thoughts of the pair, along with their friends, disintegrating into nothingness at the colonies processing station. At this he broke into fits of convulsive laughter rising deep from within his black heart!

"Mr. Sinclair," came the smooth voice of his secretary. "Alistair Blakely on line one. It sounds rather important."

Sinclair fixed his tie, combs is disheveled hair back into place, sat at his desk and tried to calm himself momentarily. He pressed a button on the console in front of him and immediately the smooth featured, dignified Minister of Human Affairs appeared before him.

"Yes sir, what can I do for you?" he said nervously.

"Oh come now< Mr. Sinclair. . . let's skip all the pleasantries. I'm afraid we have a little situation on our hands. . . do we not? Just days before Mr. Pierre DuMonde was to be presented to the world as it ultimate ruler. . . we have a little security problem, followed by the ravings of this young Zack Murphy. . . broadcast round the world, creating a terrible public relations problem!" he paused for effect. "Mr. Sinclair. . . just how do you account for this. . . uh. . . situation?" The old gentleman waited as Sinclair searched for an answer, obviously enjoying the sight of the head of Altrex squirming.

"Sir. . . I can't explain it. One of our most loyal men. . . Sam McDermott. . . just went off the deep end . . . He locked himself in the control room. . . started the broadcast, and then committed suicide. I don't understand it at all."

"I see. . ." Again there was silence as Blakely chose his words carefully. "What are we to do, Mr. Sinclair? Security has been breached. . . we need someone to shoulder the blame."

"Everything is taken care of. I have seen to it myself. All those involved are in custody and on their way to the disintegration chamber at Aurora. Everything is under control." Sinclair fidgeted before the cold stare of the white haired old man.

"You don't get it, do you Sinclair? I've consulted with the chief . . . Your services are no longer needed . . . You've become an embarrassment to us and we certainly do not need that at this time."

"What do you mean? After all these years of faithful service, you're dumping me? You can't. . . you just can't!" screamed Sinclair.

"No need to pack your possessions, Sinclair . . . We'll have someone there to pick you up momentarily . . . Dump you? I wouldn't exactly say that we're dumping you. . . goodbye Andrew." Then the screen in front of him was dark. The whole room seemed dark. . . filled with demons scratching and clawing at him in his mind.

"No!!!!!" His secretary jumped from her desk, finding his office door locked from within.

The next day the headline read, "Executive Takes Own Life After Failed Attempt to Extort Funds by Discrediting WCC."

CHAPTER THIRTY ONE

Zack learned a new use for the privacy switch on his seat as all of the prisoners sat in darkness for the duration of the entire shuttle flight. Their hands and feet had been secured firmly in place, not allowing for movement of any kind.

The past few hours seemed a nightmare as he relived the murder of Brice Fulton over and over. It haunted him. The only thing that took his mind off of the horror of that scene was thinking of Andy. He wanted to cherish every moment they'd shared together, every detail about her. He even recalled the smell of her perfume.

"No. . . wait!" he wasn't recalling it. . . he could smell it! That meant that Andy was with them on the flight. Oh how he longed to rush to her. . . to hold her in his arms. . . and to make all of this madness go away. He had to find a way to see her.

Immediately a plan formulated in his mind. If he could get one of the guards to let him go to the bathroom. . . maybe then he could catch a glimpse of her and somehow let her know that he was there.

He got the guard's attention and asked to be taken to the bathroom. Reluctantly the NSP trooper returned with a stewardess. As she bent over him, securing the weighted vest in place he whispered, "Please miss. . . find Andy Wilford. . . and tell her Zack is here. . . and somehow it'll be alright."

The young woman hesitated for a moment but then replied, "Sure I will."

Making their way down the aisle Zack craned his neck inside the dark bubble helmet, trying to catch a glimpse of her. And then. . . there she was, two seats behind him on the aisle. He recognized the shoes she was wearing. . . all that could be seen outside of her privacy module. As they passed he gently reached for her hand inside her dark little space, found it, and squeezed reassuringly for a brief second. As he continued past their fingertips lingered for a moment in a tiny, yet powerful touching embrace.

"She knew. . . she knew. . ." he said to himself through thankful tears.

The rest of the trip was uneventful and they soon found themselves being ushered off of the shuttle in single file into the space station. As there were some thirty prisoners on the flight, they were broken down into smaller groups for transport to the processing station.

There was something different about the station on this day. It wasn't just the different situation that he was in . . . . It seemed as though clouds hung over the place. No one smiled . . . Gone were the genialities he and Andy had witnessed just days before. Had his broadcast reached even Aurora Station. . . and were these people. . .definitely fewer in number than he remembered, reeling from the realization that their "big brother", the WCC, was not so benevolent after all? He hoped and prayed so!

Gratefully, Zack realized that his group contained all of his friends. . . including Andy Wilford. They must have wanted to put them all together to make sure they got all of them in first. Zack was feeling more and more hopeless until. . . he noticed, off at the other end of the large bay, a familiar face . . . It was Sydney! He seemed to be staring directly at them. Just then the five fugitives were hustled into a van for the next leg of their journey. Zack was beside Andy and, though their hands had been bound after the escape attempt and the helmets kept them from being able to talk, at least they could gently rest their shoulders against one another.

He had to find a way out. . . somehow. . . he prayed to God for a miracle. . . some way of escape. The guards all carried phased stun-guns, which could do everything from deliver a mild shock to break every bone in a person's body. They weren't things to mess with. Still. . . if it meant his last dying breath he would fight . . . Somehow, he had to.

A short way into the trip their vehicle stopped suddenly. All of the guards piled out to see what the problem was. In all there were five NSP troopers including the driver. No one in the back of the van could hear what was going on . . . There was only silence for a long time. Then, all at once, the strange, quirky head of an android appeared at the rear door of the vehicle. It was Sydney!

He swiftly set about unlocking the wrist-cuffs on Zack, Andy, and the others, and then, producing a small black controller from his pocket, he deactivated all of the helmets.

"Sydney!" Zack exclaimed as he pulled the black bubble from his head.

"No time to talk, sir. . .another vehicle should be along this way within five minutes. Could you and the others help me to load these guards into the truck?" Zack's jaw dropped as he stepped out of the van and around toward the front to find all five NSP troopers in a neat stack along the side of the road.

"How. . .what. . .I don't understand," Zack choked upon finding them. By that time the others joined him, and after a very brief celebration, helped to load the five unconscious policemen into the back of the truck. That task accomplished, James and Dr. Noah joined Sydney in the front of the NSP truck while Zack, Andy, and Dr. Wilford jumped into the small vehicle that Sydney had been driving, all the while hugging each other as much as possible without slowing everyone down.

What followed was a whirlwind drive, somewhat akin to the fabled Mr. Toad's wild ride, up and down the clear roads of Aurora. Zack was shocked to see that within moments they were descending into the very module that housed the Colonies Processing Station. Was this some kind of cruel trick? Were there dozens of NSP troops waiting for them to arrive to snatch away what brief freedom they'd known?

Once inside, Sydney turned into a kind of back alley, leading to what seemed to be a maintenance building of sorts. A huge door swung open and both vehicles disappeared into the bowels of a dark, unpolished warehouse, obviously not for the eyes of tourists. The android stopped at a little office, popped out of the NSP truck, and proceeded back to the little vehicle that Zack was driving.

The five somewhat stunned fugitives stepped into the dim light of the building and immediately fell into each other's arms like little children dancing around a May pole. They finally were able to relate the stories of the past day to one another, stumbling over each other's words in a frenzy to share their experiences.

Zack took Andy by the hand and moved to one side momentarily.

"I thought I'd never see you again," he said, looking into her eyes.

"Oh Zack," she fell into his arms. Both held on tightly as though trying to compensate for almost loosing each other. "I love you so much." Finally they loosed their embrace, slowly pulling back just enough to cherish the sight of one another. After a long moment their lips moved softly together for a gentle, loving kiss, which lingered as the last pedal of a rose hangs gently to the bud before lilting softly to the ground.

"Excuse me sir. . . sorry to interrupt you," came the mechanical voice of Sydney from behind them. "There is someone that you should meet." Zack and Andy turned, still holding gently to each other.

CHAPTER THIRTY TWO

From the tiny office came an odd looking little man in his late fifties, with a slight hunched back. He looked like an ordinary maintenance man, wearing greasy overalls with a pocket protector overflowing with pens and small rulers. A broad smile split the homely little face below a crooked, broken nose and beady little eyes. Individually his features were near ugly. . . but as a package they came together in a quaint manner, giving him an almost loveable look.

"Hello. . . my name is Clinton Bosley. I'm very pleased that you're safe. There will be time for explanations momentarily. Our first task though, is for you to exchange clothing with the NSP troopers. We'll put your security helmets on them. . . and send them in to the processing station. By the time they discover their error. . . if they do. . . we'll be long gone."

Without a word the small band did as the little man had suggested. Within ten minutes Dr. Wilford, James, Dr. Noah, Zack, and Sydney had donned NSP uniforms, dressing the unconscious guards in their clothes. They drove the short distance to the processing station just as the guards began regain consciousness. Clinton followed behind with Andy, pulling in to the rear parking area.

At the door they were greeted by four CPS security guards who hustled the NSP troopers out of the van and into the building. It was obvious that the policemen were attempting to communicate the real situation to the security guards. . . but to no avail. One, in fact, attempted to make a break but was quickly harnessed by a strong electrical charge. Within moments the desperate NSP troopers and their captors had disappeared into the building.

"Now. . . for the next phase!" chirped Bosley, "Follow me."

The small band fell in line behind the little man who guided them to the rear door of the station, which led into the atrium overlooking the shuttle bay. He produced a little card from his pocket, which he slipped into a slot beside the door. It swished open immediately. After the group had all entered and the door behind them had closed, Bosley turned his attention to the door to the shuttle bay itself.

"Now when we get to the bottom of the stairs, I want everyone to head for shuttle number four. Use your stun guns if anyone challenges you. . . but only if necessary. I should be able to get us aboard with no problem." Seconds later the little band was at the bottom of the stairs heading straight for shuttle number four.

Sydney went directly to the supervisor and spoke to him.

"I'm afraid we're going to have to inspect your shuttles," he said confidently. "Seems someone has been bringing contraband into the station. . . and we want to rule out any possibility that it could be your crew. You wouldn't happen to know anything about this, would you?" spoke the android with a purposely suspicious tone.

"Uh. . . no. . . I don't know anything . . . Go right ahead . . .inspect to your heart's desire!" retorted the shift supervisor defensively.

Moments later, everyone aboard the shuttle, Mr. Bosley climbed into the pilot's seat. "Hang on everyone!" he said, firing up the engines. The rest of the little band found seats, strapped themselves in and awaited take off. There was a small jolt as the craft leapt upwards and then, leaving a puzzled flight crew behind, the fugitives were off into the flight tunnel. It was only moments before they found themselves in free flight. . . leaving Aurora station and their death sentences behind!

At Aurora Station, hurried preparations were being made for the five fugitives to enter the annihilation chamber. According to instructions sent on ahead of them, the normal formalities were to be skipped. All five were to be sent to the chamber immediately upon arrival.

The head security officer of the processing station read the report with interest. It said that one prisoner had already attempted to escape and had been shot. The rest were extremely dangerous so no chances were to be taken. They were to be disintegrated without even the removal of security helmets. This explained the agitated state of the five as they were led into the processing station.

Finally, after a major struggle, all of the captives had been strapped down in the chamber. The Lieutenant just wanted to get things over with, so he personally went to the control booth overlooking the tiny room. He made the correct preset adjustments and poised his hand to pull the lever to his right, thus starting the process. Just as he began to pull the lever one of the prisoners below managed to free his hands. He tugged at the helmet on his head, screaming in agony as the electric shock began. The helmet came free a full two seconds before the final sequence finished.

With horror the young officer looked below him. He saw, not the desperate fugitive he read of. . . but one of his own friends, a

National Security Police trooper. . . "Oh my God. . ." he said, trying frantically to reverse the process. But he was too late. . . his friend and the four others simply vanished under the powerful ray.

CHAPTER THIRTY THREE

Fifteen minutes out from Aurora the passengers of shuttle number four finally relaxed enough to converse. Looking around Zack saw that Andy and her father were huddled close together to the rear of the cabin. Dr. Noah sat quietly, looking out a small window, deep in thought. He and James were seated close the front, making it possible to talk with Bosley.

"Mr. Bosley. . . can you fill us in? Somehow it's hard to believe that we're actually safe . . . What's going on? Where do you fit into this jig-saw puzzle?" James questioned.

"Well. . . I guess I should start at the beginning," began the little man, realizing that he had the attention of everyone in the little craft. I was born in 1976 in Scranton, Pennsylvania. Early in my life it became clear that I had an. . . elevated I.Q. By the age of twelve I had graduated from M.I.T. in computer technologies. I had spent the first part of my life surrounded by publicity, so by my early teens I had grown very tired of the public eye. I was never comfortable with it. Well, my parents and I moved to France where I was offered a job at a computer firm. . . in research. There, in my element, I experienced an incredibly joyful period. I could create to my heart's content and never worry about taking credit for any of my inventions . . . The company did, and that was fine by me.

"While I was there I developed some rather. . .advanced computer systems. My intentions were to create a computerized system, which would help man to order his life. What I found was that it was incredibly easy to link up with systems from all over the world. . . even governmental systems. What's more. . . I tapped into a network of brilliant individuals from around the globe. . . a handful of men and women, so far advanced above others in the field that they were able to move around, unnoticed, anywhere in the computer world, and access any system. There were no locks that could keep us out.

"Innocently we played games. . .games with the computers of the major powers of the world. We manipulated global events, created them out of nothing. . .in small ways at first, but soon we realized that we had the ability, if we chose to do so, to bring the world to it's knees. . . in essence to become puppeteers with the world as our stage and it's `so called' leaders as our puppets. That was not what I had in mind. I immediately put my project on hold, shelved it where I figured no one could stumble on to it.

"I went on to another `pet' project, the Wrist Implanted Identification Chip."

"You invented the WIIC?" asked Zack incredulously.

"Yes. . . but soon I realized the potential for evil even with that project. Unfortunately I realized it too late. The company grabbed onto it and, in a crude way, made plans for implementing it as soon as they could market it.

"I had a co-worker. . . not very skilled in computer science, but none-the-less brilliant in his own way. You may have heard of him. . . Mr. Pierre Dumonde." Nodding heads around the cabin indicated their familiarity.

"Well, somehow. . . he got hold of my program. . . and next thing I knew he had risen to the top of the company. He was heralded round the world as the brilliant creator of this computer system that would revolutionize the world. It was very soon after this that the World Council of Corporations came into existence, and within a very short time. . . it had taken over the world. You probably have heard the way that the WCC claims to have come into existence. Well, I happen to know that. . . it was by the use of my program that that evil organization came into power.

"I decided to become a mole, to keep an eye on what was going on under the surface. This was not hard as the WCC employed few, truly intelligent people. I found that I could move in and out of most situations and places totally unnoticed by merely tapping into the program that I created. I could access the modest amount of funds that I needed for living.

"In time I moved to Switzerland. The Swiss had always remained neutral in war. . . and, oddly enough, this same conviction of independence and neutrality make them the last country to enter the WCC's umbrella. There was freedom there in the early parts of the century to be found nowhere else on the globe. In addition, it was easier to access worldwide systems from there as every major power had a direct link to the Swiss banking industry.

"I settled in the little city of Wohlen and bought a little chalet outside of the city. From there I have monitored world affairs ever since, occasionally leaving to inspect a situation more closely. I must say that for the past twenty years I have agonized over the true state of the world! It has not been as it has seemed. . . and of course you know that.

"Mr. Murphy, I have known of you for quite some time . . . You see, my plan was to carefully select someone. . . a journalist with the right kind of moral fiber and in a situation of some prominence. I planned to somehow feed him information, a little at a time, until such time as I could bring him fully into my confidence. It was my hope that my journalist ally would then reveal to the world the true nature of the WCC.

"Zack. . . your father was my man. I calculated right when I selected him. He was a man of deep integrity. At first I gave him bits and pieces of the puzzle, but it wasn't long before I knew I could divulge the whole ghastly situation to him.

"On the last day that you saw him. . . I had given him enough information for him to be gravely concerned. We planned a meeting in Munich, Germany. Unfortunately, somehow. . . someone got wind that your father had certain information. Through my systems link I learned that an official of the WCC. . . a Mr. Sinclair, had personally arranged for an accident to take place for your father. They did this sort of thing all the time, and still do for that matter. A bomb was planted on your parents' airliner, set to go off when the plane was over a very remote part of the German Alps. I frantically tried to contact your father, but to no avail. . ."

"Then. . . their plane did go down over the Alps," asked Zack sadly.

"Yes. . . and I grieve to this day for the loss of all those innocent people. If there were only some way to have gotten them all off the flight!"

"What do you mean, `all'" off the flight?" James chimed in.

"Well. . . I was able at the last second to change the flight plan a bit. . . to have the plane land in Zurich. . . for some bogus maintenance check. Through my computer link I arranged for an electronics crew to meet the plane to check over it's landing systems. As they swarmed onto it after touchdown, I was with them . . .with two extra technician uniforms. I was able to get your folks to the rear of the plane. They slipped into the restrooms as passengers, and emerged. . . electronics technicians. In moments we were off of the flight and it was on its way. . . to its fiery destination. The reason they found no wreckage was that the bomb on board was so incredibly powerful. Not a shred of evidence would be left behind."

Zack's eyes grew wide in amazement. "My parents. . . are. . . alive?"

"Why yes," was Bosley's simple reply.

There was a stunned silence in the tiny craft before the little man continued. "I know that you haven't heard from them. Your mom especially has agonized over that. But it just wasn't safe. It was far better for you to think that they were both dead. Then one day. . . when the timing was right, we hoped we could bring you on board."

"But where are they. . . where have they been all this time?" pleaded Zack almost indignantly.

"Well, for the first few years your parents were my guests. Your mom still lives at my chalet most of the time, taking care of it for me while I'm away. Your dad and I have been undercover all over the world for the past decade or so, trying to keep an eye on things. . . waiting for an opportunity," he became thoughtful. "Uh, you should know that your father's been quite close to you many times. You haven't known it. . . but he's been there, watching over you. He's become quite adept at disguises . . . In fact. . . do you remember an old porter at JFK?"

"You're kidding me!" Zack exclaimed, delighted at the thought. He looked back at Andy who giggled as she recounted how the old man had saved their lives.

"Oh, and by the way. . . your grandparents didn't get on that flight after all. It seems that your granddad and an old spaceport worker got into a conversation just before they were to board their flight. Somehow your folks just. . . changed their minds at the last second. It was your grandfather that got into the station and broadcast your story."

"I don't believe it! But. . . is he safe? Did he make it out alright?" pleaded Zack, reeling from the news.

"Yes . . . HE did. . ."

"Why do you say it like that? What happened?"

Bosley paused a long moment before he answered. "I'm afraid that Sam McDermott is dead." He allowed the shock to ease a bit. "He gave his life. . . to protect your granddad. . . and to make sure that your broadcast got out."

The cabin of shuttle number four grew silent for some time as everyone felt the grief in Zack's heart. He thought back through his life. How Sam had cared for him, loved him . . . He felt ashamed for the anger he'd held toward his boss the past few days.

Sensing the need to move on past the latest news he'd shared, Bosley continued. "For the past twenty years or so I've been working on biosimulations. . . uh. . . androids. Sydney is my creation. He and a small army of others are used throughout the Corporate Space Program. Again. . . the company I've worked for took all the credit for their development, leaving me comfortably in the shadows, even still under an assumed name.

"Sydney is the only android I've stayed very close to. He's become somewhat of a great friend over the years. When you and Miss Wilford visited the station. . . it was an easy matter to have him assigned to you.

"Sydney. . . wasn't that a clever trick of Mr. Murphy. . . locking you in his hotel room?" he smiled toward his animated friend in the copilot seat.

"Why yes sir. I found it rather. . . entertaining," spoke the android with a quirky smile.

"Mr. Murphy. . . Sydney could have torn the door off at its hinges. He is rather strong. . . but we really did want you to pay a visit to the processing station."

Just then Bosley's eye caught one of the gauges on the control panel before them. "Oh no. . ." he said.

"What's wrong?" came the unison reply from the passengers of the little craft.

"I checked this thing earlier this morning. It was fully charged then . . . It must've gotten used for one of the fake colony runs. Yep. . . those flights take about half an hour. . . and that's just how much charge we are short. The tough thing is that these little buggies just pack enough energy to barely make it back to earth . . . I'm sorry folks. . . without enough juice, we won't make it back."

"Precisely what are our options?" came the voice of Dr. Noah.

"Well. . . we could stay out here in space. . . until our oxygen runs out. . . or we could head back to the station. We're sure to be caught if we do, though. . . there are very few incoming flights and each one is monitored closely. By now they've probably figured out that we weren't with the NSP."

"Couldn't we try to glide into earth's orbit and save enough fuel for just before we land?" asked Dr. Wilford hopefully.

"No, I'm afraid not. . . the bulk of our power will be needed as we enter earth's atmosphere. We'll burn up if we don't approach it correctly." He shook his head sadly. "I'm sorry folks, I guess I'm not as smart as I thought I was."

Again there was dead silence in the little cabin. No one wished to go back to Aurora . . . It would mean sure and certain death at the hands of the NSP. The little band didn't want to give them the satisfaction. A full fifteen minutes passed as each pondered the question.

Zack and Andy looked at one another. At least this time they'd be together. She leaned forward, touching his cheek. He placed his hand over hers and then kissed it gently.

"If we drift in space until we run out of oxygen. . . at least the end will come in a somewhat less dreadful way. We'll all slip into unconsciousness. . . and die peacefully," Dr. Noah said with resignation in his voice. "I, for one. . . am ready to meet the Lord." Again there was silence.

"Sir. . . if I might add. . . there is another option," came the voice of Sydney.

"What do you mean, Sydney? I don't see how there could be."

"That option would be. . . to drain my power cells into those of the shuttle . . . This would still would not be quite enough but, if the shuttle were lightened, there is a very good chance that you could be successful. According to my calculations. . . if we were to jettison all excess cargo and. . . if my drained body were to be also jettisoned. . . it should be enough."

"Sydney! No!" Andy protested.

"It's the only way, Madame. If it's any consolation, my memory disk could be placed in the shuttle's computer. I would be with you in. . . spirit. . . sort of."

After a long moment Bosley spoke up. "He's right. It's the only way." He looked lovingly at this machine that had become his best friend for the past ten years. "Old boy. . . I'll try to rebuild you. . . and I will keep your memory disk," he choked on his words. "Thank you. . . my friend."

"Yes sir. I wish all of you the very best. I, being an android, could never experience knowing your Christ, but I do so wish you a joyous reunion with him one day. And in the meantime, prosper in all that you endeavor to do." With that he produced a small wire from a hidden panel under his arm. Looking back one last time he said "Goodbye. . . friends." He plugged the wire into the console and almost immediately slumped forward in his seat.

The tears were very real throughout the little craft as Sydney's final wishes were completed: his memory disk were removed, and his body was jettisoned along with other non-essential items.

Bosley watched as the limp body of his best friend floated off into the darkness of space. "Goodbye, old pal." As Sydney floated off, it almost seemed as though he had a slight, quirky smile on his face and one hand slightly raised as if to say "Goodbye."

CHAPTER THIRTY FOUR

Preparations were being made throughout WCC headquarters for the upcoming promotional campaign. . . to formally introduce Mr. Pierre Dumonde to the world. Endless meetings planned every detail of every moment of the campaign. Top advertising executives, art directors, fashion designers, cosmeticians, and holovision producers all gathered round the clock to make this the biggest production that the world had ever seen.

Alistair Blakely had just come from the Meditation chapel where he spent the first two hours of each day. He had an aura about him. . . there was an eerie peace. . . almost an absence in his eyes. He moved through the plush upper floor of the WCC building in a pious trance arriving at his office as a regal monarch would sweep into his throne room.

"Sir. . . there is an important call for you in your office," crooned his secretary, an elegant, silver haired woman.

"Thank you very much, Eleanor." With that he disappeared through massive oaken doors, which once adorned a European cathedral.

"Mr. Blakely. . ." spoke a young man over the pictophone. "The honorable Pierre DuMonde will be arriving within the hour. Plans are established for his appearance at JFK. Will you be in attendance as scheduled?"

"Why certainly . . . I'll be there within thirty minutes. I trust you'll arrange an escort for me when I arrive at the airport."

As the line went dead, Blakely eased back in his deeply cushioned leather chair with a deep, satisfied smile. He reveled in the thought of the upcoming events. How long they had waited and planned. . . how they had anticipated the final step in the master plan. . . of his master's plan. A cold, evil snarl appeared on his lips as he thought of the death blow that had nearly ruined everything. . . ZACK MURPHY. . . and his foolish band of saboteurs! They'd nearly killed the plan. . . nearly made it impossible for the great Pierre DuMonde to emerge as. . . the Savior of the world . . . the Christ! Blakely knew that, had it not been for his brilliant work. . . all would have been lost. He had healed the mortal wound. He'd turned the tide of battle with an exquisite manipulation. . . by turning the tables and discrediting this idiotic band of . . . Jesus freaks! The very name made him . . . shudder!

No one spoke a word in the shuttle until just before reentry to earth's atmosphere.

"Where will be touch down, Mr. Bosley?" asked Dr. Noah, leaning up toward him.

"Well. . . the plan is to get to a spot in the mountains, get off, and then send the shuttle on to another far away destination to crash. Hopefully that'll convince the authorities that we're all dead. . . if they have are not persuaded of that already. The spot we're headed for is the cabin you sent Peter and the two young ladies to."

"You knew about that?" asked James incredulously.

"Yes. . . in fact we were the ones that made it available to you in the first place. Do you recall a Mr. Johnson?"

Noah nodded, "You mean Tom Johnson? Why yes, he volunteered at the clinic often . . . In fact, as I recall. . . it was him who gave us the keys to the place . . . He said it had been left to him and he had no way of using it."

Bosley gave a wink. "Our plan all along. It wasn't hard to guess where you'd send people to be safe."

"They got there safe then?" asked James, deeply concerned.

"Yes, they did. . . and they're with one of our best men. They should be expecting us . . . Now everyone hold on, it'll be somewhat turbulent when we enter Earth's atmosphere."

Bosley pulled the nose of the little craft up until the brunt of the friction upon re-entry was to the heat-shielded bottom of the shuttle. It was quite a bumpy ride for a good ten minutes until they were sailing free below the stratosphere.

"I'm going to send a message to the main-tracking station in New Mexico, so that it perceives us as a cloud of space particles which will harmlessly fall to earth. Then we'll make our descent into the Allegheny mountains in southern Pennsylvania and to our rendezvous with your friends."

Crowds of cheering people filled every available inch at JFK as Pierre DuMonde's shuttle liner glided smoothly down the runway toward its final resting place under the huge hanger. The scene resembled a gigantic sporting event as bleacher seating stretched from one end of the building to the distant other end. Colorful balloons, streamers, and other bright decorations filled shining rafters as Beethoven's Ninth Symphony was played by the New York City Philharmonic Orchestra and Choir.

"Spectacular!" thought Alistair Blakely as he was shuttled into the hangar by way of a sleek limousine. "Better than even I could have done!" he said humbly to an aide at his left.

They stopped at a large, regally adorned platform where throne-like seats awaited DuMonde, Blakely, and those few others fortunate enough to have been chosen as assistants directly beneath them. At precisely the correct moment Blakely and his entourage took their seats. The shuttle moved in close so that a special ramp could be connected directly up to the platform.

Lights in the huge building began to dim as spots fixed themselves on the place where this powerful new world leader would emerge. From seemingly nowhere, fog began to immerse the spot where the shuttle platform joined the stage as deep blue lights created a majestic aura around the whole area. All at once a blinding light seemed to burst from the center of the mist and the silhouette of a man could be seen ascending smoothly through the fog as though coming directly from the light itself. A thunderous, deafening, cheering applause came from spectators as the man raised his right hand in greeting. In perfectly timed choreography the symphony and chorus reached the climax of their piece just as Pierre DuMonde, wearing a shining, elegant suit, came into full view of the crowd. He came to edge of the platform. . . both arms raised in triumph as hysterical cheers lauded his arrival.

"Perfect," thought Alistair Blakely with a seething smile. "Perfect!"

A heavy mist rose from the deeply forested hills as shuttle number four glided smoothly toward its first stop on earth. The passengers all craned their necks to peer out the little windows at the landscape below unfolding before them in a collage of deep green, brown and yellow. Fall in the Allegheny Mountains was spectacular, almost erasing from the minds of the tiny crew the dread seriousness beyond this paradise of trees.

Soon a small clearing appeared marked by the smoke of a stone chimney. In the clearing a large log hewn cabin emerged, quaintly nestled on a flat spot in the hillside. A neatly tended garden patch ran along one side of the building, which reminded Zack of his grandfather's farm. Several smaller buildings bordered the little open spot in the forest, some with fenced corrals revealing a number of horses, goats, and chickens.

As the little craft gently set down behind the main building, excited voices could be heard. Opening the side hatch, James saw Peter loping toward him, with a huge grin stretched across his gleeful face. He was followed by Jenny and. . . beyond her, James saw, leaning on the corner of the house, a lovely dark haired woman. As Peter and Jenny smothered him with hugs his gaze went beyond them to Rachel. Their eyes met, speaking in silent words.

Zack was next to emerge from the shuttle, helping Andy out after him, and then Dr. Wilford followed by Clinton Bosley. Rachel gasped, hand to her mouth, sure that her father had not made it when he stepped out into the sunshine also. She ran to him, weeping for joy at his safe return.

Just then an old couple came around the corner of the building. When they saw Zack their pace quickened. He looked up as they reached him. "Son. . . it's so good to see you . . . We were so worried!" came the trembling voice of Gramps as he and his wife smothered their dear grandson in hugs.

"Gramps! Gram! I thought I'd lost you" came his choked reply. Zack felt as if he were a little boy, once again safe in the arms of his loving grandparents.

After long joyous moments the excited group began to relate the experiences of the past two days. All were saddened to hear of Brice Fulton's death. "He was a brave man. . . and a good friend." Noah said solemnly.

Zack had his back to the main barn but the bulk of the others were facing him. He noticed at one point that the attention of the group was directed toward something behind him. Puzzled, he turned . . . There, coming out of the old building came a tall, lean man in his fifties. At first, though there was something very familiar about him, Zack couldn't make the connection. And then a shocked look gave way to heartfelt tears. Tears that had waited fifteen years to surface . . . He was looking at his own father . . . Josiah Murphy. The two stood silently, just watching the other, as if waiting to wake up from a dream. And then, slowly each began a steady walk toward one another, picking up speed until, the last few yards they nearly sprinted into each other's arms. There they remained a long time. . . unashamedly weeping joy-filled, bittersweet tears.

The rally ended as it had begun, with a grand explosion of activity and special effects. DuMonde's triumphal entry was seen live round the world. . . and round the world, in every major language, he was extolled as the new King of the earth, the first king in many centuries to really have power and authority. He was God's own son!

As he finished his short, powerful speech the fog machines kicked in again, gradually immersing the stage in a soft blanket of blue glowing mist. Waving to a frenzied crowd he slowly disappeared from sight, as though eased away by the mighty hand of God.

A limousine waited beneath the platform. Blakely was waiting inside already as DuMonde entered. His face showed clear irritation as the demi-god stepped into the long sleek vehicle.

"Blakely! You do such a wonderful job at creating illusions! Why is it that, when it comes to the real thing, you tend to fall short!" DuMonde snarled.

"What are you speaking of, sir?"

"You obviously have not been keeping informed. It was our plan to remove these little pockets of resistance before today. I understand there is a large group of radicals in Israel fanning out over the whole country preaching their antiquated faith! Why was this not dealt with before it got started?" his evil stare let Blakely know he better have an answer.

"Sir. . . uh, we're on the situation." Then a thought came to him. "There could be some advantage in allowing this. . . uh, radical movement to go on for just a bit. You see. . . I believe that this could set the stage. . . for something quite interesting. If you'll give me a day or two, I'll have a plan detailed for you, a plan that will secure you. . . permanently. . . in the position of king of all the earth."

DuMonde became thoughtful for a long moment. "Very well, my friend. . . I will trust your judgment. . . and await your. . . plan."

CHAPTER THIRTY FIVE

The large living room of the cabin, made warm by a crackling fire in the huge fireplace, seemed packed by the group. There they met to discuss the situation, but more importantly. . . to pray. Long minutes filled with thankful praises seemed more and more filled with a sweet presence. It was that same presence that they'd felt in the little storefront chapel, and had been gently in the recesses of their hearts ever since, even during hard times.

After all words were said, all petitions shared, all songs of praise sung, a peace-filled silence gently engulfed the room. As if initiated by some unseen hand everyone in the room looked up, ready to move on to the next order of business.

Bosley spoke first. "Folks. . . it's imperative that we understand our situation. . . and the situation of the world. . . so that we can act accordingly."

"I'm ready," burst in James, "to lead a group to destroy the `real' heart of the WCC! They need to pay for their crimes against the world."

"NO!" came the deep voice of Josiah Murphy. "There will be no more killing! That is not the way!" He spoke with authority and strength. "The battle is not ours. It is Gods. . . and if we're to fight it we must fight. . . His way."

Shuttle number four was picked up over lake Michigan, streaking low above the water. Five TASCOM jets streaked toward the little craft, closing in from all sides when, with a blinding flash, it blew up before them with such heat that it left nothing but a vaporized cloud of metal momentarily hanging in the air.

"The shuttle disintegrated," reported the squadron leader to his base. "No one got out alive. Returning to base."

The report came from TASCOM headquarters, reaching an anxious Alistair Blakely pacing his office. He'd been incensed over the fact that somehow Zack Murphy and his cohorts had escaped from Aurora Station, leaving five NSP troopers to perish in their stead. The head technician had been arrested and charged with treason.

Now a satisfied smile spread across his face. He'd finally be rid of this band of trouble makers. He gloated over their escaping Aurora just to perish in a fiery explosion before they could reach earth!

Now he could concentrate on more important issues. Utmost in his mind was the situation in Israel. He'd need to do some master manipulation to orchestrate his plan for a huge battle, where finally and decisively the forces of the WCC would destroy the enemy, announcing to the whole world that Pierre DuMonde WAS really king of all.

"Get me the CEO of Mediterranean Technologies in Tel Aviv," he spoke over the intercom to his secretary. Moments later the face of a dark skinned middle-easterner appeared before him.

"Good afternoon Mr. Anrabbi" crooned Blakely coolly.

"Good afternoon sir. . . how may I be of service to you?" spoke the middle aged CEO with a slight accent.

"I understand that there is quite a movement afoot in Israel, evangelizing people toward Judaism. . . and I might add, a form of Christianity."

"Yes sir, we've noted the rapid spread of Judaism amongst young people here. . . even a movement to initiate ancient temple sacrifices and such. Simultaneously, others appear to be following the ancient teachings of Jesus Christ. . . that movement is growing stronger also. We've been gravely concerned about this revival of these ancient religions . . . It may pose a threat to the WCC as more and more of our population falls under the spell of these radicals. What are your instructions, sir?"

There was a long pause. "For now. . . do nothing."

"NOTHING? But sir. . ."

"I said. . . do nothing. Let them grow and flourish for awhile. But. . . keep me posted. . . AND. . . you are to download any classified information to the main center here in New York. Under no circumstances are you to have ANY sensitive information in your systems at all."

"I don't understand sir. . . but as you say." With that, the screen went blank.

The plan congealed in Blakely's mind as blood coagulates in a wound. He'd let the so-called revivals go on, unchecked, but closely monitored, until they overthrew the country. He knew that many lives would be lost at the Tel-Aviv offices, but. . . that was the price which needed to be paid. Then, at a precise moment, he and Pierre DuMonde would arrive on the scene with legions from all over the globe, to crush this evil rebellion. Judaism and Christianity would be wiped out, and once and for all Mr. Pierre DuMonde would step up to his rightful throne to become king, the savior of the world!

Josiah Murphy slowly and thoughtfully paced across one end of the room while the others watched him, waiting for him to speak.

"During my stay in Switzerland I was able to travel to LaBris, where Sir Francis Schaefer, a famous twentieth century theologian, built a colony some years ago for study and prayer. The WCC succeeded in pressuring them out of business round the turn of the century, and most of his writings were destroyed. We came on some though, that had been preserved beneath the rubble of a landslide. There I learned of Christ. . . of his reality. . . of his desire to bring us all into fellowship with God. I was taken with the great love that he had for mankind. . . that He sacrificed himself for a world filled with. . . selfish, and sinful people. Even for those up to their necks in the WCC.

"He could have taken the world by force. . . if He'd wanted to. But that was not His plan . . . He came against the evil of the world. . . not with violence and warfare. . . but with love. He attacked the lies of the evil one, not with angry words, but with truth. Folks. . . that is our mission. . . to attack the evil of the world with love. . . and with the truth, not with violence. The bible says, "He who lives by the sword, dies by the sword."

"But. . . what can we do?" asked Dr. Wilford. "We're not many, and we're certainly no match for the NSP. If they find us, we'll be arrested."

"Don't worry, Doctor. Mr. Bosley and I have made plans to infiltrate computers all over the country. Instead of blowing them up, we'll use them as platforms. . . . platforms from which to share the gospel of Christ. It's our plan to flood information systems all over the world with messages of hope. The truth will stand any day against lies." He looked around gravely. "There will be danger involved . . . The Doctor was right in that we'll be arrested and probably worse, if we're caught. Therefore, all of you will have the opportunity to abstain from these activities if you choose. No one will think the worse of you." As he looked at each face he could tell that each person there had committed themselves already to the task, whatever that might entail.

"We'll lay out specific plans in the morning. In the mean time, please get some rest."

The moon was high over the deeply forested mountainside casting a silvery glow upon everything it touched. James sat in a porch swing in front of the cabin with Rachel at his side quietly drinking in the still coolness of the evening.

Zack and Josiah Murphy walked along a wide path, side by side. So much needed to be said that each wondered where to start. Instead they just walked. . . quietly savoring the presence of the other. After a mile or so the path opened into a small meadow shining silver beneath the moonlight. A fallen log lay at one end of it. The two men sat down, finally ready to talk.

"Son. . . I'm really glad you're safe. I want you to know how proud I am of all that you've done."

"Thanks Dad. . ."

"Your mom and I have missed you so . . . It nearly killed her not to get back to you. But we knew that if we had resurfaced, we'd be arrested. . . and you would have been placed in some corporate foster home. We never would have seen you again. . . and who knows how you'd have been raised. At least we had the comfort of knowing that you were with Sam. . . and close to my folks. I hope you understand. By the time we were able to work out a way to travel undetected, you were already working at the network. We knew then that it was just a matter of time . . . we'd see you one day. In the mean time, I could comfort myself in being close to you. . . in disguise."

"It's okay Dad. . . you did the right thing," Zack said patting his father on the back. "But how's Mom? Is she okay?"

"She's fine . . . You'd be very proud of her, son . . . SHE was the strong one all the time. There were many times that I would have given up if it weren't for her . . . She was always there with a comforting and strengthening word. You know something. . .

even in my worst times. . . she believed in me," he said with tears welling in his eyes. "When you find a girl to marry, I hope she'll be half as wonderful as your mom."

"Where is she? When will we see her?" asked Zack hopefully.

"She's still in Switzerland. You see, over the years we've developed a small network of allies around the world, coordinated mostly from our little home in Wohlen. She's the hub of the whole thing. . . but we're hoping she'll be able to come soon, even though overseas travel is pretty risky."

There was a long silence before Zack spoke again. "Dad. . . I have met someone. . . that is pretty special. In fact. . . I'm going to ask her to marry me. You've met Andy. . . what do you think?"

"I've wondered when you were going to get around to asking her. I've known about Miss Wilford for a long time. You see, I just happened to be having coffee at my favorite restaurant a while back and. . ."

"You were at Barney's that night?" Zack laughed with delight.

"Yes. . . how else was I going to find out about your high school football career? I'm glad for the opportunity to see you two together. I want you to know. . . she's great. . . I'm very happy for you son," Zack hugged his dad, and then the two made their way back toward the cabin. . . back toward Andy. . . to ask her. . . a certain question.

"James. . .I'm so happy you're here," Rachel said without looking at him. "I worried that I'd never see you again. . . that I'd never be able to tell you. . . how I feel."

James looked at her for a long moment, cherishing her beauty, finding himself hopelessly drawn to her strong, sweet nature.

"How do you feel?" he finally asked quietly.

"When I first saw you. . . I almost hated you. You were the embodiment of the WCC to me. And then. . . the more I was with you I realized that you were different. You weren't what I expected an executive of the WCC to be. I couldn't hate you."

"Well. . . now I know how you don't feel!" James teased.

"When you and my father didn't make it back that day. . . I felt that my life would end. . . because the two men I loved more than anything in the world. . . were both gone." Tears filled her eyes as she relived that horrifying time.

James put his arm gently around her shoulder and softly pulled her close to him. "I think I heard you say. . . that you loved me. Well, I love you. . . only I've loved you since the first time I saw you." Rachel looked up, meeting his eyes. Through her tears she smiled a sweet, tender smile. There was nothing more to say for the time. They sat for a long time, together, looking at a beautiful moon. A precious gift of God, specially given to them to celebrate the sweet realization. . . of their love for one another.

Zack and his dad found Andy reading a book, curled up at the end of a huge upholstered couch next to a crackling fire in the fireplace. As they entered the room Josiah gave a wink to his son, patting him on the back.

"I'm real tired son. . . I'm gonna turn in. See you in the morning. G'night Andy."

"Good night Mr. Murphy," she said, glancing up from her reading. "Oh, Zack. . . hi. Did you have a nice time?"

"Yes. . . a really good time," he said, finding a spot to sit at the other end of the couch. "Uh. . . Andy."

"Um Hm." She smiled a pretty inquisitive smile at him.

"I. . . um. . ."

"Yes?"

He stammered "I. . . uh. . . well. . . there's something I want to say to you."

"Yes. Go ahead Zack. . . You know you can tell me anything." It was obvious that she didn't suspect a thing.

"Well. . . I like that book you're reading," he finally burst out, grasping for an easy way out.

Andy held the book up. The cover said, "Knitting Made Easy." "Is that what you wanted to say to me?" she said with a puzzled turn of her head.

"Um. . . um. . . no," he said while nodding his head "yes!" "I mean. . . well, uh. . . what I really meant to say was. . ." He looked so sheepish and helpless that Andy began to chuckle.

"Yes. . . I'm listening."

"Well. . ." He stood for a more dramatic effect and then sat down again. "You wouldn't. . . hate it. . . if. . . you happened to uh. . . be my wife. . . SOMEDAY. . . I mean. . . would you?" He forced a pathetic smile at her.

"NO!" came her emphatic response.

"What do you mean? No you won't marry me, or no you wouldn't mind?" he blurted nervously.

She looked at him sitting there like a big bumbling teddy bear, and it was all she could do to keep from laughing out loud.

"No silly!. . . I would love to marry you, but. . ."

"Oh, I knew it. . . there's something. . . you haven't taken a vow of celibacy or anything, have you?" he stammered out, rising to his feet again.

"No!" she said, grabbing his arm and pulling him down to the couch. "No. . . I was just going to say. . . I'd love to be your wife, but. . . I haven't been proposed to yet."

His mouth dropped open slightly, but he had nothing to say for a long moment. The foolishness of the past few minutes all became obvious to him at that moment. He shook his head, chuckling.

"I'm sorry. . . I'm new at this." With that he slid one knee to the floor, took Andy by the hand, and looked into her eyes.

"Andy. . . I love you more than life itself. You can't know just how much." He didn't know why, but tears began to appear in his eyes. "I don't know how long we'll have together. . . it could be days. . . but I want those days to be spent as your husband." He paused to search every detail of her pretty face. "Andy. . . will you marry me?"

She couldn't respond except to nod her head as trembling, joy-filled tears filled the space that words might have. She ran her fingers through his hair and then softly caressed his cheek with her hand. She was, she thought, the happiest woman alive.

Three weeks later there was a triple wedding at the little cabin officiated by the captain of shuttle four, Clinton Bosley: Peter and Jenny, James and Rachel, and Zack and Andy. The little band of friends gathered in the large fireside room to celebrate the beginning of these new lives devoted to one another, and most importantly to the Lord God.

Zack looked at Andy, dressed in her mother's wedding dress that they'd managed to smuggle out, tears streaming down her face. He loved her so. As he looked into her eyes he saw someone beyond her at the side of the room. She seemed to be waving gently to him. As he recognized her, a woman in her fifties with a radiant smile, tears of joy filled his eyes. This day would be complete. His mother was there, finally, after all these years, to share his joy!

The ceremony continued with songs, readings from scripture, prayers, and short messages of encouragement from various friends and family gathered. Someone put on a recording of Beethoven's Moonlight Sonata, it's deep dark tones pulsing sadly for moments and then weaving into subtly happier strains, always resolving as their lives had done, into a better place than before. The service was perfect, their lives seemed better than ever, as three new families emerged to go on into life together for however long they might have.

CHAPTER THIRTY SIX

Things in Israel progressed as Blakely had planned, in fact, they'd gone much faster than anticipated. The small revival was turning into a massive movement adding hundreds to its ranks each day. It soon became apparent that there were not two separate movements but really only one. The form of Judaism being preached and received by more and more each day was in itself actually Christianity. These people called themselves "completed Jews".

By November there were huge, albeit peaceful, demonstrations outside of the WCC corporate buildings all over Israel. Even members of the "token" parliament had been swept up in this craze and were pressing for independence from the Would Council of Corporations.

The only time that this became a concern at all to the Minister of Human Affairs, or the "Prophet", as some called him, was when they took open verbal "pot-shots" at Pierre DuMonde or himself, calling them the anti-Christ. That was a title that he despised. Why, DuMonde WAS the Christ, the savior of the world. They'd all see soon enough.

Blakely had been in contact with WCC officials in China, Russia, the middle east, Europe, and in North Africa. Large contingents of armed forces were being massed in a circular pattern around the tiny nation of Israel.

Soon, at the right time, there would be a battle, or at least the pretence of one. The end result would be a testimony to all the people of the world. They would see armies from round the globe powerfully united to destroy the enemies of the WCC and its glorious sovereign, Pierre DuMonde. As the battle ended, these armies would sweep into Jerusalem itself, placing their grand leader on the very throne of the temple, accompanied by the strains of Handel's Messiah, proclaiming once and for all that Pierre DuMonde was king of kings and lord of lords. There would be no question after that!

The plan had been laid carefully by Josiah Murphy and Clinton Bosley. Most of the group was to go out two by two. . . the main goal being college campuses. There they would find typical young people. . . open to new ideas, radical ideas. . . and many at a stage where they were discontent with society as it was.

With the understanding that youths go through these times of pseudo rebellion before falling back into line with society, the

WCC left radical groups in colleges alone. Their feeling was that to pay too much attention would add far too much legitimacy to any one group, leaving the potential open for radical ideas to spread beyond the bounds of the college.

This gave the little band the perfect opportunity. They would go into a university, distribute pamphlets announcing a rally, and then just hours later gather in some public location where someone would stand on a high place to share a message of hope beyond the hope that the WCC offered. They were always careful not to attack the Corporate system outright, but would come just short of doing so, leaving the rest to be figured out by the imaginations of the hearers.

Always there would be an invitation for prayer, counseling, or more information. Quite often someone would come forward who was already a Christian. These were encouraged to form small cells for the nurture and encouragement of new converts.

The results were slow at first. . . but then, as if ordained by the hand of God, the crowds began to grow, and the responses more and more filled with those open and ready to know a deeper truth: The truth of Jesus Christ.

Peter and Jenny worked south of the little cabin, venturing into Virginia and west, hitting every big and small college they came to, returning home every two weeks or so for a short rest.

James and Rachel worked north and east in a similar fashion. They were particularly careful not to spend much time in larger cities for fear of being recognized.

Zack and Andy headed due west, through Ohio, Michigan, and the whole Great Lakes area. They especially found success at a small college, which had been the site of a tragedy many years earlier during protests over the Vietnam conflict. At Kent State University they found a student body ripe for their message. The response was astounding. Hundreds and hundreds of young people hungrily received the news of Jesus Christ, of His love for them, of His death for their sins, and of the new life that He offered. So extreme was the response that the newlyweds soon felt compelled to move on, or risk being caught. Behind them though, they left a solid movement, which flooded the University and spread like wildfire out into the surrounding area.

Dr. Wilford and Dr. Noah searched out college professors in all disciplines who showed signs of interest as the others visited colleges. They very rarely met with much success, but when they did, they knew that the results would be exponential as these professors would have the opportunity to have an impact on many, many students.

Bosley and Josiah Murphy had a different objective. They would locate strategic information centers, gain entry through computer manipulation, and plant messages, which usually went out, undetected by corporate officials. Before many weeks went by, they had infiltrated nearly all the major media sources with subtle, yet effective spiritual communications. They never really saw the results of their work, but trusted in the mighty hand of God to use their work for His purposes.

Amanda Murphy stayed at the little cabin, doing what she'd done for so many years in Switzerland, coordinating their efforts, and keeping the home fires burning. She also spent blissful hours caring for a little guy that had finally been reunited with his family. Nathaniel Noah finally had a mother.

Rich and Sarah remained behind too, Gramps doing what maintenance work that needed to be done around the place while Grams helped Amanda with the cooking, cleaning, and caring for their new little one.

CHAPTER THIRTY SEVEN

As Alistair Blakely looked out his massive two hundredth story picture window he surveyed the skyline of New York City. The past weeks had changed his feelings for what he saw immensely. He no longer gloated over the seemingly complete control he had over this city and cities all over the world. There was a mass movement afoot, one that he seemed utterly powerless to control. From colleges and universities around the globe came reports of revivals of Christianity just like the one overtaking Israel. He wanted Israel to become infested with anti-corporate sentiment, it was part of his plan, but the rest of the world, why that was another issue! His power base would be eroded if he waited too long. He must do something, something quickly, something quiet to hold back the tide of this menacing movement, until the day, that final step in his plan.

Blakely turned sharply and angrily toward the intercom on his desk. "Eleanor!" he barked. "Send for the chief of the National Security Police."

Everyone met at the cabin at the end of November for the purpose of celebrating Thanksgiving. It was the first time that they'd all been together for weeks so there were stories to share of their experiences on the road. As the picture began to unfold it became extremely clear that God had gone before them to prepare the way. Peter and Jenny had reached a little farming community in Georgia where a tiny college had its home. So dramatic was the impact of their simple message that on the second day of their ministry to the place nearly the whole town came out to hear them.

Despite the fact that neither Peter nor Jenny had much experience at public speaking, somehow their words hit a chord. Their plain words sank deep into the hearts of the townsfolk and before the week was out, there were multiple daily meetings for prayer, sharing of testimonies, and hearing God's Word read aloud. Peter and Jenny were taken into the homes of the people who fed and cared for them during their stay. The day quickly came though, when they knew that they were no longer needed. Leaders emerged daily from the ranks of the people, taking over meetings and somehow, supernaturally gaining the ability to teach the Word of God.

James and Rachel found most success at Cornell University. Incredibly, Cornell had become a hub for the corporate world, turning out leader after leader to fit into high positions with the WCC. Not in all of their travels did the pair find a more ready audience. Somehow James' demeanor, his corporate training, came through. They found students and professors alike enamored with their messages. They stayed as long as they dared, nearly being recognized by a former colleague of James' who had become a teacher at the college. They left a large group of hungry people, wanting more of what they heard. James promised that they'd return, even though, in their hearts, they knew it not the best of ideas.

The two had other news as well. They waited until everyone was there to make their announcement. Rachel was with child. If the Lord didn't return before spring, there would be another Alton in the world, the first for many generations born to Christian parents. Everyone was ecstatic over the news. Rachel, Jenny, Andy, Amanda, and Grams Murphy hurried off to another room in the house to discuss plans for the new little one.

Bosley arrived just a bit into the happy announcement, silently apologizing for being late. After the women had disappeared from the room he made an announcement to the men, who remained seated.

"I've finally gotten some of my equipment delivered from Wohlen. I'm going to need some help to finish up a project. Could I interest any of you?" Curious about the nature of the little man's work, all of the guys fell in line behind him and out to one of the sheds, which had been converted into a makeshift workshop for the brilliant inventor.

It was the night before Thanksgiving and soft blanket of snow covered the little settlement, giving it a magical quality. Andy stared out the window at a shaft of light coming from the little shed. "Wonder what those guys are doing?" she asked, turning to the other ladies engaged in various activities throughout the warm fireside room. "They've been out there all day. . . they even missed dinner. That's not like my father!" Something though, kept the ladies inside, leaving the men to whatever they were doing. Somehow they all knew that it was something special.

Amanda Murphy was first to rise on Thanksgiving morning. She wanted to begin early preparations for their feast. As she descended the large staircase she saw the living room filled with men who must have plopped down exhausted sometime during the night, sleeping where they dropped. What she failed to notice though, was that there was one more than usual. She tiptoed past them and on into the kitchen, shaking her head lovingly at some of the odd positions she found them sleeping in.

Andy came down next, chuckling to herself as she wove her way through unconscious bodies. She was all the way to the kitchen before she stopped, realizing that there was something strange behind her in the living room. Before she could turn around a whispered voice greeted her from across the room.

"Good morning Miss Wilford. . . er excuse me . . . I understand that it is now Mrs. Murphy. Congratulations."

Andy nearly fainted as she recognized the quirky voice of Sydney! He'd been sitting bolt upright at one end of the room as she'd made her way through it. He looked marvelous, almost identical to his former self, although he had a different hair color. Andy ran across the room to him, kicking sleeping bodies on her way until she reached him.

"Oh, Sydney! We've missed you so much," she said, throwing her arms around him.

"Thank you Madame . . . I missed you too." Andy could have sworn she saw a little twinkle in his eye as he spoke.

CHAPTER THIRTY EIGHT

While Captain Earnest Smithlin stood uncomfortably at attention, Alistair Blakely paced back and forth, fuming. Every so often he would stop as though deep in thought, and then angrily stomp away.

"Smithlin. . . I can't believe what I'm hearing. You've let these dissidents just run amuck on college campuses all over the east!"

"Sir, our policy has been to allow radical groups to blow off steam on college campuses. We left them alone because most of these groups just fizzle out on their own. We've never had a problem like this before."

"We have a problem now, Mr. Smithlin! The timing on this could not be worse for the World Council of Corporations and for the new world order. Something must be done. . . at once!" His tone told Smithlin that the conversation was over, what's more. . . he had better get the situation under control.

Thanksgiving was a joyous experience for all in the little cabin headquarters. Grams and Amanda Murphy, Andy, and Rachel put together a wonderful feast while the rest of the little band enjoyed a spirited conversation in the living room. Everyone was glad to see Sydney in their midst. Even those who hadn't met him before knew him well from the stories of others.

Nathaniel sat on his lap, poking at the gawky android, prodding and examining his synthetic features. Sydney sat like a faithful family dog would, patiently allowing the little boy to crawl all over him.

"Know somethin!" the little guy blurted out after some minutes. "You're my best friend!" With that the dirty faced munchkin buried his head in Sydney's chest, hugging him with all his might. Then he laid down on his lap and promptly fell asleep, comforted by the presence of his newfound buddy.

Soon everyone was crammed in around a large table, ready to share a precious supper with one another. Josiah looked at the little family gathered round the table for some time before he spoke.

"My brothers and sisters, let us share this bountiful feast with thankful hearts. . . as a similar feast was shared many, many years ago. The days to come are going to be difficult. . . and to be honest. . . there may be some who share with us today who will not do so again. . . at least in this life. Let us cherish this time. . . cherish one another. . . and the great love that has brought us all together. For when we were quite unlovely, we were loved . . .

When we were quite undeserving, we were made worthy. When we were faithless, there was One who remained faithful to us."

James indicated a desire to speak. He stood, thoughtful for a moment, and then said, "Folks. . . it took me some time, longer than most of you, to really come to grips with. . . my need for Jesus. I was very satisfied with my life before Christ. I was satisfied with. . . so little, when there was so much to be had.

"I want to tell you though, that now. . . I don't know how I ever survived without Jesus. . . without Rachel. . . without all of you." He paused, as tears came to his eyes. "I just want to say thank you. . . and thank You," he said, looking upward.

It was a long time before statements of praise and deeply, heartfelt prayers gently subsided. No one noticed that the food was very cold. . . for the fellowship was very warm.

James and Rachel stood on the little porch saying goodbye, hugging each of the others warmly before moving on to the next. They'd received a call from Cornell again, an urgent request for them to come back to meet with a group of people hungry for the Good News of Christ. Though they were hesitant, they had to go. How could they turn down someone who was hungry for Jesus?

"Be careful, James," said Zack, gripping his hand firmly. "We want to spend time with that little one, come spring. Who knows?

You guys may have started and epidemic!" He looked at his own wife who promptly punched his arm.

CHAPTER THIRTY NINE

Professor Paul Richards hung up the phone struggling with mixed feelings in his heart. He was loyal to the WCC. . . and yet he'd always liked James . . . He had nothing against him. Why would such a promising young man leave the security of the corporate system and a sure position high up in the ranks of corporate officials? He couldn't understand it. James was not the typical fanatic that was drawn to these ancient, antiquated religious movements. He was well educated, from a good family. He had so much potential.

Anger welled up inside him as he thought of the idiotic speech he'd heard James give some weeks earlier. "Well. . . if he was foolish enough to be drawn into a subversive organization which preached such anti-corporate doctrine, he deserved to. . . to. . ." and then he thought. "What would the authorities do to him? To his wife?" He pushed these questions out of his mind, busying himself with correcting student assignments. Something inside of him though, had decided to be present. . . to hear James' last speech. . . before. . ."

"Who was it that contacted you, James?" asked Rachel, cuddling up beside him as they drove through the night toward Ithaca, New York and Cornell University.

"Do you remember a young man by the name of Fred? He's a chemical engineering student. Well, he got word from a number of other people that they very much wanted us to come back. I'm not exactly sure what more we can do there, but. . . I'm sure God has plans for us."

"I don't know. . . something just doesn't feel right. What if we run into that old friend of yours?" she snuggled down closer to him as she spoke. He felt a shiver go through her.

"Why don't you try to get some sleep, sweetheart . . . Things will be just fine . . ." He groped behind him in the back seat for a blanket, which he draped over her. He didn't know why, but he felt the same way . . . Something wasn't exactly right.

CHAPTER FORTY

Captain Smithlin of the NSP arrived in Ithaca sometime after midnight, checking in to the police headquarters there before retiring to a local motel. He planned to be at the next meeting to see first-hand this young defector from the corporate ranks. Just before retiring, he phoned a report to headquarters in New York City.

"Captain Smithlin of NSP Command Force Number Six reporting from Ithaca, New York. Plans are to apprehend fugitive corporate defector James Alton Jr. with the help of local authorities at a rally to be held on campus at Cornell University tomorrow morning. Will incarcerate individual at local facility and then complete executive order number 467 as per orders." He then spoke the name of his motel and his room number into the phone before disconnecting and retiring for the night. He fell asleep with the hope that this arrest would curb the radical new movement, and get Blakely off of his back!

An alarm sounded in Bosley's lab, waking him from a fitful sleep. He too had felt strangely about James and Rachel returning to Cornell. He'd put a lead out to search the NSP computers for any correspondence, which contained the names of either James or Rachel. After staring at an inactive monitor all evening and late into the night he'd sunk into a nightmarish sleep. In his dreams he saw James and Rachel standing, arms raised in surrender, in front of five NSP troopers. The troopers had dark helmets on, but somehow he recognized them. They were the men, he'd since found out, who had been disintegrated in the place of his comrades. He was horrified as the gentle, steady "beep, beep, beep" slowly dragged him to wakefulness.

He removed his glasses and rubbed his eyes, trying to bring the screen into focus. And then, all at once he saw it. "Oh my! OH MY!" he yelled, running from the room to gather the others.

"Can't you do anything, Clinton?" spoke an anxious Peter as the group gathered in the living room heard Bosley's report. "We just can't sit here and let them be arrested!"

"Peter. . . please, sit down. Let us think for a minute." Josiah said in as calm a tone as he could muster. "What do you think, Clint? What should our first move be?"

The little man was thoughtful for a moment. He paced back and forth, squinting as if scanning some invisible computer screen for a hidden phrase.

"We'll need to go to Cornell immediately. I should be able to pull up the code for the computers at the Ithaca Police Station.

Even if they are arrested before we get to them I think I should be able to fake a release order. But we'll need to be ready to scoop them up quickly after they get out." With this he disappeared into his little office, reappearing five minutes later with his laptop case and a little slip of paper containing a hastily scrawled code number.

"Let's go!" he said hurrying out the door. He was followed by Josiah. As the two men reached the service van they'd secured from a local WCC subsidiary, Peter appeared on the porch.

"Hey you guys. . . I want to go," he said with an intensity that made it hard to argue with him.

"Alright Pete . . . Get in."

The three were careening down back roads moments later. It was a long, three hour drive at top speed. Each prayed silently in his own heart for James and Rachel and for the new little life, which she carried within her. A little more than an hour into the journey they reached the main highway, which allowed them to increase their speed considerably.

"Let's just hope we don't attract any NSP troopers. That'd be all that we need," said Peter, showing his concern over the breakneck speed they were traveling.

"No problem there, son. I've got everything under control," Bosley responded calmly.

On they sped, into the night, racing against time to reach James and Rachel before . . . Forty five miles outside of Ithaca the inevitable happened. The white corporate van crossed a speed trap and within seconds the lights of an NSP patrol car could be seen in the rear-view mirror.

"Oh no!" cried Peter, turning around to see their pursuer.

"Son. . . I said it was not a problem." Bosley was more than a little annoyed at Peter's obvious lack of faith. He reached for a little box mounted on the dashboard, made an adjustment in its readout, and then pushed a button.

Without the van slowing down one iota, the NSP car broke off the chase, turned its lights off, and turned around, returning in the direction from whence it came.

"What happened?" asked Peter incredulously.

"All those NSP troopers are the same. They train em to be techno-junkies. No matter what their eyes tell them, they'll believe their instruments. This radar jamming device merely sends a message to his portable unit telling him we're not traveling over the speed limit and that he should return to base to have his speedometer recalibrated . . . Works every time," he smiled smugly at the young Alton seated to his right. "You really can trust me son. . . I know what I'm doing."

James and Rachel arrived at their motel around one a.m. They checked in hurriedly so they could get a couple hours of sleep before their early morning rendezvous at a local coffee shop. Before going to sleep they knelt together beside the bed. There was an urgency about their prayer and a felt need by each to somehow cherish the other. . . to savor and to appreciate anew the wonderful gift that God had given them both. There was a deep sense that they were no longer two, but a family of three. . . kneeling together, loving one another, and loving God.

CHAPTER FORTY ONE

The large clock in the town square showed four a.m. as the white van pulled into town. Bosley was fairly certain that they'd arrived in time. The problem they now faced was finding James and Rachel. Ithaca was a fairly large town, as towns go. They would have to split up to search the area around the college looking for James' car. They prayed together before separating, asking God to allow them to find their endangered brother and sister.

Peter took the area north of the university, starting two miles out and weaving his way back and forth until he reached the campus. He searched every motel and restaurant parking lot that he came to, looking for a black Mercedes.

Josiah combed out west of the school in an area filled with many motels and coffee shops. Glancing at his watch told him he'd better hurry. It would take some time to search this honeycomb of businesses.

Bosley covered the south and east in large sweeps with the van. If he failed to see James' car he planned to crisscross back and forth across the university itself.

At five a.m. Captain Smithlin was in the lobby of the little motel checking out. As he signed for his room he caught a glimpse of something interesting. Under his name where he'd signed in the night before was another name, James Curtiss, party of two, one a.m. On a hunch he got a cup of coffee, picked up a newspaper, and waited in an inconspicuous corner of the lobby.

Thirty minutes later he was ready to abandon his hunch when an attractive young couple made their way quietly into the lobby to check-out. Smithlin reached for his briefcase, unlatched it, and stared down at a picture. It was him, James Alton Jr! He could hardly believe his luck. Of all the motels in the city, they'd chosen his. With a smug nod of his head he prepared to follow the pair, waiting for the right moment.

James and Rachel abandoned their car to enjoy a brisk morning walk to the nearby coffee shop. Rachel clung tightly to her husband's arm, huddling close to him in the cold darkness of the winter morning. He bent down as they walked and kissed her tenderly on the cheek. "I love you Rachel. . ."

She snuggled even closer as he put his arm around her shoulder. As they finished their way to the little shop both had a feeling that, in the midst of all the evil in the world, life was good!

The warm little diner cast a friendly yellowish light on the snow lined street as the pair gladly stepped inside out of the cold. Off in a corner booth sat a nervous looking young man. It was the student that had called them. Sliding into the booth, Rachel and James greeted him.

"How are you?"

The young chemical engineering student was fidgeting terribly as he answered, "I. . . I. . . think I've made a terrible mistake."

"What do you mean?" asked James with growing concern.

"I was contacted by a professor from school . . . He asked all sorts of information about you. . . and, well. . . I told him most everything that I knew. . . except how to get hold of you. When he told me how anxious he was to get together with you, and that there were many others who were really interested in what you had to say. . . well, I sent for you right away. I didn't piece things together until the next day. I didn't realize who this guy was."

"Well. . .I don't understand . . . Who was he?"

"Do you know a man by the name of. . . Paul Richards?" he asked with trembling voice.

James sighed. "Yes. . . yes, I do . . . So in other words, this has been a set up."

"I believe so sir . . . I'm so sorry." The young man looked broken before him.

"If you'll excuse us. . . we need to be going," James said, trying to hide the panic that gripped his heart.

"No, Mr. Alton. . . I don't think so," came a deep voice from behind them. The trio looked up to see the face of Smithlin, his beady eyes laughing down at them, with two uniformed NSP troopers at his side.

CHAPTER FORTY TWO

Bosley cruised slowly through a neighborhood business section, eyes searching every nook and cranny for any sign of James' car. Just as he pulled up to an intersection he caught a glimpse of something darting from an alley toward the white van. A moment later Peter was sitting in the passenger seat, totally out of breath.

"I found them!" he said through gasps of air. He leaned forward to get his breath. "I located James' car outside a motel just on the outskirts of the university. They'd already checked out but the desk clerk told me which direction they went . . . I got to them. . . just as they were being led out of a coffee shop by the NSP."

"I'm sorry son . . . We'll get em out. Don't you worry."

It was twenty minutes before they were able to locate Josiah, and another ten before they were parked outside and across the street from the Ithaca police station. Bosley donned a pair of WCC overalls, picked up a clipboard and crossed the street, entering the small station house. Walking up to the front desk he got the attention of a uniformed officer.

"Excuse me sergeant, can you tell me where I might find the phone company?" he said with a southern accent. He pretended to listen as the NSP trooper gave directions. Nodding intently he gazed around the station, taking mental note of everything that he saw. Then with polite thanks he made his way out of the building and back to the white van and his partners.

"Well. . . things are a little more complicated than I thought. I caught a glimpse of someone that I recognized. Captain Smithlin from main NSP headquarters. Things have to be pretty drastic for him to be here personally. He's the top guy of the whole eastern force . . . We'll have to wait till he leaves. . . hopefully without James and Rachel, until we try to get them out. It should be no problem to get a release order into their computer, but it'll never work while Smithlin's around. If he leaves for even an hour we should be able to pull it off." So the three men waited, hoping and praying for their opportunity.

"Don't worry, honey. . . everything will be alright," James said to Rachel as they sat in the back seat of the patrol car heading for the police station. "Clint will figure some way to get us out." He squeezed her hand.

She patted his arm. "I know, James . . . What I'm worried about is. . . giving the others away. We can't give them away."

She put her hands lovingly over her mid-section. "Oh, James," she said, giving way to frightened tears. Lovingly, he put his arm around her and pulled her close, praying for strength, for protection, and for courage to face whatever their fate might be.

They arrived at the rear of the Ithaca police station, were hustled through the back door and into a cell. A few minutes later, Smithlin appeared at the door. He stood there, looking down at the couple for some time before he spoke.

"I don't know what's worse. . . a religious fanatic, or a traitor. I want both of you to know something. I have no pity for people like you. . . there's no place in the world for your kind. You just think about it for a few minutes . . . The only thing that MAY save you is the information you provide about the others." He looked disgustedly at the couple, shaking his head as he turned to go. "Oh, and by the way. . . I kind of hope you refuse. Then I'll have a reason."

"You're an animal!" Rachel screamed as he disappeared from sight. He acted as if he didn't hear. . . but he did. The reality was that he heard all too well. He wasn't the blood-thirsty villain he'd made himself out to be, but he was desperate. He knew all too well that his job, and maybe even his life, was on the line.

Smithlin made his way into the main lobby of the station to prepare himself for the upcoming interrogation. It'd been a long time since he'd been so personally involved in any case, but this one was too important to trust to anyone else. The look in Blakely's eye at the end of their last meeting communicated the grave seriousness of situation. He dared not fail, even if it was distasteful. He poured himself a cup of acrid coffee, trying to collect his thoughts while pacing around the nearly empty squad room. He passed a little maintenance man in coveralls that quickly scooted out the front door.

Fifteen minutes passed. Enough time, he thought, for the pressure to do its work. These were not hardened criminals, not even professional agitators. They were just a couple of people, untrained and unprepared for the psychological pressures they would experience. It should be short work to obtain all that they knew. And then. . .

After slowly making his way back to the cell, he found the couple kneeling in prayer. He decided to start with kindness. Waiting for the pair to finish, he quietly entered the cell.

"Folks. . . please forgive me for my harshness . . . I'm under a lot of pressure. . . and, well. . . I need to get hold of this. . . movement. I need to. . . understand it. You see, the WCC would like to work with. . . uh. . . Christians. . . to keep them from having to resort to covert activities to accomplish their goals. You'll help me, won't you? I just need the names of your associates, and where they can be contacted." He stood and turned toward the cell bars for effect. "If you will help me. . . you'll be out of here before you know it." There was a long silence.

"And if we don't?" James' voice was steady.

"Let us not discuss the negative . . . Please, James, for the sake of your wife. . . give us the information that we need."

"Sir. . . I know the opinions of the corporate world regarding Christians. You're asking us to pronounce a death sentence on others." He looked at his wife, so very precious to him. "We've resolved that, no matter what, you'll not get a single name from us." With that they knelt to pray again.

Smithlin fumed for a long moment. "You fools! I have your very lives in my hands." He grabbed James to throw him backwards. He did not expect so meek spirited a man to be so strong. James immediately had him by his thin wrist with one of his muscular hands.

"You don't have our lives in your hands," he said calmly. "The fact is. . . you don't even have your own life in your hands. You're owned, lock, stock, and barrel. . . by a corrupt system, an ungodly system."

A nearby trooper brought the butt of his pistol down hard, rending James nearly unconscious. He fell forward at Rachel's side.

By this time Smithlin was in a rage. "You'll be very sorry, my friend, very sorry!" He turned and disappeared, leaving James and Rachel huddled in a corner of the dark little cell.

Passing the front desk, Smithlin barked, "Order number 467 for those two, Sergeant." With that he took his coat from the rack, laying his gloves on the table. He angrily donned his heavy black overcoat, placed his hat upon his head, and disappeared through the front door, leaving a bewildered desk sergeant fumbling at his computer terminal for the definition of order number 467.

Even in his anger Smithlin did not like having to have James and his wife killed. It was the only way, though. It would be the way that Alistair Blakely would want it done, he'd known him too long to believe anything else. Still, he could not come right out and say the words. Somehow, giving only the order number sanitized the situation and put the local guy in the hot seat.

"Now's our chance!" Bosley chirped, jumping from the driver's seat into the rear of the van. Everything was ready. All he needed to do now was to make the final command to tap into the local police computer. Within a minute everything was set.

"Here goes nothing!" Bosley said, keying the final sequence. There was a barely audible "beep," signaling that the transmission had been completed. "Now we wait."

The desk sergeant scratched his head in disbelief as a priority message came over his monitor.

"Of extreme importance: Prisoners James and Rachel Alton are to be released immediately. A grave diplomatic error has taken place. In addition. . . Captain Earnest Smithlin is to be apprehended at once and held for questioning.

"Again. Please comply immediately! No response message required."

Somewhat confused at the big picture but unwilling to challenge higher headquarters, the old policeman called for an officer.

"Release the young couple immediately!" he barked.

"What Sarg?"

"I said release them. . . now! And after that. . . go out and pick up that Captain Smithlin. We're supposed to hold him for questioning."

The young policeman scratched his head but complied. He went to James and Rachel's cell, opened the door and announced,

"You're free!"

"What?" James said holding his bruised head.

"I said you're free to go . . . I don't understand it any more than you do sir. . . but. . . you are free."

The couple hurried out the door in disbelief. They cautiously passed the front desk where the old sergeant gave James an envelope with their personal effects in it.

"Have a pleasant day, sir. Uh, you want something for that bump on your head?"

"Uh. . . no. . . no, I'll be fine, thank you." They moved out the door and into the street walking briskly away from the little station. They hadn't gotten ten yards when James looked back to see Smithlin's car pulling up to the front door just as the young officer came out. They were still close enough to hear the Captain say something about forgetting his gloves. Then he noticed the young couple.

"What's going on? Why are they free?" he screamed. Before the officer had time to say anything he pulled the weapon from his coat and fired four quick shots. The young policeman tackled him before he could fire again, wrestling the gun from his hands and yelling for back-up from inside the station. Almost instantaneously, other officers burst into the street to subdue Smithlin and drag him inside. By the time the young man got back outside, James and Rachel were nowhere to be seen.

"What is the meaning of this?" Smithlin shrieked as he was dragged toward a cell.

"Orders from headquarters, sir. You were to be arrested and held for questioning," replied the old sergeant.

"I don't believe this. . . you fools! I demand to talk to headquarters!"

"You will. . . all in due time. . . you will. Now lock him up, fellas."

CHAPTER FORTY THREE

The white van rolled steadily onward toward their mountain headquarters. Bosley was silent as he drove, staring straight ahead, deep in thought. Peter was in the back, cradling James' head in his lap while Josiah did the same with Rachel.

"Peter? Is that really you?" James said, straining to raise his hand to his younger brothers face.

"Yeah, it's me, big brother. I'm here."

"Rachel!" he tried to get up but couldn't. "Where's Rachel?"

"She's here, James. . . right next to us . . . She's asleep."

He turned his head painfully just enough to see his wife next to him, her head cradled in Josiah Murphy's lap. She was breathing. He turned his head back, collapsing in relief.

"What happened?"

"You guys were just about to get clean away when that psycho Smithlin opened fire with a fazed stun pistol. You must have stepped in front of Rachel. She was only knocked unconscious." Peter's voice cracked.

"What's wrong Peter? She is alright, isn't she? And the baby?"

"They both seem to be okay. . ." Peter looked away.

James knew then. "Then it's me . . . I'm pretty bad off, huh?"

Peter didn't answer. He didn't need to. The tears that flowed down his cheeks told James everything.

Smithlin had missed with his first two blasts, allowing James time to block Rachel from the further shots. The third hit James' shoulder and glanced slightly off of Rachel's head, rending her unconscious. The fourth shot hit James dead in the back, causing massive internal damage. He had only minutes, at best, to live. There was nothing that anyone could do.

James began to loose consciousness as Rachel came to. As soon as she was able to sit up she knew the reality of the situation.

"Rachel!" James gasped.

"I'm here my darling . . . I'm here. . ." She moved into the position that Peter had held, gently cradling her husband's head in her arms. "James, I'm here," she said, choking back tears.

He opened his eyes long enough to see his pretty wife looking down at him. "Rachel. . . you're safe. . ." he gasped. "I love you so much. . . tell the baby. . . I love . . . him." He smiled weakly and then, little by little, he gently closed his eyes.

"Sleep my darling . . . One day. . . we'll meet again." Rachel cradled him all the way home. Home, where he'd find his final rest.

CHAPTER FORTY FOUR

The situation in Israel was coming quickly to a head. The Christian movement was sweeping like a huge tidal wave over the ancient land. Town after town became seedbeds of evangelism. Archeological sites, held sacred until decades ago, regained their spiritual significance, turning them from museums into shrines of intense, living worship.

Even droves of local WCC officials changed their first loyalty from the Corporate Council. . . to Christ and his people. Many possessed "top secret" information regarding the inner workings of the WCC and, in particular, the Utopia Project. Holovision and radio stations aired broadcasts exposing the evil of the World Council.

It was time to make a move. Blakely began to put final details together for the "great war" which would finally place DuMonde in his rightful position. In the meantime, the future monarch of the world remained safe and comfortable at a large estate recently vacated by a former WCC executive. The Alton manor was a perfect place for DuMonde to rest and make ready for this, the most important moment of his life.

"Mr. DuMonde. . . all but the final details are in readiness. Shall we meet to discuss them, sir? I can be out there some time tomorrow afternoon." He waited as the Frenchman took his time to answer.

"Very well, Blakely. . . and Alistair. . . please bring with you information regarding the Royal Russian Cavalry. Are you familiar with them?"

"Yes sir, they're a brigade of horsemen used in ceremonial events. I believe they use coal-black Arabian stallions."

"Precisely . . . I shall look forward to our meeting." DuMonde pressed the disconnect button and leaned back in the huge leather chair. An evil grin began to form on his face as he envisioned himself riding triumphantly into Jerusalem mounted upon a beautiful, spirited, black stallion, with every home in the world a witness. "How dramatic!" he thought.

CHAPTER FORTY FIVE

The sun was just beginning to set over the mountain leaving deep crimson streams streaking through an evening sky as the little band gathered to say their final farewells to James. Dr. Noah read from the old leather-backed Bible. "Let not your hearts be troubled. . . believe in God, believe also in Me. In my Father's house their are many rooms . . . If it were not so I would have told you so . . . I go to prepare a place for you, and if I go to prepare a place for you. . . I will come to take you with me, that where I am. . . you may be also."

There was definite sadness in the hearts of those who loved James. . . but there was also joy. James was in a far better place. He was with Jesus. There were tears, but through them there was an understanding, and a hope. James would be missed, but someday he would be with them again. Their hearts were wounded, but in that day all wounds would be healed and broken hearts mended.

As the sun shed its last rays over the winter scene, a lone grave marker adorned the crest of a little hill, overlooking the valley below as if watching, peacefully watching, waiting for spring to come, bringing new life and hope to the barren landscape.

Back in the little cabin everyone was settling in for a long winters night. Amanda sat in a chair near the large stone fireplace, knitting baby clothes. Most of the others had long since gone to bed. Peter stood at the fireplace, poking a stick into the fire absently.

"What're you thinking dear?" Amanda asked, sensing an unsettledness in the young man.

He looked up, drawn from deep thought. "I was. . . uh. . . thinking about my sister. She doesn't know about James."

"Do you know where she is?"

"If I know Sondra, she's not far from home. She's probably even living there right now. . . although. . . I don't see how she could be keeping the place up."

"Have you thought about going to find her?" Amanda said softly.

Peter took a deep breath, shaking his head. "It's too dangerous. I'd probably risk all our lives going back there."

"Peter. . . talk to Josiah and Clinton. They'll know a way." She rose from her chair and went to him. "And. . . I want you to know something . . . We love you."

Peter looked at Amanda and saw the same look that his mother had. He felt something break within him like a dam bursting its walls. As tears began to flow he moved to her, burying his head in her shoulder. She held him like a little boy for a long time, allowing the emotions to surge. She knew why he needed to find Sondra. They were the only ones left.

The next day Peter, Zack, Josiah, and Bosley met together to discuss the situation.

"Pete, I want you to know I support your wanting to find Sondra . . . You just have to be careful," Zack encouraged him.

"Yes Peter, Clinton and I have discussed your situation. We should be able to get you into Alton Manor. You did say there were security switches around back of the place?" Josiah asked.

"Ya, it's where the service trucks came onto the property. You can control the whole system from a box near the back gate. I used to use it to sneak in late when I was in high school."

Bosley looked gravely at the young Alton. "It's crucial, Peter, if you encounter any NSP personnel, you'll need to get out of there quickly. We don't know if it's being used by the WCC or not. There's no information on it on the main computer link at the NSP."

"Well, if it's not on the computer, then they're not using it."

"Not necessarily, Pete. There have been times when the top brass leave certain actions of theirs out of the computer file, depending upon what they're doing."

Peter nodded. "I understand. I'll be really careful. I feel somehow that Sondra's at home . . . If I can't convince her to join us, at least I can tell her about James. She deserves to know." Everyone nodded agreement.

The night was thick black due to a cloud cover, which conveniently descended upon the area some days earlier. The white WCC van crept slowly down a back road near the Alton Manor until it came to a large iron grate fence. Massive ivy covered walls went out in either direction from where they stood, adorned with barbed electric wire and flood lights every fifty feet or so.

Peter felt his way for a metal box, obviously not often used as it was covered with ivy. It took him some minutes but finally he located the small square metal door in the brick. A rusty screech let the others know that he'd pulled the door open.

"Peter! Come here!" whispered Bosley. He was looking through the wrought iron gate toward the rear of the house.

"Someone IS in the place. I saw lights going on and off in an upstairs room. And look." He handed Peter the pair of night vision binoculars he'd been using.

"There. . . you can just make it out between the trees."

Peter squinted to locate what Bosley had seen. Finally he made out the form of a van, a WCC van.

"I don't think you ought to try it, son," Josiah said gravely.

"Look, I know this place inside and out. I can get in and out without anyone knowing it . . . I'll be okay!"

Bosley and Josiah were silent for some moments. They sensed the desperation in Peter's eyes.

"Alright Peter. . . go ahead. Clinton and I will be waiting over there amongst the trees with the motor running. Get in and out fast."

Peter went back to the rusty metal box, punched a series of buttons, and waited for the gate to open. Immediately there was a slight clanging and the gate swung open wide, allowing Peter to slink inside, keeping to one side of the road. He disappeared from sight, leaving a concerned duo behind and praying for his safety.

CHAPTER FORTY SIX

Ahvram Mayer had been an orthodox rabbi for nearly thirty years when the WCC came to power. He subsequently had been exiled to a remote area of the Sinai Peninsula. There, in a little settlement, he was forced to live side by side with Moslems, Hindus, and worst of all, Christians. He could deal with the others, but something about Christians he could not abide.

For years he practiced his faith in as pure a manner as he could with the few remaining faithful who shared his convictions. Most of them were very old, though, and one by one they all died off, leaving him alone with the gentiles! He remembered traveling to the Dead Sea, to Kumran, where the Essenes, an early group of Jewish monks, had lived. There he cried out to Jehovah God! Was he the last faithful one? He knelt on the windswept, dry stones the once bore the feet of the noble Essene monks and he cried bitter tears.

In the depths of his despair a section of scripture from the Torah came to his mind. He saw the prophet Elijah complaining to God that there were none save him who had remained faithful to God and not bent their knee to Baal. And then he heard, a still small voice from within him saying, "Ahvram. . . rise. . . for in your settlement you will find those who are faithful to me . . . They are named for me. . . for I AM the Christ." He was devastated. If this voice WAS the voice of God, then he was saying that Christians were His people. How could that be?

He rose, as if lifted by a supernatural hand, and made his way home. He prayed through the whole journey, asking God to lead the ones He'd talked about to him, without any kind of search. He wanted this to be initiated totally by the Lord, and not a creation of his own heart out of a desire for companionship.

He waited in his little apartment for days, expecting a knock at the door at any moment, and then expecting nothing.

He searched the scriptures night and day for some sign, some confirmation, and then, one morning as he read Psalm 51, it became clear to him. He'd read the Psalms hundreds of times before. Why had he not seen it? There it was, a beautiful picture in words describing the death of Jesus Christ. He agonized as the words took shape in his mind. This was Yeshua, the Messiah, the coming One of Israel, only, he had already come some two thousand years earlier! He had come, had lived, and had died for the world, even for this old Rabbi who had been caught up from birth in a religion that had looked for his coming, but had somehow missed it.

His heart broke, and he knelt weeping bitter tears for the hardness of his own heart, and for those who'd passed through his life who he could have REALLY helped, had he known the truth.

"Forgive me, God! Forgive me, Yeshua . . . You are the Christ!"

Suddenly there was a knock at the door. The rabbi rose slowly, moving toward the front entry to his tiny home. Opening the door he found a young woman in her late teens or early twenties. She had a look of desperation in her eyes.

"Rabbi, I'm so sorry to disturb you. . . but you're the only holy man around. All of our men have gone to Jerusalem for a rally. It's my baby . . . I think he's near death." Tears streamed from deep brown eyes as the young woman spoke. "Please, will you come to pray for him. . . please!"

The old rabbi had the heart of a shepherd. He could not refuse such a request, even if it was from one of another faith. But did his prayers have any power? He strongly doubted it.

The woman led him down a narrow street and into a little hovel. It was tiny, and obviously constructed of used and discarded bits of lumber. There was an open fire at one end of the little room, which filled the ceiling area with smoke that escaped only poorly through a little vent in the roof. The Rabbi coughed as he followed the young mother to a tiny bed in the corner of the room.

There lay the lethargic little body of a toddler, not more than two or three years old. He gave a pathetic little glance at the old gray bearded man before his eyes rolled back in his head as he slipped into unconsciousness. The scene gripped the old man's heart.

"What is the child's name?"

"He is called Peter."

Ahvram remembered another Peter. He'd always felt disdain for him. He'd left his Jewish roots for a heretical religion, or so he'd thought. Now, as he looked over this tiny one also named Peter, he found himself praying to his new savior that this boy would live, and become great, like his namesake.

He laid his hands upon the baby's head, looking upward.

"Oh God. . . my Father. We bring this little one to You. We lift him up into your arms of love and compassion. Bring healing to his tiny body that one day he might grow to be a man. . . to serve you and your Son. . . Jesus Christ." He felt a surge of coolness flow from his innermost being, through his hands.

The young mother's mouth dropped as he ended his prayer.

"Sir. . . you are a follower of Yeshua?"

He looked at her for a long moment, and then nodded his head.

"Yes, dear child. . . I am a follower of Yeshua . . . He is the Messiah." He could hardly believe his own words. He'd now made a public confession of a revelation that he'd only just had. But it was right. . . it was RIGHT. Joy surged into his heart like he'd never known before . . . Yeshua WAS the Messiah. . . He was HIS Messiah!

There was a little stirring beneath his hands. Startled, the rabbi pulled back. There, staring at him, rosy-cheeked, was little Peter. He had a broad smile and a twinkle in his eye. He seemed totally healed as he squiggled around in the tiny bed.

His mother, tears of joy streaming down her cheeks, rushed to him, embracing the little one. As she picked him up though, he reached out to the old man.

"Pop, pop," he said, reaching with all his might for the rabbi.

Ahvram slowly stretched forth his hands to receive the little one who tumbled into his arms, burying his face in the old man's long gray beard.

That evening, the others returned to find little Peter, the picture of health, bouncing on the old rabbi's knee. When his mother, Madeline, explained what had taken place, the whole group gathered around him.

A young man in his early thirties spoke finally. "We are few in number, Rabbi, but we've been praying that God would send us a leader. . . a wise man. . . who would lead us, teach us, and help us to live for Yeshua. You are God's answer. We praise His name."

Ahvram had been welcomed into the little family of believers and became a grandfather to little Peter, who grew strong in the nurture and training of Christ. The little family grew also, until late in 2029 they numbered nearly one thousand, all jammed into the little settlement on the Sinai.

By this time Peter was nearly twenty. He'd grown up beside Ahvram, totally devoted to him, learning all that he could from the now very old man. The young man was zealous in his love and commitment to the service of Yeshua and hoped one day to follow in the footsteps of his beloved Rabbi. For now though, he was content to stand beside Rabbi Ahvram, to help him in any way, and to learn.

One quality evident in the old rabbi was his sensitivity to God. Probably because of the way he'd come to belong to Yeshua, he did nothing without clear direction from God. He remained the monarch of the little community, which based its loyalty to him on his obvious wisdom. Its people honored him as teacher and shepherd.

For years Ahvram had sensed God saying to his people to stay where they were, to grow strong in wisdom and knowledge and to multiply their numbers by sharing Yeshua with any who might pass by. By the spring of 2029, though, there was a growing sense that it was time to move out, to reclaim the holy land for their King. As he sought the Lord's guidance, the old rabbi was given a vision. In it he saw his people moving boldly out over the whole land of Israel, fighting a holy battle, but fighting it God's way, through prayer, praise, and most importantly, obedience to Christ. He saw armies of praying warriors leading millions to Yeshua and to the life that he offered. Without a shot, without a single sword, without a drop of blood being shed, the nation would fall to its rightful sovereign, the King of Kings, and Lord of Lords.

He gathered the band of believers at the little marketplace of the settlement. He then had Peter and two other men lift him onto a high platform where he could address the whole assembly.

"It is time, my brothers and sisters, for us to go out in the strength and power of our God and to reclaim this land for Him. We must go as the ancient armies of Israel went into battle, with worshippers at the lead of the battle, and with prayer as our weapon. God has prepared a harvest. Let us go now, as each is led by the Spirit of the King, to do the work that He has called us to."

Within a week nearly all of the community had gone, some individually or in pairs, and others in small groups, to share the gospel of Christ. Ahvram and a few others waged the war from their little settlement, spending many hours a day in prayer. None had much of an idea of what they'd be up against but all went joyfully, trusting God, the Lord of the harvest, for results.

Soon pockets of believers began to appear all over Israel. They remained small for some time. Ahvram's army had learned some invaluable lessons in sharing the Gospel. They knew that the best evangelism is costly. It costs time and commitment to those who are to be reached. They needed to invest themselves deeply in the lives of those they ministered to if their work was to have any lasting value. And this they learned well.

Approximately eighteen months later it began, at first in isolated areas, but soon the whole nation was reeling in the throes of a massive revival of Christianity. WCC officials didn't know how to respond. There were no acts of sabotage or terrorism, only thousands upon thousands of people, corporate people, were being swept up in this movement. At first local WCC officials sought to imprison those that seemed to be leaders in the revival but soon droves of NSP troopers, and even WCC executives, were falling victim to the influence of these gentle warriors.

CHAPTER FORTY SEVEN

Peter made his way through rows of neatly trimmed shrubs, crouching low so as not to expose himself to spot lights, which adorned various points of the ornate garden. Within moments he was next to the house feeling his way for his old "secret entrance." Years earlier he'd disconnected this old servant's entrance from the alarm system. It was never used, as the kitchen had been moved to another section of the house some fifty years earlier. Now it opened into an abandoned series of passageways which once allowed servants to move around the house unseen to appear in various rooms to tend to dinner parties and the like.

Again Peter felt through the ivy covered wall of the house until he found his old passageway. Putting pressure on the top corner of the door, while pulling on the handle, he finally had it free a couple of inches. It took some time for him to pull the overgrown ivy away enough to create a portal adequate to fit his body into. Finally he was in. He reach into his pocket for a small flashlight which allowed him to make his way through the cobweb filled passageways.

Within a few steps he was outside his father's office. He found the latch on the old entrance panel, which opened in, leaving the panel totally flush with the wall when closed. Peter cautiously lifted the latch and pulled a very slight bit. There was a tiny "creak" and then a crack of light appeared, enough to survey the room. The light was on, but it was empty.

In a moment Peter was in the room. It all seemed the same, the books on the shelves, the pictures on the walls, the things on the desk, except for a large envelope labeled "TOP SECRET".

He stood over for a few minutes, debating as to whether or not he should open it.

Then movement caught his eye. He looked up to see Sondra, dressed in an evening gown, passing the large double doors of the office. He moved to the door and cautiously looked around. Down the long hall in the living room, Sondra was pouring herself a drink. He watched her take a drink and then curl up on a sofa, thumbing through a magazine.

As the young woman finished looking through her fashion journal, she felt the presence of someone behind her. Startled, she spun around in her seat. The look on her face told Peter that he was the last person she expected to see.

"Hi, sis. . . good to see you again."

For a moment Sondra forgot how angry she'd been at Peter. She jumped up and threw her arms around him.

"Peter, where have you been? I've been worried sick about you and James . . . You two just disappeared after. . ." and then she went cold, pulling away from him. "After daddy died." She turned away.

"We had to get away, Sondra. . ."

"What do you mean? Where's James? Why did he have to get away?"

"The WCC is not what it claims to be. . . it's a front for evil."

"Peter. . . you never change. The WCC is responsible for all of this, for you and I, and James to go to the best schools . . . By the way. . . where is James?!" she was becoming adamant.

"Sondra. . . James is dead."

His sister gasped, sitting down on the couch.

"The WCC is responsible for his death. . . and for father's. Don't you see?!"

"You're wrong Peter. . . you're wrong . . . I don't know how James died. . . but it couldn't have been the WCC." She buried her head in the couch, sobbing.

"Sondra? What's the matter darling?" came the voice of a Frenchman from somewhere behind them.

Peter turned to find a man in his early fifties, with coal black hair and dark eyes, dressed in a silk smoking jacket, coming toward them down the circular staircase which led from the living quarters upstairs. At once Peter recognized his face. This was Pierre DuMonde himself. He continued down the stairs and arrived at the couch, putting his arm around the sobbing Sondra.

"What's the matter, my darling . . . Who is this?" he looked at Peter with a cold steel stare.

Sondra looked up, first at DuMonde, and then at Peter. She was silent for a moment.

"I'm sorry Pierre, this is a friend of mine from school. . . he just stopped by to tell me that a mutual friend. . . died. It was a shock . . . I'm sorry my love. . . I didn't mean to worry you."

DuMonde rose, smoothed his jacket, and gazed intently at Peter. "I feel that I have met you before, young man . . . Your name is?"

"Uh. . . Sydney. . . Sydney Morrel," he blurted out, immediately knowing that his choice in names was weak.

"Well Mr. Morrel, thank you for coming. I think that Sondra needs some time to herself now. Goodbye."

Peter nodded politely and turned to go. He looked one more time at Sondra. . . she glanced up quickly.

"Goodbye Sydney. And. . . thank you." There was a quiet desperation in her eyes and Peter noticed that the side of her face, though well covered with make-up, was badly bruised. As he left the room, she waved weakly, mouthing the words, "Goodbye Peter. I love you."

DuMonde had his back to him so Peter slipped into the office again, planning to take the secret passage. There on the desk was the envelope. Peter took it, tucked it into his jacket, and slipped out the passageway.

It was a short sprint for Peter, weaving his way through the lush garden, out of sight from the house. The anger and disgust built within him with each step. How could Sondra sink so low as to become lover to Pierre DuMonde himself. The very embodiment of the WCC and the evil it represented. What made matters worse was that the creep was beating her. It would be just like a worm like DuMonde to beat a woman. It probably made him feel good.

Josiah and Bosley were deep in prayer when a tap on the window of the van startled them. They looked up to see Peter waiting to get in the van, a grave expression on his face.

"What'd you find son? Was your sister there?"

"Yes, Mr. Murphy. . . she was." That was all that he said. He moved to the back of the van, sat down, and looked out the window. The three drove home in silence, the older men respecting the younger's need to be alone. In time he would share his experience.

DuMonde was in a rage. He'd torn the office apart looking for the envelope. Sondra appeared at the door, drink in hand. Looking at her, he finally put two and two together.

"It was that friend of yours, wasn't it, Sondra?" he growled.

"I don't know what you mean!"

DuMonde grabbed her by the hair and pulled her close to him. "You little fool . . . Either you were in on it. . . or you allowed yourself to be used!" He made ready to hit her when he noticed some pictures on the wall behind her. DuMonde dragged her the few steps to the wall.

"I don't believe it! Sydney Morrel, eh? You little tramp! That was your little brother. . . Peter is his name, I think!" His evil stare bore into Sondra. She broke down hysterically.

"I'm sorry Pierre. . . he just showed up! He told me that the WCC had killed my brother, James. I was upset, I didn't know what I was saying. . . and. . . I'm so sorry!" DuMonde was so angry that he was speechless. He stepped back from the sobbing young woman shaking his head.

"You're nothing. . . NOTHING!" He wheeled around and disappeared, leaving Sondra a whimpering mass collapsing to the floor.

R. Norman Johnson

CHAPTER FORTY EIGHT

Ahvram was in his little apartment deep in prayer when there came a gentle knocking at his door. He opened it to find a group of very dignified individuals along with one of his trusted friends Yosef.

"Yes, may I help you gentlemen?"

The obvious elder in the group spoke first. "May we come in? We have some very important things to discuss with you, sir."

The old rabbi, glad for the company, opened his door wide, making way for the distinguished entourage.

"We're sorry to disturb you Rabbi. . . but these men have some things that they need to tell you," spoke Yosef.

"Very well my sons. . . tell me."

"Rabbi. . . we are from the WCC. . . the World Council of Corporations. We have all come into faith recently. . . and we're not sure how to deal with certain information that we have."

The men began to explain to the old rabbi about the Utopia Project. He listened intently, looking out a window. They tried to speak in as diplomatic terms as they possibly could, but the news was nevertheless shocking. For over an hour they alternately peeled back the layers of corruption that gilded the

330

WCC. Still the rabbi sat motionless, but soon a single tear appeared on his cheek. When they were finished there was a long silence.

"My sons. . . you bring grave news indeed. What do you plan to do with such. . . tidings?"

"We though of broadcasting the truth over the airways. . . what do you think?"

Again there was a long silence. Ahvram closed his eyes, intently praying.

"The truth is always powerful . . . It is the thing that defeats the lies of the enemy. It can also be used as a sword. Outside of God's will it can be cause much harm. I recommend gentlemen, that you pray long and hard before making your broadcast. Be sure that this is what God wants . . . If you're sure, then do not let anyone turn you away from your duty. This is all I have to say on the subject. Thank you for coming."

The group left, a little bothered that they did not receive more clear direction from the old monarch. But pray they would, and hope that they would hear correctly.

Peter had almost forgotten about the envelope he'd slipped into his jacket. The three men were almost half-way home when he finally remembered it and pulled it out.

"Say. . . Mr. Bosley. Is this something you might want? I found it on the desk in my dad's office." He handed it up to the front of the van.

"Oh my . . . Josiah, will you open this?" The senior Murphy complied, gently breaking the seal and pulling the documents from inside.

"Clint. . . these are going to take further study . . . Peter, just who did you see inside the house?"

"That jerk, Pierre DuMonde! He's got my sister wrapped around his little finger. . . and what's worse. . . I know he's been beating her. I saw the bruises on her face. If I ever get my hands on that guy. . ."

"Peter. . . we've got to get your sister out of there . . . I don't think that you, or any of the others, realize just who Pierre DuMonde is." The rest of the trip home was spent in total silence, broken only by the occasional turn of a page as Josiah examined the documents before him, dread growing steadily in his heart.

Arriving home late in the evening, Bosley, Josiah, and Peter met with Dr. Noah in a back room before the whole little community was called together in the fireside room. Josiah stood in their midst. It was hard to read his frame of mind. He seemed troubled, and yet somehow exhilarated.

"Brothers and sisters. . . during our visit to the Alton Manor, Peter found this." He held up the envelope marked "Top Secret".

"What this is. . . is a detailed plan for a battle. It will take place in Israel. . . on Christmas Eve of this year. You see, Pierre DuMonde, the head of the WCC, has plans to be proclaimed king of the whole earth after sweeping down upon the defenseless people of Israel, wiping them out with an immense army he's been amassing all around the tiny country." Everyone was spellbound as Josiah continued.

"This would be just another of the WCC's atrocities. . . but the situation is very clearly spelled out in the Bible. I've not been one to jump to conclusions about. . . the anti-Christ. But this document confirms very definitely what I've suspected for quite some time. Pierre DuMonde. . . and in many ways the WCC, is the anti-Christ. . . the servant of Satan sent to deceive the whole of mankind, and to ultimately attempt to conquer the world for his master.

"It's also been clear that Mr. Alistair Blakely is the false prophet sent to promote the Anti-Christ." Zack shuddered as he thought of the personal interview he'd had with the white haired gentleman.

After a thick silence Bosley added, "Two things seem quite evident. One is that we must get Peter's sister away from DuMonde. It seems that he's temporarily moved into the Alton mansion and taken over more than just the house. He must have found her there and somehow. . . well, suffice it to say, she's not safe with this fiend . . . The next issue is that we feel we are no longer safe here. When we got home I checked the NSP wires. DuMonde knows that Peter was in the house. . . and he's ordered an all-out search for him and has ordered a comprehensive dragnet out to find him. Like never before they're searching for him. . . for us. They have surmised that there are more than just Peter involved.

"We have consulted with Dr. Noah, and we all agree. Our work here has come to an end. We feel that Israel is the where we ought to go. There's been a dynamic movement spreading across the whole country. In fact, we have just learned days ago that nearly the whole country has pulled away from the WCC. Jews, Arabs, and many others are joining together in Christian brotherhood. This document clearly spells out DuMonde's intention to wipe Israel from the face of the earth. We feel that we should get to the leaders of the movement to warn them of the WCC's intentions."

At this point Dr. Noah stood. "It's clearly laid out in the Bible. There was to be a great revival. . ." He began to read from his well worn Bible. "I do not want you to be ignorant of this mystery, brothers so that you may not be conceited. Israel has experienced a hardening in part until the full number of the Gentiles has come in. And so all Israel will be saved." He smoothed the pages gently.

"Folks, the revival in Israel now. . . is the same one written of here in Romans 11. And this awakening of faith. . . is to just precede a couple of. . . major events. One. . . a huge battle on the plains of Megiddo . . . You've probably heard the term Armageddon. It is coming."

Rachel stood. "Most importantly though, is what happens following the battle. . ."

The next day Zack found Josiah standing out back of the cabin, looking thoughtfully over the valley below.

"It's beautiful up here, isn't it, Dad?"

"Yes son, it is." He looked at his son for a moment. "How're you doing?"

"Fine, Dad. . . I have an idea to discuss with you."

"Go ahead. . . shoot."

"Well. . . I heard you and Bosley talking last night. . . how you feel it might be difficult to work out the details on moving everyone, and getting them all to Israel."

"Yes son, the net is closing tighter all the time. Even Clinton is feeling hindered in his ability to maneuver around in the computer system."

"I have a couple of friends. . . from school. . . who could help us, I know."

"Are they corporate?"

"If I know them, neither of them has much love for the system. I've been wanting an opportunity to find them. . . and to share Christ with them anyway. I think that. . .if they can be brought on board, they could help us a lot."

"Let's get together with the others and pray about it, son. We need God's wisdom on this one."

CHAPTER FORTY NINE

Later that evening, Zack and Andy cautiously made their way down the mountainside in the white WCC van. Bosley sat at his console in the rear, constantly monitoring NSP transmissions and computer dispatches. The attention that he focused on these tasks told the pair in the front seat just how perilous their situation was. Once Bosley barked, "Pull it over fast!" They waited in a grove of trees for thirty minutes before he announced. "All clear. . . there was a ten vehicle patrol heading for us. They passed without noticing us. That was close. . . I'm sure they're slowing honing in on our position. We've got to hurry. . ." It was an hour before they were entering the New York City limits and another ten minutes before the van was parked down the street from Stu's home.

Zack took a deep breath as he stepped out onto the street. Andy would remain behind in the front of the van while Bosley continued his electronic watch. Zack came around to her side of the van and leaned in to kiss her goodbye.

"Be careful, sweetheart. . . Just be careful." He could see the worry in her eyes as she spoke.

"I will. . . I will. You just make sure to take off if. . . well, you know." He kissed her warmly and then made his way down the snow lined street.

Fifty yards away from the van Bosley, said, "Zack, say something, I want to make sure we're picking you up okay."

The tiny earpiece worked all too well as a passerby heard Bosley loud and clear.

"Turn it down Clint . . . You want to whole world to hear? Do you read me okay?"

"Yeah. . . and sorry. I forgot how sensitive these things are . . . Remember to cough twice if something goes wrong. And then once again if you want us to pick you up. If you don't. . . we'll take off. And dear friend. . . be careful."

Zack found his way to the familiar, modern looking apartment building where Stu lived. Seeing his car on the street he figured his friend must be home. He looked around and then pressed the button next to Stu's name at the entrance to the building. It took just a moment before his old friend groggily responded.

"Uh, yeah?"

"Stu. . . this is Zack."

"Hey. . . where've you been? Come on up!" The door buzzed and Zack walked to the elevator which took him to the twelfth floor where Stu owned a very spacious condo. He made his way from the elevator down a long, plushly carpeted hallway, seeing his old friend standing in the doorway ahead of him.

"Zack! Man, is it good to see you! I thought you must've dropped off the face of the earth. Where've you been?" Stu was slapping him on the back as he entered the spacious flat.

"It's a long story . . . I'll tell you everything. . . but first, I'd like to ask you a favor. A big favor."

"Well, you can ask."

"You still own your distributorship, don't you?"

"Ya. . . we're the biggest distributors of beverages in the whole state. Why? What can I do for you?"

"Well, I need you to help me rescue someone. . . someone who's trapped against her will at James Alton's house. You remember James, don't you?" He paused, allowing Stu to process what he'd said so far.

"Yeah. . . but I don't understand . . . Rescue someone from James' house?"

"It's his sister. . . she's being held there against her will. I'll fill you in more later. Can you help me?"

"Yeah, I guess so. . . but how do you propose we do our little rescue job? We're not secret agents, ya know."

"If you will arrange to make a delivery out at Alton Manor, we can get her into one of your trucks . . . What do you think?"

"Sounds easy enough. . . but Zack, you've got a lot of explaining to do. I've had NSP troopers here two or three times looking for you."

"If it's okay, I'll explain as we drive. Okay?"

"Yeah. . . let's go. I didn't have much going this evening anyway. Just a minute, though." Stu went to the window, looking out rather suspiciously for what seemed a long time.

"What're you doing, Stu?"

"Oh, nothing. . . I uh. . . I've been waiting for a package to arrive . . . The postman should be here any minute." Then, seeming to perk up all of the sudden, he disappeared into his room.

Something wasn't right. . . Zack shifted nervously in his chair. His throat began to feel dry, making him want to cough something terrible. He didn't want to send a false signal to Clint and Andy, though.

"Clint. . . can you hear me still?"

"Yeah. . . loud and clear. What's up?"

"I don't know exactly. . . but," and then Stu reappeared in the room. He walked directly to the door, a serious look on his face.

340

There was someone in the hall. Zack could hear the door handle being turned from the outside. His heart went into his throat. Had he been turned in by his own best friend? He had to cough so bad that it hurt, and the more he thought about it the worse it got.

Zack decided to take the earpiece out before he let loose. Fumbling at his ear his fingers finally located the little capsule-like piece just as he began to cough uncontrollably. The earpiece popped out, but as Zack's body convulsed in a fit of coughing, it slipped through Zack's fingers and dropped to the floor and out of sight.

"Oh no. . ." Clint looked at Andy, holding the earphones closer to his head. "He was about to tell me something . . . Then he coughed. All I heard after that was loud bumping on the mike and muffled voices."

"He's in trouble . . . I've got to go to him."

"No, Andy. . . wait. If there's anything we can do he'll signal us . . . And if not. . . there's no use for us to play into the WCC's hands. We can do more for him if we get to safety." Andy stared at him in disbelief. How could he be so calm? Her husband's life was in danger!

Five minutes went by without a sound from Zack. Clint looked at Andy. She was curled up in a ball in the front seat, softly crying. She knew. . .

Without a word he moved up to the front seat, turned the ignition switch, and pulled into the street. He drove past Stu's building, hoping against hope, but there was nothing, not a sign of life inside or out of the building. Half a block down the street Bosley began to speed up.

All at once he slammed on his brakes and put the van in reverse, driving backwards down the street. Andy sat up, dazed. And then a familiar face appeared at the window of the van.

"Zack! You're alright!" she said, opening the door and throwing her arms around him.

"Yeah. . . I thought I'd never convince these jokers that you'd be heading down the street any minute! Sorry. . . I'm sure you were both really worried. I lost the little earpiece just as Stu was letting Pat in. Andy. . . you remember Pat, don't you?" Andy saw that Stu Smith and Pat Erwert stood behind them like a couple of schoolboys, pushing and punching at each other.

Pat stepped forward and pulled Andy from her husband, giving her a big hug. "What did I tell ya Zack. . . you two were meant for each other." Zack just shook his head as he ushered the others into the back of the van.

"We've got a lot to talk about, guys. Shall we get going?"

Later that night a Standard Beverage van pulled up to the Alton home. The service entrance had a speaker which signaled the house. An NSP trooper came onto the intercom as the driver of the van buzzed.

"Yes!"

"I've got a delivery from Standard Beverages. Sorry we're so late. It's been a long day and I kind of got lost trying to find this place."

"You're right, it is late. I don't know."

"Look pal. . . my boss'll have my head if I miss this delivery. It'll take no more than a couple of minutes. . . you can supervise the whole thing if you want."

There was silence for a moment before the speaker crackled again. "Okay. . . but make it quick. I'll meet you at the delivery ramp. And. . . keep the noise down!"

"You got it!" There was a buzzing sound, followed by the clanging of the gate as it swung open to allow the van to enter. Stu noticed a camera on a pole alongside the narrow driveway, obviously monitoring them as they entered the ground.

"There's a spot up ahead where the cameras won't be able to see us for a moment. Just slow down a bit. We'll jump out there. I'm hoping we'll be back in the van before you're finished. Just take your time!" Peter said, preparing to open the side door of the van. Zack and Pat were right behind him. . . all three dressed in black.

"Here we are. Let's go." The door swung open and the three men tumbled out and into nearby bushes. They made their way in the shadows to Peter's secret entrance. It was only moments before they were ascending a ladder in the dark labyrinth of passageways that threaded through the old mansion. Peter led the way to a spot in the upstairs wall that contained a narrow passage covered by a plywood panel. It led into a closet in the sitting room adjacent to Sondra's bedroom. He prayed that they would find her there, alone.

Zack and Pat waited in the passageway while Peter crawled through the tiny opening. It took him just a moment before he was able to gently open the closet door to survey the room. It was dimly lit and empty. Padding silently, he made his way into the sitting room and to the door when opened into Sondra's room. Just as he was reaching for the door knob he heard the voice of a man.

"Look Sondra, I'll be leaving in the morning . . . While I am gone, you get yourself together. You're a wreck! I don't know why I even bother with you!" Peter clenched his fist and grabbed the door knob, ready to burst into the room when he felt a hand on his shoulder.

"Easy Pete. Don't do anything stupid." He turned to find Zack standing behind him. Collecting himself, Peter finally nodded. They stepped back into the darkness of the closet just as the door burst open revealing a seething Pierre DuMonde. The Frenchman stomped through the room and out the door, slamming it as he left, hurling curses in French all the way down the long upstairs hallway.

They could hear sobbing from the other room as the two men crept from their hiding place. Peter entered the room to find Sondra, obviously bruised and beaten, laying across one end of her bed. He crept near her and knelt down, touching her hand softly. Startled, she nearly screamed. Peter gently put his hand across her mouth until she recognized him.

"Peter. . . oh Peter!" she fell into his arms sobbing.

"Sis. . . I've got to get you out of here . . . Pack some things and let's go." She began to protest meekly. "Sondra. . . please. .

. let's go. I've got to get you to safety." His older sister looked at him intently. . . and finally nodded her head.

Five minutes later the three men and Sondra were hiding in the bushes adjacent to the loading dock waiting for an opportunity to get into the van. Stu stood on the dock with a clipboard in his hand while Sydney, dressed in overalls bearing the name "Standard Beverage," shuttled loads of containers into the house. An NSP trooper stood at the door, watching intently as Sydney passed him.

"Psst!" Stu nodded, obviously understanding.

"Uh. . . Sydney?" He yelled into the house after the android. Immediately there was a huge crash from within the building. The NSP trooper abandoned his post, dashing into the house. With muffled yells in the background Peter and the others hastily slipped into the back of the van. Soon everyone, including Sydney, was back inside, and the van was moving toward the back gate.

"How did I do sir?"

"A fine performance, Sydney! You deserve an Oscar," smiled Bosley.

"Oh. . . thank you sir!"

CHAPTER FIFTY

DuMonde was furious as he paced back and forth awaiting the arrival of Alistair Blakely. Not only was Blakely late to pick him up, but he knew what the white haired gentlemen's reaction would be when he arrived. He'd be cool as a cucumber. That infuriated DuMonde even more!

He was mad at himself also. Why, when he was on the verge of the greatest moment of his life, was he so bothered by the disappearance of a meaningless young woman. He was obsessed with what he'd do to her when he found her and to her brother, the whole family for that matter!

Finally the long, sleek limousine appeared, coming down the long driveway. As it pulled up, DuMonde stomped out the large oaken doors.

"What took you so long, Blakely! Don't you realize that we should be in the air NOW! I need to have time with the Russian brigade. . . to get used to the horse! WELL?"

Blakely was not his usual calm self. As he strode from the car he looked unusually rumpled. His normally cool demeanor was a mere thin veneer covering a deep strain from the depths of his being.

"What is your problem, Blakely? You look a mess!" Disgust showed in his voice.

"It's my meditation times . . . They've been horrible lately. There's something very. . . very wrong . . . It's as though there's some sort of powerful. . . spiritual movement afoot."

"We have no time for your silly emotions, Blakely . . . In fact, I could care less about your idiotic `meditation times.' We have work to do. The world is waiting! Let's go!" The pair disappeared into the long vehicle which sped them away toward JFK International.

"Its hard to believe that for all these years. . . I've been working for the Corporation without knowing what was behind the whole thing. My dad warned me when we joined the WCC that something wasn't right about it. All I can say is, I'm glad he died before he got a chance to go to the so-called retirement colonies." Stu shook his head in disbelief.

Crammed into the little shed workshop, Zack, his father and grandfather, Stu, Pat, and Bosley all sat facing one another. They'd been there for more than three hours, each man in turn sharing with Pat and Stu from their perspective on the WCC and its evils.

"I can believe it . . . I've never trusted the organization. Lucky enough though, I didn't have to spend much time under their thumbs. My work as an architectural consultant allowed me to pop around all over the world avoiding a lot of the bureaucracy. . . but I've seen so many people who would live and die defending the WCC. It's pretty pathetic!" Pat scoffed.

After a moment Josiah spoke. "Pat, Zack tells me you have some pull with the airlines. We've just about used up our cover. Somehow we need to get this whole group out of the country. Do you think you could arrange it for us?"

"No problem getting spaces on flights. . . but I don't know how we're gonna get around the wrist scans. There are just too many of them at the airport."

"Mr. Bosley has worked out a temporary solution for that. You see, he was the original inventor of the wrist implant. He has developed adhesive strips that contain chips that we. . . borrowed from a little mortuary in the Appalachian mountains. They should provide us with at least a short time of use."

"Very ingenious . . . Well, in that case we should have no problem at all. Just fill me in on times and places. I'll take care of the cost. . . its the least I can do."

Later that evening, after supper, Zack and his two old friends took a walk along a snow covered path. The moon shone brightly on the surprisingly mild winter night, creating a magical feel to the mountainside trail. Smoke from unseen fires filled the air with a sweet, warm aura filling their minds with memories of winter scenes in days gone by.

"We've never really spent much time talking about serious things," Zack said, finally breaking a long silence. "I want you guys to know what's happened to me. . . beyond all the WCC stuff." The silence let him know he could go on.

Zack spent the next hour sharing from the depths of his heart about a change in his life, about the realization that he'd come to about his need for Christ, and about his reasons for going on and living, even in the midst of a corrupt world. As he spoke it was as though flashes of light could be seen faintly in the night air and a warm glow seemed to fill each man's heart.

"Zack. . . I'm with you all the way on the corporate stuff. The rest of it. . . well. . . I just don't know . . . It's a lot to swallow in one day," Pat said, getting up from the log they were seated at. He moved across a little opening in the trees to look out over the valley below, covered in a blanket of white. Zack knew Pat. . . he knew to leave him alone.

No words needed to be spoken by Stu. Zack could sense his friend open and searching for what he had come to know. The three old pals just sat, silently drinking in the sights and smells of the evening and enjoying each other's company. There was the quiet sense that this might be the last time all three would be alone together, and yet. . . it was okay somehow.

CHAPTER FIFTY ONE

There was no fanfare at Beirut International Airport as Pierre DuMonde's private jet taxied down the runway. In fact there was an intense lack of any activity at the large middle eastern airport. It was odd. Since the WCC brought peace to the region, this airport had become one of the busiest terminals in the world. Lebanon, as well as most of the surrounding Mediterranean countries, had become incredibly busy with tourist trade especially in the last two decades.

Suddenly DuMonde saw the reason. Far off in the distance, surrounding the whole area, were military vehicles and aircraft of all types. The leer jet stopped in the center of the runway and was immediately surrounded by a small convoy of military vehicles including a black limo flying a WCC flag from its antenna. A stocky man wearing a headdress stepped up to the ramp as DuMonde and Blakely descended to the tarmac.

"Where is Mr. Achib?" Blakely was obviously agitated.

"I regret to inform you, sir. . . he has joined the Israeli movement . . . He resigned his post yesterday. I am Jamil Docar, his deputy. I will assist you, gentleman. Will you follow me?" He led the way down the rest of the ramp and into the waiting limo.

"The Russian Brigade is awaiting you north of the city. Once we join them you will have some days before . . . Well, you'll have plenty of time to accustom yourself to horseback. All is in readiness for December 24th."

"Very good. . . very good. You have done your work well, Docar. There will be a reward for you after. . . after our business here is completed." The convoy moved out swiftly toward its destination, staying clear of the city and the turmoil that brewed even there, and on toward the huge horse brigade. . . and to glory!

"Wake up everyone!" Bosley yelled, running through the cabin. "Wake up . . . We've got to get out of here now!" People began appearing from bedrooms all over the building donning bathrobes, combing back tousled hair.

"What's going on, Clint?" Josiah was at the top of the long staircase, Amanda at his side.

"I picked up an NSP bulletin. They've located our general vicinity. I don't know how, but they'll be here in less than an hour. We've all got to get out of here right now!"

Most were already packed for their flight the next day so it took only a few minutes for the whole group to get on the road. Zack and Andy joined Stu and Pat in Pat's car, while Rachel, her dad, and the elder Murphy's rode in James' Mercedes. Jenny, Amanda, and Sondra rode with Peter in Zack's Merc, while Bosley, Sydney and Josiah led the way in the white van, scanning the road ahead for NSP cars.

Once out of the general area, the little caravan took the long way to get to New York City, trying to arrive as close to flight time as possible. It was about four a.m. when they finally stopped at a rest area to stretch their legs.

"Son. . . got a favor to ask of you," Gramps said, pulling Josiah aside. "We've got till four p.m . . . Why don't we stop by my house? I'd kind of like to say goodbye to the old place again. Your mother can fix us all something to eat, too . . . What d'ya say?"

"Dad. . . that sounds like a good idea. We could use a good meal before we take off. . . and. . . I guess I wouldn't mind seeing the old place again anyway."

A stark winter sun was just peeking over the horizon when the little caravan pulled into the long curving driveway that led to the Murphy farm. Zack remembered the last time he'd been there and felt a bit of the pain again as he relived the circumstances that brought them there.

Soon everyone was seated around the large kitchen table, sharing a wonderful breakfast summoned up by Sarah and Amanda Murphy. Josiah sat at a window seat in a corner where he could keep his eye on the road outside. From his perch he could see everyone in the room. What a wonder it was. . . this odd assortment of characters had become a family. Even Sondra, who'd kept to herself pretty much for the first few days of her stay with them, was beginning to interact with the others as though she'd known them all her life.

"Thank you Lord," he whispered under his breath. "Give us all strength for the days to come."

"How many troops are gathered?" DuMonde asked, gazing out the limousine window.

"Well over a million sir. . . and the Chinese force hasn't arrived yet. Who knows how many they'll bring . . . It will probably as least double the size of our army." Docar was fidgeting in his seat.

"Stop here!" DuMonde scrambled out of the car as it swung into a scenic lookout along the mountain road. He gazed out over the valley below where a large contingent of the middle eastern force was assembled. "Spectacular! Look, Blakely. . . all of that. . . for ME!" The valley floor was literally covered with military units stretching out for miles like a huge green flag ruffling in the wind. DuMonde took a deep, seething, prideful breath.

"All for me!" he muttered sliding back into the limo.

Ahvram prayed more these days than ever before as though drawn to his knees by the very hand of God. He had the sense of something powerfully significant in the air, as though the whole atmosphere was charged with some kind of heavenly electricity. He even noticed tiny bursts of light occasionally streaking the air.

"Lord, make us strong. . . give us wisdom."

One morning a knock came on his door, finding the old rabbi kneeling beside his bed, as he had been all night.

"I'm sorry, Rabbi. . ." came the voice of Peter.

"Yes, my son. . . come in."

"We've just received word from the United States. There is a delegation of non-corporate people coming to Israel. . . today. They wish to speak to the head of the church in Israel . . ."

"And you assume that is me?"

"Everyone does, Rabbi . . . Everyone does."

"Very well. . . gather elders together from as many towns as you can. We will meet in Jerusalem this evening. Whatever place you choose will be fine."

There was a sense in the old man's heart that this meeting was ordained of God. He would go, for he knew it was right.

CHAPTER FIFTY TWO

John F. Kennedy Airport loomed ominously before the little band. They had parked some distance away and approached on foot the last mile or so trying to act as casual as possible.

Pat and Stu led the way with Andy and Zack right behind them while the others spread out in a random fashion for a block or so. Zack could see that, while Pat was his usual calm, carefree self, Stu was noticeably worried. He had chosen not to accompany the group on the plane, feeling the weight of running his business.

"You okay, Stu?" he finally asked.

"Yeah. . . I'm just. . . concerned about you guys. In a way, I'd like to be with ya . . . You understand though, don't you?"

"Sure Stu. . . it's okay. We'll miss ya, that's all." Zack reached forward, patting him on the back.

Entering the passenger terminal group by group, they approached the check-in station. Thankfully, there was only one station actually monitored by a human being, and she was noticeably bored, not checking anyone very closely. Everyone managed, somehow, to board the plane without incident.

As was usually the case nowadays, the flight was full of tourist types, anxious to get away for some sunshine and relaxation. Zack, Andy and Dr. Wilford found themselves quite some distance from the others who seemed to be bunched together over a couple of adjoining sections.

It seemed an eternity before the flight finally got airborne. Andy noticed her father was sweating a great deal and obviously uncomfortable.

"Are you okay, Dad? Did the take-off bother you?"

"I'm fine. . . just a little. . . indigestion or something. I'll rest a bit." With that he put his seat back and closed his eyes.

Andy heard what he said but still kept an eye on him, checking with him every once in a while through the whole four hour flight. His discomfort seemed to continue steadily, though he tried to deny it.

Arriving at Tel-Aviv International Airport the group disembarked individually. One by one, each was admitted without incident. Zack, Andy, and Dr. Wilford brought up the rear. Andy was scanned without incident, followed by Zack, again without any problem. When the Doctor's wrist was scanned, though, the attentive technician scowled. He asked him to pass his arm over the scanner again, and then one more time.

"I'm sorry, sir. . . you'll have to come with me," he said curtly.

Dr. Wilford went white, looking at Zack and Andy pleadingly. Zack pushed Andy along into the waiting arms of Rachel, who'd waited just the other side of the scan station for them.

"I'm with him," he said, chasing after the technician who had Dr. Wilford firmly by the arm.

"Then you both have some explaining to do!"

The scowling man led them into a small interrogation room where he motioned them to take a seat behind a table. He left the room, locking it behind him, and was gone a little more than five minutes.

"I don't feel very well, Zack . . . It's my heart." Dr. Wilford clutched his chest, looking more gray with every passing second.

"Hang on Doc. We'll get some help for ya." Zack began to stand, intending to call for help when a middle aged man came through the door followed by the young technician.

"I scanned him three times. Here's the readout. It says he's a woman, in his twenties. . . named Heidi. You can see for yourself . . . He doesn't look like a Heidi." Both Zack and Dr. Wilford sank their heads, realizing that somehow, the chips must have been switched. They were in serious trouble. . . trouble that could cost them their lives. Wilford looked very pale, coughing deeply. "Hang on Doc," Zack whispered.

"Thank you Moshe. I'll handle this from here." The older man looked gravely at the pair. "Well. . . what have you to say for yourselves?"

Satisfied that things were being taken care of, the young technician headed back to his post. As he shut the door, the elder official looked at Zack and then Dr. Wilford.

"Welcome to Israel," he said in a chipper voice. The two Americans looked up in disbelief.

"I don't know your real names. . . but we've been expecting you. My name is Yoseph. From the looks of you, sir, we'd better get you to a hospital at once. Please, follow me. . . and please, do look frightened. . . for the sake of Moshe." Yosef smiled and opened the door, allowing the two men to go out ahead of him.

He directed them past the scan station, pushing Zack just a little for effect, and then on into the main terminal where the others were waiting.

Yosef gathered the whole group together and hustled them into a small tour bus for the trip. By the time they got outside of the terminal, Dr. Wilford was feeling a bit better so they decided to get to their destination before seeking medical help. The road was packed with cars of all types, all traveling the scenic, two hour drive to Jerusalem along the Israeli Freeway.

Yosef had arranged to use the traditional site of the Garden Tomb, just a few blocks outside of the old city, for the meeting. It was surrounded by high walls and dense foliage and had an ample amphi-theater-type seating area for the fifty or so men and women to meet. The place began to fill at six p.m., a full hour before the meeting, many spending long minutes praying in this holy place. After leaving Andy and Rachel with Dr. Wilford at a little hospital near their destination, the group hurried on toward the gathering.

It was right at seven when the small group, led by Yosef, entered the grounds of the Garden Tomb. Nearly all of the others were seated already waiting for their visitors. As they approached the front of the meeting area an old rabbi with a long flowing beard and sparkling deep blue eyes stood in greeting.

"You are our friends from America?" spoke the old monarch.

"Yes sir, you must be Rabbi Ahvram Mayer . . . I'm very pleased to meet you, sir . . . I am Josiah Murphy."

"Josiah. . . a very good name, young man. And your friends?"

He introduced the others one by one, allowing the gentle old man to warmly greet each one, pausing to look deeply into their eyes for a moment.

"You've been through much, I sense," he said, "Now tell us your news. . . please. These people are leaders from cities around our country. They are very interested in what you have to say."

Josiah took a large envelope from his briefcase. He spread the document with maps out on a table set up in the front of the meeting place.

"These are top secret documents of the WCC detailing a plan to sweep over Israel on December twenty fourth, Christmas Eve, destroying everything in their path. They've been monitoring the revival that you've been experiencing here and have been waiting for it to reach just the right point. Then, claiming that the country has entered into rebellion against the WCC, they will sweep in with a massive army to destroy everything.

"They will be led in battle by Pierre DuMonde, the head of the WCC. . . and a peculiarly evil man. He will ride into Jerusalem on a black stallion, move into the temple area, and be crowned king of all the world as he sits on a throne of gold. He will claim to be God."

There was a momentary uproar as the people gathered began franticly to discuss what Josiah had shared. Ahvram sat silently though, eyes closed, for a long time. Finally he stood, gazing intently into the small crowd, and silently raised a hand. The garden became silent almost at once.

"My children. . . we should not be surprised at what our friends have shared with us. For some time we have known. . . that the end was near. . . the end of suffering and pain. . . of sadness and tears. Most importantly, the final foe. . . death, has seen his last days. This news is startling, yes. . . but only for a moment, for you see, it is all spoken of the Word of God . . .

"Shall we run and hide from these terrible armies? Shall we take up arms in a futile attempt to fight them? Yes, they are dreadful. . . their power is awesome. But do they come close in any way to the wondrous power of our Father? Are their armies any match for the heavenly hosts?" He looked at them radiantly for a long, silent moment. His words were more than the words of an old rabbi. They were anointed with power. They struck every heart like a mighty shaft of light.

"If our Lord did allow us to be stricken down by the sword, of what consequence would it be? Will the sting of death be any longer than a moment before we are drawn into the glorious

Project Utopia 2030

presence of our Yeshua?" The old rabbi folded his hands behind his back and turned from the crowd, walking to the tomb. He leaned against the stone face of the sepulcher caressing it with his hands.

"These stones. . . saw the face of our precious Lord . . . They cradled his lifeless body. . . and witnessed His glorious resurrection . . . I feel very strongly in my heart. . . that we too will see Him, face to face, not many days from now." He walked back toward them, face radiant, and a firm, deep conviction in his voice.

"My brothers and sisters. . . let us gather all of our people at the valley of Megiddo, as prophecy states. There we will fight a battle. . . a mighty battle. Not with the weapons of man, for our real warfare is not with flesh and blood. We will fight our battle with the weapons of God . . . We will go out with joy, and be led forth with peace. At the front of the battle will be our singers of praise, and our ranks will be filled with warriors of prayer and thanksgiving. We will stand, and see the salvation of our God!"

With that the old man sat down, leaving an inspired assembly, unable to talk but keenly aware that God had spoken through His vessel Ahvram.

365

"Daddy, there's someone here who'd like to meet you," Andy said, gently rousing her father from half sleep.

An old man a with a long, gray beard, entered the room.

"At last. . . someone a little closer to my age!" he said softly. "My brother. . . I am no prophet, no healer. . . but I do wish to pray for you. I know that your heart is very bad. The doctors give you only a few hours to live. Somehow though, I feel that God would have you witness the events of the next few days. Would you allow me to pray for you?"

Dr. Wilford nodded meekly, a broad, kind smile spreading across his old weathered face as he gripped Andy's hand, looking at her lovingly. A single tear rolled down his cheek as he saw in his little girl a beautiful woman.

"Daddy. . . I want you to know something . . . You're going to be a grandpa. . . even if Jesus comes back tonight. . ." He placed a feeble hand over her stomach and winked at her, too weak to speak. And then he was asleep.

CHAPTER FIFTY THREE

DuMonde spent his first days with the Russian brigade getting used to being on horseback. He often stopped, admiring the beautiful animal he was perched upon, and thinking that he resembled the great Napoleon. How majestic he would look, riding down from the hills, leading the horse brigade into battle. All the world would see the greatness of their new king.

Finally, the day came, December twenty-fourth, two thousand thirty. He rose early to meet with the commanders of the various units which would take part in the mighty battle to end all battles.

"Sir. . ." spoke an Iranian general, "The Israelis are doing something very strange. They know that they are outnumbered many times over, and yet they have not scattered at all. They have not retreated within the walls of Jerusalem . . . In fact, they are massing. . . in the valley of Megiddo, thousands of them. They must know that it will be nothing for our armies to sweep down to destroy them. . . in a matter of hours."

"I have long since given up trying to understand the minds of Christians. They obviously have a death wish. . . well. . . we won't disappoint them. It will make our triumphant entry into Jerusalem all the sweeter!"

Blakely was in the room. He was sitting in a corner of the room, a sweating, disheveled mass of nerves. DuMonde passed him on his way to the stables.

"You look very bad, Alistair. . ..you really should see a doctor. Or is it your meditation times. . . not too good, eh? Well. . . that's a shame, old friend . . . But you have been useful . . . You've fulfilled your role. . .Now, you're not needed anymore. . . Goodbye." Moments later there was a single shot heard from the direction of the meeting room. DuMonde looked up with an evil, knowing smile. He mounted his horse and took his place at the front of the formation.

The brigade rode two miles in ceremonial fashion to the railhead where the horses where loaded onto stock cars which would take them to the edge of the battle. There the brigade would form up again to lead the charge through the valley of Megiddo.

"Are the camera crews in place, Mr. Docar?"

"Yes, Mr. DuMonde. We have over a hundred portable crews as you requested. They have orders to cover every angle of the battle. The signal will be processed at our Beirut station and then sent out over the whole world on WBC affiliate stations."

"Excellent." DuMonde stepped aboard the specially outfitted rail car which would comfortably transport him to the forward edge of the battle where he would mount his beautiful black stallion and take his place at the head of the Russian Cavalry. A delighted chill ran up his spine as he pictured the event!

CHAPTER FIFTY FOUR

Three men walked together through ancient winding streets as a full moon rose overhead. The crisp night air caused their breath to come in tiny clouds of vapor as they ambled slowly down ancient walkways of cobblestone.

Zack, Josiah, and Rich Murphy were alone together for the first time since they'd all been reunited. In fact, it was the first time for over fifteen years. Amidst the turmoil of the world situation, somehow there was a deep, abiding peace which surrounded the trio. Zack reveled at the thought of the three Murphy's together again. He couldn't help but look often and long at his dad and granddad together. This was a perfect place for a family to be reunited, this ancient city of the Jews for whom family heritage was such an integral part of life.

Not knowing exactly where they were, the trio contentedly ambled along. Finally, after some time, they found themselves in a large courtyard area. There were hundreds of people standing near an ancient looking wall. . .

"This must be the Western Wall," Josiah said, marveling at its immensity. "It used to be called the Wailing Wall, for Jews down throughout history have come here to lament the plight of their people and to place prayers on little slips of paper in the cracks of the wall." The prayers being said this night were anything but wails. Many knelt silently while others, arms lifted in joyful praise, spoke whispered, thankful prayers. It was obvious that the wall no longer symbolized the plight of the Jews, but the faithfulness of their Savior, Yeshua.

"Tomorrow is the twenty fourth . . . I've been wanting to talk to each of you about what will take place." Josiah had a serious tone to his voice.

"There are two places of significance for the events that will surely lake place tomorrow. One is on the Mount of Olives, just outside the old city. If we are correct. . . this will be the place that Christ himself will descend. If we are not, then DuMonde's forces will be easily seen as they enter the area, allowing for some hope of escape.

"The other is on the plains of Megiddo. It will be there that the great battle will take place."

"It doesn't sound like it will be much of a battle, Dad. All that Ahvram's people plan to do is pray. They'll all be wiped out."

"Son. . . sometimes the ways of the Lord are very different than ours. I believe that Ahvram has heard from God. I don't understand how things will pan out . . . It may be, in fact, that it will be a suicide march. I trust in God, though. . . somehow He will prevail at that battle, even if every one of us is killed in the process."

"You don't mean that you're going to be with Ahvram's people? You're going to be on the battlefield?"

"Yes, son. . . your mom and I. . . and also Gramps and Gram."

"DAD, GRAMPS! I've waited fifteen years to finally be with both of you. . . and now you're going to. . . leave again. . . probably to your death!" Zack turned away from his father in anger.

"Zack. . . I don't know how to quell your fears, or to make our parting any easier . . . All I can say is that we know this is what God wants. Please. . . understand. . . and go to Him. He'll give you peace."

Zack knew that his father was right. It was just so hard to think of loosing both his parents and grandparents. . . again, after he'd just found them. He turned to look at them and slowly walked toward them, holding his hands out. . . his heart breaking. The three men embraced, weeping both sad and joyful tears for a long time.

"Zack. . . I think it wise that you and Andy stay here in Jerusalem with Sondra and Dr. Wilford," his father spoke after some time. "Sondra is not settled in her faith yet, and the Doctor cannot travel. The others can choose according to how they are led." Zack nodded compliance.

"Josiah, Zack. . . you boys don't know how much it means to Sarah and I to have you both with us. . . I mean really with us, in spirit as well as body. Now, we'll never really be parted. . . never." Gramps patted them both on the back as they continued to walk.

They walked on, out of the city, through the Kidron valley and up to the Mount of Olives. They continued silently upwards, walking the same trails that Jesus himself had walked. Finally, after an hour, they reached a place, nearly at the top. There they sat, looking back at the city before them, totally illuminated by floodlights all around its perimeter, its yellow stone shining as gold.

None wished to return to their hotel to sleep, but instead they clung to every moment, cherishing each as it came, like a dear old friend, until slender golden shafts of light let them know that their time was over. . . at least for the moment.

CHAPTER FIFTY FIVE

A two hour drive brought the remnants of the family to the plains of Megiddo. As they followed the road which entered from the south, a spectacular sight burst before them. All across the valley floor, in ranks of thousands, were huge battalions of warriors, both male and female. . . prayer warriors. . . already kneeling for battle. They were as ordered in their ranks as any army on parade but displayed no sign of weapons of any kind.

At the front of each battalion were rows of banner-carrying worshippers interspersed with musicians quietly singing and playing songs of praise. The banners were a bright red, and as they waved in the wind created the effect of a great churning sea.

At the extreme front of the whole army was a small band who knelt in prayer, arms extended upwards. Josiah recognized Rabbi Ahvram, the young man Peter, and Yosef, along with some of the others who'd been at the meeting.

Each of the members of his group fell in toward the rear of the massive formation, joining the others already engaged in supplication. Peter and Jenny knelt beside both the elder and younger Murphy's, followed by Dr. Noah and Rachel, with Clinton Bosley at the end of the row.

As they knelt they all simultaneously looked upward to the hills around the valley. There, surrounding them on three sides began to appear the ominous sight of a massive army of tanks and weapons of all types. The hills were literally covered with what seemed millions of foot soldiers, their weapons glinting in the nearly noonday sun.

Off at the very northernmost horizon one could barely make out the shapes of horses, thousands of coal black horses snorting and stomping impatiently. From the same direction the strains of Beethoven's ninth symphony began to blare from some hundreds of unseen speakers. The sight was dreadful. . .

"We will attack at the very strike of noon, General," DuMonde shouted cockily. "We should finish this task and be in Jerusalem by sundown! Look at those pitiful wretches! It is their wish to die. . . and I want no prisoners . . . Everyone MUST DIE!"

"Yes sir! We await your command!" Even as the Iranian general spoke, though, there could be heard a terrible rumbling as if from a huge earthquake.

"Listen to the glorious sound of our army. When they move the whole earth shakes!" DuMonde laughed a hideous, evil laugh. "I will be King within the hour!"

The air seemed electric, as though there were invisible, living creatures swarming through it. From behind, DuMonde heard a low, squealing whine which increased more and more with each second. He looked upward to see a thick, dark cloud swarming over his massive army and down the hill toward the legions of pathetic Christians.

And then, from the south, directly over the throng in the valley, shafts of light began to appear, gliding gently over the kneeling Christians as if to honor them. More and more filled the valley until the whole region was bathed in a brilliant light. It moved swiftly once past the front of the formation toward hills, fanning out in three directions.

"What! What is happening?" DuMonde screamed, but his generals could only stare in amazement.

"ATTACK!" he screeched with a demonic fervor. "Attack. . . attack. . . attack. . ." The order was passed until the whole army began to move forward into the valley below.

CHAPTER FIFTY SIX

Zack, Andy, Sondra, and Dr. Wilford had been shown to the home of a faithful old saint who lived directly at the top of the Mount of Olives. One had merely to cross a quiet street to reach the crest of the hill and to view the spectacular old city below.

Andy and Zack stood arm in arm looking over the hill at the massive, ancient city of David. There was so much there to see, not only with the eye, but with the heart; so much history, so many powerful stories of people wholly dedicated to God. The golden sun was beginning to burn away the last mists of morning.

"Can you believe that it was only four months ago that we met?" Andy felt as if they'd been together all their lives. Memories of all they'd been through together in the short time filled the minds of the young couple. How they'd changed. How the world had changed. And now, they knew that the change that was coming would be much greater still, beyond anything they could imagine.

"Andy. . ." Zack said after a long time, "Do you. . . think that Jesus. . . will be back today?"

She looked at him, her face showing the deep joy in her heart. "I think so, my love."

"I wonder. . . how it'll be. I mean. . . when we're all with Him. I can't even picture it . . . All I know is that it should be. . ." He searched for a word to describe his thoughts.

"It'll be wonderful," Andy finished. Zack just nodded. "One thing, though. Zack. . . do you think we'll still be together, I mean as man and wife?"

He grinned a mischievous grin. "I don't know. . . but it not, it's been nice knowing ya!" he said in an nonchalant manner.

She punched him in the arm. "You creep!"

Just then Sondra burst from the house. "Zack, Andy. . . come inside quick. It's on television! The battle is being broadcast!"

In moments, everyone was huddled around the old man's ancient television set. It was all there. The valley of Megiddo, the throngs of believers kneeling and praying while, at the head of each group, people loudly praised God waving banners, playing instruments and singing songs.

The camera panned upwards to the surrounding hills where hordes of men and equipment from all around the world were slowly advancing on the army of gentle warriors. Above them was a churning dark cloud unlike anything that those in the little house had ever seen. It surged forward and then recoiled as it advanced like a snake taunting its victim. As the cameras panned the sight, deep gargled shrieks could be heard from the midst of the blackness on all sides. It was horrible.

And then the shot changed. The picture switched from the evil dark cloud to the air above the legions of praying Christians in the valley. There a myriad of beautiful lights in many hues streaked through the air, slowing every so often and seeming to bow in honor before a group of believers.

At the edge of the group in the valley, the lights burst forth in all directions toward the churning black cloud. From the camera angle high above the formation it appeared that the mass of people in the valley had a halo of brilliant light totally surrounding them. A wonderful deep and rich chordal sound proceeded from the glowing spectacle, as though a million beautifully rich voices joined in harmony.

The armies of men were still some distance from the group in the valley when the dark cloud encountered the army of light. The brightness surged forward, tearing a deep gouge into the murky haze as a terrible screeching could be heard. Then, finding a gap in the light a mass of darkness surged forward only to be driven back again by reinforcing legions of light.

The sounds of the battle were spectacular. Massive crescendos of thick rising harmony were interspersed with hideous shrieks and long guttural wails. Any human sound from either side was totally drowned out except for short moments here and there.

As the battle wore on, those viewing the spectacular sight began to make out more distinct shapes as the dim outlines of grotesque demonic beings clashed with powerfully beautiful angelic beings. As weapons clashed it was as thunder rolled through the valley.

The human army of DuMonde soon stood dead still, staring in awe at the campaign being waged above their heads. Whole companies of men fell to the ground crying out in fear, and pleading with God for mercy. Others writhed in agony as the demons that possessed them awoke in agitated fury.

DuMonde, face contorted with rage, barked out orders to the cavalry that followed him, riding back and forth like a civil war general railing on his troops for their cowardice.

"Attack! Now!" At first no one moved other than to try to control the frightened animals on which they rode. Then, one by one they moved ahead, bracing themselves against the dread terror that gripped every heart.

DuMonde galloped ahead urging the brigade onward, faster and faster until they moved down the hill at a dead gallop, thousands of men aboard terrified stallions. The northernmost slopes leading to the valley seemed to flow as a massive, black torrent pouring onto the valley floor below it.

Sondra stood in the little room, horrified. "It's DuMonde! He's there!" She was pointing to the television screen that showed a close-up of the horsemen as they made their descent. There, hair blowing wildly in the wind, face contorted in an heinous battle yell, was Pierre DuMonde leading his men toward the mass of praying Christians.

As they watched, they saw the horse brigade nearing the edge of the black cloud of demonic warriors. At a breakneck pace the whole regiment of horsemen, now spread out in a mile long line, hit the ranks of angelic soldiers. It was as though they ran headlong into a brick wall. The agonized cries of men mixed with the terrified squalls of horses and the whole line stopped dead in their tracks. All, that is, save one. As Pierre DuMonde hit the ranks of angels they simply moved to the side, creating a gap in their line which immediately closed as he passed through.

It was nearly a mile before DuMonde realized he was riding alone through the valley. The army of gentle warriors was but one hundred yards ahead but his own army was far off in the distance. The demons within him screeched in rage, driving him forward, alone, toward his mortal enemies. Just ten yards from them he stopped his horse, angrily dismounted and drew a ceremonial sword from his side.

"You pathetic creatures. . . do you not know who your king is?"

A dark shape began to rise from within the depths of DuMonde's body. For a moment he began to convulse uncontrollably but soon this gave way to seething angry strides. Before him an old rabbi stood, looking him directly in the eyes without a word.

Simultaneously DuMonde and the huge demonic being which had seethed from within him burst forward toward the old man. They let out a bloodcurdling cry as one, DuMonde raising his sword over his head.

CHAPTER FIFTY SEVEN

By this time the camera had closed in on DuMonde, catching every detail of the event as it took place. Andy grabbed Zack's arm squeezing tightly as the evil man before them was poised to strike down the beloved old rabbi Ahvram. "Oh dear God. . . help him," someone cried from the little room.

The sword came down with a swoosh of air. . . stopping inches away from the old man's head. Ahvram had not flinched a bit. The strong hand of Peter, though, had caught DuMonde's arm as he brought it down.

"Forgive me, Rabbi," he said, twisting the Frenchman's arm until his sword dropped to the ground.

The old man looked at his beloved boy and smiled gently. "You're forgiven, my son."

Above them they immediately saw the black, demonic gargoyle in the strong immobilizing embrace of a majestic angelic warrior. The demon squealed but to no avail. The mighty angel looked at the men below and seemed to bow a bit, smiling as he dragged the ugly monster off and out of sight.

The enormous battle continued to rage at the fringes of the little valley, filling the air with a deafening sound. All of the human warriors were still though, either kneeling in prayer or staring in awestruck amazement at the sight above them. On the fighting continued...... for what seemed hours.

And then from the eastern sky a stunning, beautiful light burst onto the floor of the valley as a deafening thunderclap mightily shook the earth. From the midst of the light came a being, more radiant than anything earth had yet seen. As he descended, light spread outward, engulfing the whole area for miles in every direction. Hideous screams were heard all around the valley as the demonic host writhed in pain before disintegrating in the radiance, allowing the angelic warriors to fan out, overwhelming the whole battle field as far as the eye could see.

"Yeshua!" exclaimed Rabbi Ahvram lifting his hands upward as if trying to embrace his coming Lord. The brightness of His face was so brilliant that even his faithful had to shield their eyes as they looked at Him, and look they did. The massive sea of believers lifted their eyes and, as Ahvram, reached upward toward their King. "Yeshua! Yeshua!" could be heard throughout the valley.

DuMonde watched in horror as the men and women in his massive army, slowly at first, and then in overwhelming waves, began to kneel, eyes heavenward in anguish. A muffled sound began to swell from their midst. He heard it in ten different languages at once at first like a faint whisper. The soldiers were saying something over and over growing louder with each time. Finally terror gripped his evil heart as he understood that their anguished cries formed the sounds. . . Jesus. . . is Lord!

Suddenly there was a noise as a mighty, growling earthquake and a majestic voice, seemingly from heaven said simply. . .

"IT IS FINISHED!"

CHAPTER FIFTY EIGHT

Peter and Yosef rose, walking cautiously toward the man curled up in a fetal position, spastically convulsing. His cries were not understandable, merely noise coming from foaming lips. The two men moved to help him when the steady voice of Ahvram came from behind them.

"Leave him alone . . . Do not touch him . . . He is in God's hands now." DuMonde gave one last decrepit attempt at speech, but all he was able to utter was a feeble "NO!", and then he was silent.

The heavenly host burst upwards like a shimmering stream of golden light encircling the King of Kings. Down over the valley battlefield the whole majestic procession flowed as each gentle warrior heard in his heart of hearts. . .

"Well done. . .my good and faithful servant."

Zack stepped out of the little house to find Sydney looking over the hill. To his right Pat sat on a large rock, quietly weeping. As Zack crossed the street, Sydney turned to him.

"Sir. . . knowing that the time was short. . . I took the liberty of speaking to Mr. Erwert. I shared with him various scriptures regarding his need for Christ. . ." He turned his head toward Pat with a jerk. "I believe I was. . . most persuasive."

Walking to his side, Zack asked, "Pat. . . is it true?"

"Ya. . . it's true. . . it's true." His normal "jokester" attitude had faded, leaving him, at least for a time, a vulnerable young man finally able to come to grips with the real needs of his heart. The two friends hugged while the others joined them, one by one, rejoicing at the news of a new brother in Christ!

After a long moment, Sydney, who'd continued looking out over the Kidron Valley toward Jerusalem, spoke.

"Mr. Murphy. . . I believe that you will be interested in what I am looking at." They all joined him at the crest of the hill looking curiously out over the ancient city. There in the distance, coming steadily toward them, was an incredible sight. It was as though the whole sky was aglow with the most glorious streams of light coming from a central point. It seemed a constant swirl of glowing embers emanated around, a being, an exquisitely beautiful being coming steadily toward them.

Sydney looked at Andy. "Mrs. Murphy. . . this world will soon pass away. . . and I am a part of it. I said once to you that I as an android could never know your Christ. Well, it seems that He is at hand. I do so wish you a wonderful meeting with Him. . ."

Tears flowed down her face as Andy hugged the gawky android. Then she took Zack's hand and, side by side with her beloved husband, waited for the most important meeting of their young lives.

POSTLOGUE

A living crystal blue stream flowed from the throne of the King and out into the lush kingdom that his beloved children dwelt in. It passed the beautiful gardens happily winding its way through fields of fragrant flowers and past a lush green meadow.

Two young boys frolicked along its gentle banks near the place where their families reclined in the cool of the day. After a long romp in the sweet smelling clover the older of the two plopped down at the lap of his mother.

"Mommy?" he said, adoringly.

"Yes, Jimmy" his mother replied stroking his dark hair.

"What was the world like before?"

"Before what, son?"

"Before you and daddy, and Benjy's parents. . . and. . . all the rest were here with Jesus."

Rachel smiled down at her sweet son, holding her husband, James' hand tightly. "Well. . . things were not nearly so wonderful as they are here. It was as though we lived in a constant shadow."

"Wasn't there anything good there?" The little boy persisted.

She thought for a moment and then looked at Benjy's mom knowingly.

"God made many good things there. . . and. . . he allowed Mr. Bosley to make one, too." Andy smiled at Rachel's son. "His name was Sydney"

.

About the Author

R. Norman Johnson lives a life full of kids. Beside his own five children he has been serrogate father to thousands of other children over the past thirty years. Teaching and coaching are his tools to reach them but kids are his focus. A teacher of twenty years he spends his life dedicated to making a difference in the lives of young people. He has a degree from Pacific Lutheran University in education and teaches music and drama, as well as history. Writing is a full time occupation for him as he fills any gaps in his curricullum by writing choral music, plays, and musical productions of his own. He has a Master of Divinity in religious education from Covenant Bible Seminary and spent over a decade as a youth and music pastor where he led numerous missionary groups to Mexico to help the poor.

Fiction is an escape from the present, but can open the door to teach the truth. Project Utopia 2030 is the culmination of five years of work aimed at opening the reader's eyes to the possible downside of our great technilogical explosion. We must enter the 21st century with excitement and wonder mixed with great fear and trembling. "With great power comes great responsibility!"

Printed in the United States
961200004B

9 781410 709691